FASTER

OTHER TITLES BY ANDIE J. CHRISTOPHER

Stand-Alone Novels

Unrealistic Expectations

To Win a Witch's Heart (Part of Dangerous Tides series)

Thank You, Next

All They Want for Christmas

*Biker B*tch*

Full Contact

One Night in South Beach

Stroke of Midnight

Dusk Until Dawn

Break of Day

Before Daylight

Night and Day

All Hours

The Nolans

Not the Girl You Marry

Not That Kind of Guy

Hot Under His Collar

FASTER

Andie J. Christopher

This is a work of fiction. Names, characters, organizations, places, events, and incidents are either products of the author's imagination or are used fictitiously. Otherwise, any resemblance to actual persons, living or dead, is purely coincidental.

Published by Montlake, Seattle

www.apub.com

EU product safety contact:
Amazon Media EU S. à r.l.
38, avenue John F. Kennedy, L-1855 Luxembourg
amazonpublishing-gpsr@amazon.com

ISBN-13: 9781662533211 (paperback)
ISBN-13: 9781662533228 (digital)

Cover design by Letitia Hasser
Cover image: © MAKSYM CHUB, © Volodymyr TVERDOKHLIB, © Brendt A Petersen, © KOTOIMAGES, © Kollawat Somsri / Shutterstock; © jacoblund / Getty

Printed in the United States of America

My books are always for the girls, but this one is for the fangirls. Especially the DTS fangirls. And fuck everyone who says that our passion for the sport isn't valid because the drivers are also hot. They can't help it; it's not like they would drive faster if they were ugly.

Winter Break

Chapter One

Cece turned the key over in the door about six times—hoping that he hadn't changed the locks—before big, strong hands took it from her and fitted it into the keyhole.

She stepped back and looked at the owner of the apartment. Every time she saw him in person, she was surprised at how handsome he was. The pictures taken in the paddock never did him justice. His strong features just translated better in person. It didn't stop millions of girls from around the world from being in love with him just based on the pictures, though. Maybe if he didn't turn the other way when he spotted her at races, it wouldn't be a shock to her system to be sharing space with him.

She never saw him around, even though they lived only a few meters apart in the Fontvieille, a Monaco neighborhood that was remarkably Soviet-looking for a principality based on unfettered capitalism. The entire country was like a small liberal arts college campus for billionaires and tax evaders—all of them packed almost vertically in an area a tenth of the size of Harvard. It should have been hard to avoid him, but he'd slipped away all the same.

"How long have you been standing there, watching me?" She wasn't really drunk, but she swayed on her feet from too much champagne and not enough food. The title of her memoir—it was going to be a sad one.

Luca narrowed his gaze at her. "What did he do this time?"

She opened her mouth, and a little belch came out. So embarrassing. Not just the belch but showing up here. But Luca was the only person in the world who would ever understand how callous Ethan could be. "They were in my bed." When that statement echoed through the hallway, she whispered, "On my side of the bed."

She didn't know why that detail of her husband's infidelity bothered her so much. She would have been enraged had she found Ethan cheating on her in the kitchen or a hotel somewhere on the road, but her bed—their bed—stung so much more.

Luca's head fell back, and he sighed. Even that small sound echoed in the hall outside his penthouse condo, along with the drops of rainwater falling from her New Year's Eve dress.

"We were having a party." She'd been making sure that no one left cocaine too low to the ground, where one of the little dogs that one of Ethan's friends from home had brought could get to it. She'd always hated the short coffee table, and that was just another reason. "He got high for the first time in ages, and I guess he lost his mind."

Luca crossed his arms over his chest. She hadn't expected him to be home. He didn't have a seat on the grid for next year, so she expected him to be in Rio or London to ring in the New Year. She'd come here to be alone, because her husband would be able to find her in a hotel when he sobered up. This was the one place he would never think to look. Not anymore.

Standing in front of this man, she realized she'd made a miscalculation. He knew everything about Ethan—things that Ethan didn't even know about Ethan. And he knew almost everything about her. The only fact he didn't know about her was that she'd been a little bit in love with him for a very long time.

But she hadn't come here with the intention of seeing Luca. She just wanted to be comforted by the fact that he'd been where she was, and he still cared about her.

Luca had promised that he'd always care for her. That he'd always be there if she needed him. But she didn't need him right now. He couldn't fix her broken marriage or pull her husband's dick out of the bikini model she'd found bouncing on top of him in her bed. On her side of the bed.

"I didn't think you'd be here." God, that sounded ridiculous. This was his condo. And he probably didn't feel like partying after being fired. That would have been an Ethan move. Not Luca. Of course he'd be here.

He turned the key in the lock and opened the door, motioning for her to go in first. "Come in. You haven't eaten."

"I ordered really good food for the party." No one had touched it. All the drivers were really concerned about gaining too much weight over the holidays. Maybe they'd indulged at Christmas, but training started tomorrow. And all of the girlfriends, wives, and "models" were on a strict Ozempic-and-blow diet plan.

Cece didn't like coke. It made her heart race and made her anxiety worse than it was on an everyday basis. Before meeting Ethan, marrying Ethan, and moving from Miami to Monaco, she'd liked weed gummies and skinny margaritas.

No one knew how to make a decent margarita in Monte Carlo.

Luca looked down at her feet. "I'm going to get you some dry clothes. I'm also going to bring you socks. You will put them on."

She didn't normally like to be told what to do, but his bossiness didn't bother her—Luca was just like this. He said something would happen and he simply made it so. It must be so frustrating for him to have his career end on something other than his own terms.

As he walked into the hallway, she felt a pang of guilt over how she was burdening him with her problems—problems he'd probably thought he'd left behind when his friendship with Ethan ended. At the time, she hadn't understood the falling-out, and Ethan hadn't told her anything other than, "He was being a dick, and I cut him loose."

Ethan was the first man who'd ever pursued her seriously. The night they'd met he'd told her that he was going to marry her. She'd been in her early twenties, and men just didn't say that kind of thing unless they meant it. And he'd been relentless in courting her—a total gentleman. That made her laugh now.

Luca walked back just in time to hear it. "If something is funny, you'll have to share it with the class, Ms. Ramos." He sounded like a stern headmaster with his British accent, and it sent a thread of heat through her veins that she dared not acknowledge. "There hasn't been much to joke about of late around here." He pushed a pile of clothes into her hands.

"I was laughing at how ironic all of this is. He tried so hard to get me—" She didn't want or need to finish that statement. Luca knew. He'd been there.

He grimaced. "Go change."

Cece looked around the penthouse as she walked to the bathroom. Everything was the same as it had been years before. Except that it was quiet and empty. Luca still had the same couch where he and Ethan had played video games until all hours, even though he'd updated his game console, and the TV was bigger.

She'd expected him to give her clothes that some girl had left in the hopes that he would call her to return them.

Instead, she was cozy in his oversize sweatshirt and basketball shorts that went down past her knees. Luca was tall for a racing driver, so they were almost pants.

"I always forget how small you are until I see you."

"I'm not that small." She'd been tall enough to model occasionally when she'd run into Luca and Ethan at a Miami nightclub. It seemed like a century ago now. She couldn't be *that* much older in less than half a decade, could she? She felt like she'd lived five lifetimes since then.

"I feel so much older than I did when I met the two of you." It probably wasn't wise to say something like that out loud. It could open doors that would be much better off closed. But it hadn't been a good idea to come here at all.

Luca ran his hand through his hair. Since she was already doing dumb things, she allowed herself to luxuriate in the way his triceps flexed when he lifted his arm. She let herself really look at him for the first time in years. She could admit it now—that she'd tried her best to avert her eyes on the rare occasions she couldn't avoid him, because loving Ethan instead of him was a mistake. She'd been thinking with her head, not her heart. There had always been too much passion in her feelings for Luca. And maybe not enough in her feelings for Ethan.

"I don't like to look that far back." He laughed, and his mouth went crooked in this boyish way that made her want to give him anything he wanted. She definitely shouldn't be here. "I've made too many mistakes since then to be able to sleep at night."

"You don't sleep at night?" She knew that because they were alike in that way. Neither of them was born into the world they now inhabited. That feeling that they'd snuck in the back door made them both restless.

"It's a good thing for you, tonight, that I don't." He rounded the counter and held out a cup of tea.

He'd made her tea. Like a friend or a parent would. "You shouldn't have to take care of me. Not right now—"

"Don't worry about it," he said in a tone that brooked no argument. "I told you that I'd always be here for you."

But those words had been said out of pain—he'd been rejected by his best friend—and she'd been so sure that she'd been making the prudent choice when he'd said them. "I never thought he'd do this to me."

"No one ever thinks a leopard is going to eat *their* face." He motioned for her to sit at the stool next to the island. "Did you sign a prenup?"

"Yeah." She'd been thinking about that when she'd quietly shut her bedroom door and walked out of the condo instead of confronting Ethan right that moment. She wouldn't get any money if she killed him. At the time, she'd laughed at that clause in the prenup. It had probably come up in the hundreds of years that Ethan's family had been rich, but she never thought it was a hypothetical that might apply to her own murderous rage.

"If you divorce him now, what do you get?" Luca didn't mince words, and Cece appreciated that about him. Still, she winced at his question. "That bad, huh?"

"I get about two pennies to rub together." Ethan's family didn't like her. She was mixed race, an outsider, an American, and nothing like what they'd pictured for their golden boy. But she'd survived on her own before and she could again. Hell, she was more popular in the paddock than her husband. Without her, he'd be seen for the petulant, ungrateful, rich prick that he was.

"You can join me in the poorhouse, then." She should be more sensitive to Luca's firing, but he had made money while racing. She'd simply been arm candy.

Cece looked around. "At least you have a house to sell. Houses."

Luca smiled at her. "True."

Her insides warmed from the way he looked at her, and she wanted to grasp this moment and keep it. This could have been her life, but she'd made the wrong choice. She couldn't go back now, but maybe they could pretend.

"You would have—"

Luca broke the moment. He shook his head and turned away from her. "We're not going to dwell on the past now." He opened the refrigerator and pulled out a carton of eggs. "Make some toast."

"I'm not hungry." How could she eat at a time like this? But then her stomach growled. Luca's low laugh awakened another primal urge she couldn't afford to dwell on.

"Make some toast."

She loved him. Not like she had before, when all three of them were close but Ethan and Luca were closer—simply from the years they'd spent together. She remembered being shocked by how intimate their friendship was. It made it so much harder when Luca exited their lives. She felt as though he'd taken a piece of Ethan with him. But there was something of the love she'd always felt for him—the friendship and comfort—that hadn't gone away. If she wasn't so strung out, she'd count it as a miracle.

So, she made toast.

Luca was vibrating from being in the same room as Cece—like his car was underneath him on a bumpy track, and he couldn't feel the racing line. He was upside down, like he was airborne and just waiting for the impact against the barriers.

He didn't know if he could mitigate the collision. He hated feeling this out of control. But there was no way he could have turned her away. Besides, when a driver is afraid of crashing more than he wants to win, it's time to retire.

Making an omelet wasn't his usual mode of winning, but he would have done anything for a second shot at making Cece his—and Ethan had just handed it to him.

He should have known it would only be a matter of time before the selfish, entitled Ethan would do something to mess up the one thing that he'd ever earned through hard work. Though he never would have guessed that she would show up at his door. He'd hoped but never expected.

"Do you want me to put something on TV?" He didn't know if the room felt as thick to her as it did to him, but they needed something to cut the tension.

Cece shook her head. "Can you put on some music? Something mellow?"

He could do that. If he recalled correctly—and he recalled almost everything about her—she liked Tems.

As soon as the beat dropped, she started swaying her hips as she buttered their toast. He shouldn't be eating this late, but he hadn't felt like going to any of the parties he was invited to. Now that he wasn't officially associated with a team, the only people who wanted him seen at their clubs and parties were the seedy bottom-feeders and con artists who wanted him to be the face of their crypto pyramid scheme.

"Why aren't you out tonight?" Cece asked. "I would have thought you'd want to forget everything happening."

For a second, he wondered if she had come here partially out of pity. But that thought didn't stick. She'd been a little tipsy when she'd walked in, though that seemed to have worn off. But she was distraught over her own situation, probably just getting around to thinking about what was going on in his life now. Maybe some of Ethan's self-absorption had rubbed off?

It kind of didn't matter to him, though. She was here, with him. And he didn't particularly care what had gotten her to break the yearslong stalemate between them.

"I didn't feel like pretending." That was the truth. He didn't feel like pretending he wasn't upset about the break with his former team. They hadn't had the car to win the championship, as they'd promised him when he'd signed. And then they'd blamed him for it instead of the engineers who designed the car. He was easier to blame than the engineers or the other driver—whom he'd beaten this season—because he didn't have an advanced degree, and he'd brought in fewer sponsors than his teammate, whose father was a powerful French politician.

"Why aren't you with your family in London?" He remembered introducing Cece to his family when all three of them had been just friends. The way his mother had looked at her when she'd sat down on the floor and played with his nieces and nephews after helping clean up the kitchen. A "good girl," according to his mother. Not anything like the "models" he was photographed with for gossipmongering Instagram accounts that covered WAGs (wives and girlfriends) and potential WAGs. His mother didn't think those women were bad, just that they didn't come from the same kind of place he did.

Cece was from Miami, but she'd fit right in his parents' cozy row house in South London. She still didn't expect everything to be handed to her, but he hated to see the way she'd hardened into cynicism. He blamed Ethan.

"I didn't want them to see right through me." They'd supported his racing career, often sacrificing greatly so he could stay karting. But they didn't truly understand what drove him. All they knew was that he wasn't as angry when he was driving as fast as he could.

When he'd won enough to grab the notice of one of the manufacturers and entered the same junior program where he'd met Ethan, his mum had cried with joy. At least he'd thought it was joy at the time. Maybe she'd cried because she knew this life would eventually break his heart.

He looked at Cece as he pushed a plate with half an omelet toward her. She'd broken his heart, but she'd come back. Maybe his career would be the same.

"I can't believe you're eating this late with me." She nodded at his plate. During the season, he had to make weight. Being tall made that difficult.

"I could indulge a bit over the holidays, even before. You were always so disciplined."

"You've always had kind of a birdlike metabolism," she said with a mouth half full of eggs and cheese. He loved the way she did everything with such passion. Eating, laughing—he could only imagine how she was when Ethan fucked her.

His mind flashed back to the morning after they'd all met at a South Beach nightclub. Ethan had secured his first win, and they were celebrating. Luca had podiumed, but he'd been on pole. It should have been him on the top step. Back then, he hadn't been bitter about his friend finding success. That would come later.

"I would kill for one of those croquetas and Cuban coffee on the beach right now." He wanted her to remember with him. How they used to be. Her eyes closed as she slipped back in time with him. A soft moan left her lips, and he stared at her mouth.

Fuck, she was beautiful. "I was so nervous taking the two of you to my spot." She laughed, and it hit the center of him like a g-force. "I was scared that paparazzi would follow you, it would become the hot place, and then I would have to wait in line every time I needed my hangover cure."

He leaned against the island, just to get a little closer to her. "They didn't. No one saw the three of us together."

She sniffed. "That started later. I remember when that so-called reporter found my mom's cell phone number and wouldn't leave her alone." He could tell by the look on her face that she was afraid of that happening again, and he wished he could protect her from the world the way her husband should have.

He looked down at her hand. She still wore her garishly large engagement ring and wedding band. Ethan had always liked to mark his territory. Once upon a time, Luca had been part of Ethan's territory. But then, they'd met Cece.

Cece pushed away her plate. He was satisfied that she'd eaten most of her food. "Thank you."

They were silent long enough that it became awkward. Luca didn't know what to say. *Stay with me, forever?* That was too much. She'd just had a shock. The man who had promised to love only her had broken that vow in a viciously cruel way.

"I can, uh, put you in the spare bedroom, if you need to sleep," was all that came out.

Cece shook her head. "Are you tired? I'm not."

He could tell by the red rims around her eyes and the fact that she kept rubbing them that she was lying. She was bone-tired, but sleep probably wouldn't help. She'd wake up tomorrow thinking that tonight had all been a bad dream. Only to get hit by a truck. The longer she stayed awake, the longer she could delay falling off that particular cliff.

"Do you want to watch a movie?" That's what he was going to do before she'd arrived.

He'd spent the entire holiday holed up in this apartment. He wasn't sure why he hadn't hired someone to pack up his place for him and gone to see his family. He might be unemployed, but he still had money. He had enough money that no one in his family ever had to work again.

But Bendettos always worked. So, he would find another racing seat, or he would go work in the auto shop with his dad. People would forget him. Did he want that? To fade into comfortable anonymity with a wrench in his hand—not much to look forward to other than a pint and a game of football on the telly at the end of each day?

Maybe it would feel good if Cece were there, if they could share a quiet home on a quiet street until they filled it with loud children. She might be worried about walking away from her marriage with nothing, but she would survive. They were alike in that way. They'd come from outside this world, and they could return to a status that didn't have them waited on hand and foot.

It had always felt strange for him to have people doing things for him that he could do himself. He didn't have a job right now, so he'd pack up his place in Monte Carlo all alone.

But he wasn't alone. He had someone to keep him company. Someone as sad as he was.

"I would love to watch hot people shoot at each other." She still remembered what kind of movies he liked. Despite the public image of the dim race car driver, racing took a lot of brainpower. When he was off duty, all he wanted to do was shut everything off. When he was younger, that involved more booze and girls than it did now. Now, he meditated and did yoga.

He still watched action movies, though.

She walked into his living room, and he followed her—trying and failing to avoid being mesmerized by the way she moved. She was so graceful and precise, and he'd somehow forgotten how much he liked that about her. She'd been waiting tables at the club when they first met.

Luca had seen her initially, weaving between tables and delivering bottles. He'd smiled when she'd slapped a guy's hand away without him even realizing she was rejecting him. That was, of course, the moment she'd looked over at Luca.

And then she'd winked.

Luca hadn't blushed since he was a schoolboy, but he'd blushed right then. Even with her in his home, years later, he rubbed the back of his neck thinking about what he'd felt when she'd first looked at him.

Cece flopped down on the end of the couch, and he had a choice to make. She was next to the remote, so it wouldn't be weird if he sat next to her. But it would be odd to cuddle up with someone else's wife. However, the husband in question had broken his vows first. And Cece had been sending him heated looks since she walked in. She came here.

He didn't want to assume that she'd come here to have sex with him. Well, his ego wanted to assume that, but his actual brain told him that she'd come here for solace and comfort. He wasn't going to ruin that for her by making a pass that he wasn't really and truly sure was welcome.

"Can you get me a drink?" A stay of execution, just as he stood in front of her. He put his hands in the pockets of his sweats, and her gaze followed his movement. She wet her lips. He just barely kept a feral sound inside his throat.

"What would you like?"

Then, she looked up at his face. For a split second, he thought she was going to say something about his dick. But then she said, "Tequila?"

He was surprised she didn't ask for more champagne. She was a sedate, married lady now—long past body shots and pitchers of too-sweet margarita. But he had a great collection of tequila that would just go to waste when he moved out, and he would do almost anything to please her.

He made them both tequila sodas and brought them to the couch. She took the seating choice off his hands when she scooted over and patted the spot she'd made next to her on the end of the couch.

There was zero space between them. Their thighs touching from knee to hip, his flank pressed up against her. He could feel every breath she took. He knew she wasn't wearing a bra under his sweatshirt.

He was either being given a gift or the universe was teasing him with everything he could have had if only he'd been born Ethan Harrow. But he wasn't going to move. If Cece wanted him, she could have him. If she just wanted to toy with him, he'd be her plaything. He was a little bit helpless when it came to her. And instead of making him angry, it felt right.

Chapter Two

Cece took a drink and acknowledged that she was playing with fire. She never let herself be this close to Luca. He'd caught her eye first out of the two friends, but there was always something a little unknowable about him. There was too much mischief in his gaze to get any real grounding. She realized now that it wasn't that he hadn't wanted her—he just hadn't known whether or not he deserved her.

Ethan, on the other hand, hadn't left her guessing for a minute. She knew he wanted her because he'd relentlessly pursued her. It took her so long to get it—that he hadn't really wanted her for the woman she was. He'd wanted a pretty trophy he could show off and a way to humanize himself in the press. If his wife wasn't one of the model/influencer/socialites that most of the other drivers dated, it would mean he was really genuine and down to earth.

Yeah, a genuine asshole she currently wanted to put six feet under.

Well, she had certainly learned her lesson about listening to popular dating advice. Sure, men loved the chase, but they still cheated when they caught you.

She hadn't been consciously thinking about seducing Luca when she'd walked the two blocks from the condo she shared with Ethan to Luca's building. Just that she'd needed someplace to be for a while. But she wondered if she'd subconsciously been planning some sort of revenge seduction.

She shook her head. "Too strong?" he asked. Why did he have to be so considerate when she wasn't sure if she was being an asshole by thinking about cheating on her husband with their former best friend?

"Just right," she said, trying another smile. It didn't work because Luca lifted his hand as though he wanted to reach out and touch her.

But then he stopped himself. Cleared his throat. Pointed the remote at his screen and asked, "This okay?"

"Yes, I need to see some beautiful, yet evil, people die."

Luca nodded and turned on a French action movie that she would have to carefully read subtitles for. Even after years of living in Monte Carlo, she wouldn't say that her French was particularly good. She might have been a bit less isolated if she was fluent.

But part of her knew it wouldn't help. The very nature of her life was isolating. She was married to one of the most famous men in the world. It hadn't always been that way, and it hadn't been what she'd intended. Before Netflix had done a documentary show that heavily featured Ethan and Luca, they could have walked down the street in most cities without being bothered by their fans.

Now, that would be impossible.

She turned to Luca, his face lit by the dim lights put off by the television. They flashed across his features. She wondered if the attention was what had broken him. He'd been so self-assured before—sure that he'd be a world champion.

"Do you regret it?" She shouldn't be waking the dead like this. He'd opened his home to her, fed her. He was coddling her like the child he had never gotten to be. She shouldn't be hunting for the ghosts of their shared past.

"I never regret anything. It's a bad habit." She could tell he was lying by the look in his dark-brown eyes.

She was most definitely going to regret the next thing she did for a long time. She knew it before she moved her face even closer to his. Before he cocked his head so their mouths would slot together. She regretted it as his Roman nose brushed against her face. She regretted it as soon as their mouths touched, and she kissed Luca Bendetto for the very first time.

He ruined her in that instant. Embers had been burning underneath her skin since she'd walked in, but they raged beyond control the instant he touched her. She was afraid to touch him anywhere but his mouth—she held her hands just above his shoulder, feeling his heat—but he didn't share that hesitation. He turned his whole body and pulled her onto his lap, so she was straddling him. He held her close to him as though he was afraid she'd get away. His fingertips made deep impressions against her upper arms.

His hardness felt huge between her legs, and she was pretty sure he could feel how damp she was through all the layers of clothes. He grunted as she settled against him, sending a shiver down her spine.

That made him pull back and open his eyes. It took her a second to catch on that he had pulled back. God, she'd kissed him. He had just reacted, and now all of this would be over. It would be so awkward if they ever saw each other again.

Her eyelids fluttered closed. "Are you sure you want this?" he asked.

She wasn't sure she wanted this, but she was damned certain she needed it. She needed to feel like she was wanted somewhere in the world. It was unforgivably weak of her to go searching for that feeling with him. She was just as selfish as Ethan for coming to Luca to fill the gaping hole that her husband had left. It was just triage for the wound that would take a lot longer to heal.

And she would definitely hurt Luca in the process. They couldn't keep each other—not permanently. They only had tonight.

"I need you, Luca." She owed him the truth, at the very least. "I need you tonight, but we can't—"

He made a hushing sound and rubbed his giant hand up and down her back. "I know. Just tonight."

She wanted to look at him sitting underneath her for hours and days. With his hair ruffled and his lips swollen and red, he looked like her very own Lucifer fantasy come to life. But they only had tonight, so she held his face in her hands and kissed him again.

He crushed her body to his, as though he wanted them to meld into one. All the drivers talked about being one with the car during a race, especially when they had a really good car. Cece had never understood what they meant. Not until Luca held her like that.

It was like he knew exactly how to kiss her, like she was made for him. He knew exactly how much pressure to use with his hands as he smoothed them down her waist and pulled her hips even closer, so close she moaned into his mouth. She felt high and almost dizzy, like all her blood was pooled at the center of her. She'd never come from dry humping. Not even close. Not even in high school, when she hadn't wanted to swap fluids with any of the boys in her neighborhood.

But she was so close now with her thighs pressed to the outside of his splayed legs. It was indecent and delicious.

He snaked his hands under her sweatshirt and found her nipples. She squirmed against him as he stroked her. He took his mouth away from hers and trailed kisses down her jaw. "Need this off, Cece."

He said her name as though he was supposed to be here with her, like he'd been born to whisper her name like a prayer. She'd wanted to kiss him for so long, and she would never let herself. Because, unlike Ethan, she was loyal. Until now.

Tears sprang up, and she tried to suppress them, but she wanted to feel all of it, everything with him.

She raised her arms, and he pulled off her top, immediately latching on to one of her nipples. She wrapped her fingers in his hair, pulling him closer. He was like silk—his mouth, his hair. The only thing rough about him was his calloused fingertips as he teased her other nipple and secured her to him with his hand on her back. She was shaking with need.

His chuckle was dark as he let go of her nipple with a lurid pop. "You're not cold, are you?"

Cece shook her head, and he pulled her hair down, so it spilled over her shoulders. "Overheated. We might need to cool down the engine."

That hadn't sounded cheesy when she'd said it in her head.

"You want to slow down?" His brow creased with concern. She guessed it was the first time he'd needed to say that in any context. Who could slow down when it came to Luca? He was a sweet she wanted to consume in one bite—a shot of high-proof alcohol that went straight into her system and made her dizzy.

"Never." She leaned down and kissed him again, grinding against him, trying to be as close as possible. The less space there was between them, the fewer crevices for thoughts to creep in.

He was almost hesitant when he pulled on the waistband of her sweats, but she raised her hips and broke their kiss, standing to shimmy out of them. She made sure that she was staring right at him, all the lust she felt beaming at him, so he would know that he wasn't just a convenient body for her to work out her anger at her husband on. She was here with him because it was almost inevitable that they would get here.

From the moment they'd met, she'd wanted him. She'd put that want in the back of her mind, just below her conscious thoughts for so long that she'd fooled herself into believing it wasn't there anymore. But it had just been buried and not as deeply as she'd thought.

His hands against the skin on her hips were electric. She couldn't get enough of him. She pushed his shirt halfway up, and he stopped playing with the sides of her panties long enough to rip the lace seams and pull them off with one hand. His movements were efficient, and his lean torso was so corded that he almost seemed more dangerous with fewer clothes on.

Cece pulled herself away from him long enough to pull off his sweats. He wasn't wearing any underwear, so his cock sprang out. He was all angles and hard planes, except for this. She licked her lips, torn between going to her knees and putting him inside her right now.

Luca took her wrists in his hands and looked at her. She wanted to blush, but she couldn't manage it. The way he stared at her body, even though she was sure he'd seen more perfect bodies, made her feel like there was nothing to be embarrassed about. It was a kind of worship that she'd rarely experienced.

"I was tested a few weeks ago," she said. She bit her lip, wondering if she should explain further. "We had vaguely talked about a baby this year. But we haven't—not since then."

There was the embarrassment. She should have known that her husband was in the mood to have sex. Just not with her. Maybe she should have gotten him high. Or perhaps she'd already been in the process of being discarded, and she hadn't even known it.

"I was tested this week. Nothing was positive. And fucking my way through Europe as a way to bury my feelings hasn't been my thing in a while." He smiled against her lips, and she wondered if he was joking. She felt an unearned jealousy, but she wanted to feel him against her more than she wanted to interrogate him.

"It's not the right time of the month for me to get pregnant." She had been looking for Ethan so they could "practice" when she'd found him. He'd always gotten horned up by cocaine, and she'd wanted to take that one small advantage from his drug use.

Luca put his hands around her head and pulled her close. "Are you saying that you want me bare?"

If she was only going to get to have him once, she was definitely saying that. She wanted him with nothing between them. If this was only going to happen once, and she wasn't sure how it could ever happen again, she wanted nothing but him.

"Yes. I want all of *you* inside me." She wanted to walk back into the condo she shared with Ethan with his childhood best friend still inside her. It was petty and vengeful, but he'd been negligent and cruel. He had to pay a price, and she wanted a prize.

Luca ran a thumb across her bottom lip. "Remind me never to cross you."

"Okay." She bit the tip of his thumb and then sucked it. He pulled it away and then put that hand into her panties. He knew she was on edge somehow, so he homed in on her clit immediately. It was almost more pleasure than she could handle.

"I want you to come first. I need it from you." His voice was rough and demanding. She would play that quiet order in her head when she touched herself for a long time afterward. Every touch—even the way he breathed and the smell of his skin—went inside her memory bank for safekeeping. Even as her body spiraled toward orgasm.

As soon as they'd made contact, she'd known there would be an explosion. But knowing that didn't prepare her for feeling like she was flying through the air, weightless, not even bothering to brace for the crash.

They told the drivers to take their hands off the wheel if they knew they were going to hit the wall. It kept their hands and wrists safer from injury during an impact. Right now, there was nothing safe about taking her hands off the wheel and giving over control to Luca.

But she found that she didn't really care.

The feeling of Cecelia falling apart because of him would never leave Luca. He wasn't dumb enough to think they could carry on an affair, so he knew this one night had to last him for the rest of his life. Maybe it was because she was the only woman he could never have—not really—but Cece's orgasm made him feel like he was ten feet tall.

Everything happened fast after she came. It was like he'd made her hungrier. She lined up his cock with her entrance in what felt like a flash-forward in time. He was dazed by feeling her, watching her.

"I don't know if I should be flattered or insulted right now." He wasn't sure why he said that out loud. He didn't usually talk a lot during sex. It wasn't usually quite this intimate. That had never bothered him until now. But, with Cece, he felt the need to share a little more of himself.

She stopped, but kept her soft, little hand on him. He twitched in anticipation. Probably should have kept his mouth shut. "Why would you be insulted?"

He loved the way she cocked her head with the question. "Because I just made you come, and you need my dick right away. No afterglow."

"I feel like you do after a podium, right now." She leaned closely and whispered in his ear. "I need more adrenaline. More of a rush. Faster. I won, but I need to win more."

If he hadn't been hard enough to cut glass before, her words got him there now. "Take it."

When she lined him up again, he pressed his hips up, and they came together. Their sweat-damp skin pressed together, and he felt her everywhere. Neither of them spoke, but they looked at each other. He didn't usually look his partners in the eye while he was inside them. Again, way too intimate. But he couldn't get close enough to Cece. He wanted to crawl inside her skin and never leave. He wanted more. Faster. All of it. Right now.

And he let himself take more, allowing Cece to press and grind against his pelvis, clutching him tight inside her. She was soft everywhere, but also impossibly strong. He let her long, dark hair curtain their faces as he kissed her again. It felt like silk against his skin, catching against his stubble. He couldn't get enough of touching her delicate brown skin, learning the curves of her body, trying to memorize this the way he could still taste the champagne after his first win.

The sweat on her neck was better than that. He wanted to bottle it. Even though he wanted this moment to last forever, he knew it couldn't. His body was impatient. He needed to come inside her, to mark her as his. Just this once.

He picked her up enough to roll her to the side and on her back. She wrapped her legs around his hips and kept him gripped the whole time. They didn't talk anymore, and they didn't look at each other. The intensity of what they were both feeling individually was too much.

All he could think about was her. She was the whole world at that moment. He hadn't been fired. He'd never been her husband's best friend. He'd never even driven a race car. There was no struggle in the past or even in the future. He was a rutting beast, and she was his mate. It was primitive and grotesque and completely ecstatic.

Her third orgasm took him by surprise, and he felt it in his bones. She squeezed him so hard and scratched his back so deeply, he might have scars afterward. It sent him over the edge. He came until he felt empty. Until he felt new and used up at the same time.

It was almost unfair how good it was with her. How could she do this to him? Why had she given him a taste of paradise that he couldn't keep? He'd come to peace with the fact that he'd never have her—that he'd never even kiss her. It was the blueprint for how he was coming to peace with the fact that his career was most likely over.

Now, he would never know peace. He couldn't let her know she'd done this to him. It hadn't been intentional. Not even her fault really. He could have put a stop to this, tucked her into the spare bedroom, or even not let her in the door.

He was the one who was weak. But she couldn't know that.

So, he smiled down at her, cleaned her up, put her in his shirt and bed, and slept with her until she snuck out at dawn.

Cece walked into her apartment with her body still buzzing. Satisfaction and shame fought for supremacy beneath her skin. So much had happened last night that she couldn't tell which direction was up and which was down. Although she'd set out for revenge, the way Luca had touched her had turned last night into something else entirely.

By the time she got out of the hired car and made her way up to the penthouse in the clothes she'd been wearing last night—this dress was definitely ruined—she was exhausted. It was only a few blocks away from Luca's, but the distance felt so much more arduous because she didn't know what she was going to find once she returned home.

She opened the door to find that the housekeeper had already been there and gone. Ethan must have called them first thing this morning. Either he was disgusted at what he'd done the night before and wanted to remove all the evidence, or he'd thought ahead and had the service come in while they would still be asleep. She tried to harden herself against the fact that he was always thinking ahead. She both loved and hated that about him.

When Cece was growing up, she'd hated waking up the morning after her father had a party. One morning, she'd stepped on a smoldering joint on the floor. In retrospect, it was a good thing that she'd stepped there—she'd probably prevented her mother's little house from burning down. But it had hurt like a bitch, and she'd had a scar for a long time. Her father had moved out about a month later.

Cece had no idea whether her tearstained face and gasping sobs had done anything to make her mother wake up to the fact that her father was a loser, but she never had to wake up and clean up after her dad's creepy friends again.

It was too early in Miami to call her mother. Graciela would know what to do. She'd probably tell her to pack her shit while Ethan was still asleep and get on the next flight to Florida. A younger Cece would have done it. She could always go home. But there were enough years between who she was in Miami and who she was now that she hesitated to go back and crawl into her childhood bed.

Her mother would make her the strongest Cuban coffee on planet Earth, and they would figure out where her life would go next. But she knew it would be smaller than it was now. It would be anonymous and safe. That's what her mother had retreated to after kicking her father out.

Cece had always craved more. She'd been searching for excitement from the moment she'd gained even the tiniest bit of freedom. And, as much as she hated the press, she loved the notoriety that came with being married to Ethan. She loved getting to go on influencer trips. She loved the free stuff. The spas that wanted her to come in just so they could say she'd had a facial there. She liked the money.

She never would have gotten this from modeling. The few supermodels who existed were either the children of supermodels or other nepo baby varietals. She was always going to have to marry someone the world actually thought mattered to live the life she wanted to live. That was the deal she'd struck when she quit college and started bartending and taking print jobs. She'd decided that she wasn't a serious person before the world could make that clear to her.

The flat was quiet, and Cece wondered if Ethan was even there. Maybe he'd gotten up after fucking that other woman and gone elsewhere to party. She walked into her bedroom, hoping that was the case.

No such luck.

Ethan sat on the bed with his hair messed up from sleep. It was getting a bit too long, and it fell over one of his eyes. He didn't look at her right away. His face had creases in it where it had been stuck to the pillow. Cece found it difficult to look at him, but she didn't flinch. She wouldn't show how hurt she was by what he'd done. She didn't even know if he remembered.

He looked up at her, brow furrowed. "Where'd you go last night?" He didn't sound as posh in the morning with his normally sharp consonants dulled by sleep and substances.

Instead of throwing the stupid sculpture his mom had insisted putting on the credenza at his stupid, cheating head, Cece clenched her fist. "Where'd the slut go?"

Ethan's face went blank and confused. Maybe he was still a little high. "Slut?"

"Yeah, the skank you were railing on my side of the bed when I came looking for you last night. You were going to miss the countdown for our best year ever as a married couple, but I guess you found someone else to kiss."

Cece watched as panic set in on her husband's face. He'd blacked out. But he'd still done enough drugs and had enough to drink that he wouldn't remember, so Cece held him responsible.

"You didn't even think about the fact that someone could show up and test you for drugs at any time."

"I was in my own house. Those were old friends." He stood up and approached her, but she backed away. His torso seemed even more lean than usual this morning—a product of dehydration probably. "That had to be more than coke."

Cece walked into the bathroom. "Don't follow me."

Of course, he didn't listen. "You have to believe me."

"I don't have to do anything." She tried to slam the door in his face, but he wouldn't let her. "I need to shower, and I need to not kill you. I need to be alone for both of those things."

"Just listen to me." He sounded plaintive—weak. In that moment, she wondered why she'd ever been in love with him. She wanted to be back at Luca's condo. She never should have left his bed.

"I don't want to hear whatever you have to say."

She took off her clothes and hoped that Luca had given her a visible hickey or bruise from his fingers somewhere. Part of her wanted Ethan to see that someone else wanted her. But that was not a smart part of her. She needed to be the long-suffering wife, not the petty, cheating bitch who fucked his former best friend an hour after finding him with another woman.

But he didn't say anything as she stepped into the frosted-glass shower enclosure. She turned on the water so hot, it would burn her skin off. Hot enough to burn her sins away.

"Are you just going to divorce me without even letting me explain what happened?" Ethan asked, rubbing the last of the sleep out of his piercing blue eyes. They could see each other's faces. He rubbed his hands through his already messy, light-brown hair until it stuck up every which way. It still looked good—it always looked good—and she hated him for that on top of all the other things she hated him for.

And he'd asked a valid question. Was she going to divorce him? Last night, her answer would have been unequivocal and affirmative. But this morning, with her own transgression still buzzing in her bloodstream, she wasn't so sure.

As she cleaned her body, she remembered Luca's hands and mouth on her, his skin against hers. And she looked at her husband, a man who'd given her so much pleasure over the past five years that he was imprinted somewhere in her DNA. She'd carry a piece of him everywhere, no matter what happened in their marriage.

But she was so fucking angry at him. Maybe even angrier than she was at herself. For trusting him and then for reacting the way she did when he betrayed that trust.

If she just divorced him, she wouldn't get much. His parents had insisted on the prenup. At the time, Cece hadn't thought too much of it. She'd known that she could make her own way, no matter what. And she'd been so in love with Ethan that the idea that their marriage would end had been fantastical to her—like the existence of dragons or orcs.

Ethan chose that moment to look into her eyes. "Stay with me."

"I don't know." She really didn't know, and she was even less sure when he walked over to the shower. She was still hopelessly attracted to the man standing in front of her. They might have gotten too comfortable in their relationship and grown apart, but the connection between them persisted. Even her cells betrayed her at that moment.

"Give me until the end of summer break. It will never happen again."

"Why the end of summer break?" If his answer was what she suspected, she might just be setting herself up to get played. He might be using the fact that she'd always wanted the life he gave her to get her to stay. It would have nothing to do with not being able to bear the thought of losing her.

"You know my contract is up at the end of the season. With the new girl coming in and taking the other seat, I need to make sure that I'm not painted as an asshole cheater in the press."

It definitely wasn't because he loved her or that he wanted to make things work. Fucking prick. "How much?" She knew he already had a number in his head for how much he was willing to pay to save his reputation. Ethan always had a plan.

"Enough so that you can live comfortably and never work again."

"I want half the money you make from your next contract."

Ethan was one of the highest paid drivers on the grid. He'd won the championship twice at the beginning of his career, and that gave him significant power in the market. She might walk away with very little if she left him now, but half of his next contract would set her up for life.

Maybe she'd buy a little cottage in a small town in the South of France. No one she didn't like would ever hear from or see her again outside of an occasional appearance at Paris Fashion Week. She'd wear nothing but silk and cashmere and have ten dogs and a couple of horses. She'd read smutty books and drink rosé in the afternoons. She would never trust a man again.

Her life would be lonely, but perfect.

"Fine," Cece said. Ethan's face eased in relief. "But don't talk to me and definitely don't touch me unless it's for the cameras."

Scuderia Lupo Car Launch

—

Monza

Chapter Three

Five years. Luca hadn't been in the same room as Ethan for almost five years. Well, not intentionally. There was no way they could avoid each other completely while they were still on the grid together.

That was the one upside of getting fired. He wouldn't have had to spend any time with Ethan Harrow. Especially since he'd fucked Ethan Harrow's wife on New Year's Eve and felt approximately zero remorse for it.

Well, he'd have had a clear conscience had he retired in ignominy as planned. This sport had a funny way of pulling people back in, though. Micaela Cartwright had planned to sign with Ethan's team, Scuderia Lupo, for this season. Everyone had assumed the deal was done, until she'd changed her mind at the last minute and signed with the upstart American team on the grid, Panther Motors.

Although the sport was rife with scandals and skulduggery, it was extremely rare to have a seat open up during winter break. Since every other team had pulled up the rookies they wanted and made the moves there were to make, Luca Bendetto became the only viable option.

Luca didn't hesitate before saying yes. Even being a last-ditch option landed him a place on the grid, and that was better than being out in the cold. The complicated past and present between him and Ethan faded into the distance when the chance to race again came knocking. He could put his personal feelings—the ones that made him want to choke the shit out of Ethan—to the side for the sake of his career.

He looked forward to beating him on the track. It might even be as satisfying as it had been to take something from him off the track on New Year's Eve.

God, he hadn't been able to stop thinking about Cece since that morning. He might have given up most of his excesses, but only one taste had him seriously addicted to her. He hadn't changed his sheets for a few days after she'd been there, not until he couldn't catch whiffs of her scent on his pillow. He still sat on his couch where she'd ridden him and imagined that she was there sometimes.

He wondered if she'd be there today at the car launch. These things hadn't involved the sort of high spectacle they now did before Netflix, American fans, and American money found their way to the sport in the way they had the last few years.

Luca could play the game—he was a fan favorite on the documentary series—but he honestly preferred the way things had been before. He'd liked talking to sponsors at the factory about how great their logos looked on the new livery rather than the flashing lights and high drama.

But those days were gone. Now that he was back in the sport, he should really look at having his management team capitalize on the sport's massive popularity. He wasn't going to waste this second chance, even though returning to racing came with a price.

He checked himself in the mirror in his new team kit for the third time. He shook his head, trying to dislodge the nerves. Then, he checked his phone. He didn't have anything to worry about. Ethan was here, but Cece was at Paris Fashion Week.

Once he knew he was joining the team, Luca had set up a Google alert for mentions of her in the press and on social media. He knew it was stupid, but he couldn't help himself. He wanted to know where she was at all times. Like a fucking stalker.

He assured himself that he could conduct himself like a professional with Ethan. There was too much at stake for him to allow his personal feelings to get in the way of what he wanted to accomplish on the track.

When he'd steeled himself adequately, he went out to the podium area of the track. Elevated above the pit lane, he felt like a king. Even with the team and primary sponsored logos emblazoned on the bunting instead of the Grand Prix branding, he could almost smell the sparkling wine mixed with sweat on his race suit and see the team cheering his victory, even though he hadn't been above P6 in two years. He'd much rather be giving a victorious postrace interview than the gauntlet he'd been through of late. The team had announced his signing three days ago, so he'd been fielding press calls and giving interviews almost continuously since.

He could say all of the right things and make all of the right noises. "I'm delighted to be with the team," in both English and Italian. "Coming to Scuderia Lupo feels like coming home," also in both English and Italian. "Ethan and I have always had a strong working relationship. I don't see how this second go-round will be any different." That part was only in English because his Italian wasn't *that* good.

All of those pat phrases left him when he saw Ethan standing next to Alessandro, the team principal. Ethan hadn't spotted him yet because his smile was the real one, rather than the fake one he gave when he was uncomfortable. He loved the marketing shit. Mostly he'd always loved being in the spotlight. Luca could tell when Ethan noticed his presence as a shadow crossed his face. No one else knew that the fake Ethan smile had come online.

He wished it wasn't like that. He wished Ethan's face still lit up when Luca walked into a room. When they were younger, they'd been each other's person. For years, it had been totally platonic. And Luca hadn't noticed precisely when things shifted to something romantic.

Probably the first time they'd had sex with the same girl at the same time. It was callous to say, but it was as though that girl hadn't even mattered. It had been like she wasn't even there, and it was just the two of them together.

They had never talked about it, but they'd started sharing girls on a regular basis. And then, they'd started touching each other during their threesomes. It probably wasn't even intentional the first few times it had happened, but then they'd started kissing.

On the track, they'd remained teammates and rivals. But, off the grid, they were something else that neither of them made any effort to define entirely.

Luca hadn't realized that he was in a relationship with—in love with—his best friend until they'd met Cece. And Ethan hadn't wanted to share. He'd wanted to win her. Suddenly, their personal relationship had started to feel like their professional rivalry on the track.

When it became clear that Ethan was serious about Cece, when he'd proposed, Luca had lost his shit a little. He'd been a jealous lover before the engagement, but he'd acted like one after. Part of it was that he'd had feelings for Cece too. And he'd thought it was going to be perfect—all three of them together. They could all just go on and pretend it was just about sex, and nothing had to change.

But apparently, Ethan hadn't liked that idea. He'd wanted things to change. He'd wanted to be in an ordinary, hetero marriage with the girl they were both in love with. And he'd wanted to end things with Luca without even ever saying what they had together.

The car—well at least the shell of the car—came up to meet the three men on a hydraulic lift.

Luca tried to tear his gaze from Ethan, but Ethan needed to look away first. Their smiles never faltered, but there were decades of history, anger, and yearning passing between them at that moment.

It was going to be a long season.

Preseason Testing
—
Bahrain

Chapter Four

Wyatt Bailey, Commentator: "And the big news this week is that silly season wasn't over until it was indeed over. Luca Bendetto is now teamed with Ethan Harrow at Scuderia Lupo. The shake-up came as Panther Motors stole Micaela Cartwright out from under Lupo. Not only is she the first female driver with a permanent spot on the grid in decades, but she's also the most controversial driver. Laura had Luca in the press pen a few hours ago, before testing started."

Laura Baxter, Reporter/Commentator: "Thank you, Wyatt. Yes, I was able to speak with Luca at the livery launch, and he seemed just as in shock as the rest of us. By all accounts, his career in this series was over, and he was just about to sign with an IndyCar series team that he won't now name. But I'll let him tell you all how he feels in his own words."

Luca Bendetto, Driver, Scuderia Lupo: "I'm just really grateful to be back in the Lupo family. In this sport, you have to grab onto every opportunity you're given. I know I'm going to get what I've wanted—forever—at Lupo."

Laura Baxter: "Do you think you'll be able to nick a World Championship off of Ethan this year?"

Luca: "That and more, Laura. That and more."

There was a real first day of school feeling as Luca walked through the paddock in Bahrain. The flat tops of the permanent concrete structures were reminiscent of the traditional coral-and-palm-frond buildings in the archipelago and felt familiar to him—as though he could finally breathe. Everything about his joining Lupo had been rushed and last-minute, but the feeling of being back—truly back—slipped over him with a sense of rightness that he hadn't realized he'd missed. A calm had come over him when his driver had pulled up to the circuit in the middle of the Sakhir desert.

During testing, there weren't as many spectators as there usually were at the track, so he made his way easily to the temporary team facilities, which housed offices and hospitality. During race week, he'd have to push his way through crowds of fans who wanted a selfie or an autograph, and he'd need his trainer or someone from the team with him to keep him from being waylaid.

Toward the end of his time with his previous team, he'd kind of resented the entitlement that fans of the sport had over his time and image. He'd always put on a good face, but he was a mostly private guy. He hadn't grown up destined to become a racing driver. His father had taken him to a karting track when he was eight for his birthday, and Luca had fallen in love with the feeling of flying over the ground.

Luca's father had seen the pure joy on his son's face and took him back the following weekend—and the next and the next. Luca had no idea how his family had afforded it. He hadn't really thought about the fact that they sold one of their cars, and his mom took the bus to work. His father had taken gig work after his day job doing accounting.

Most of the kids he competed against had fathers who were in the racing world. Or they came from so much money that their families could afford the expense. Once they were old enough, it was normal for posh families to send their kids off to boarding school. So, it totally made sense for them to send their racers off to Europe once they'd graduated from karting around the UK.

His family had wrestled with it, but Luca's desire to continue racing—and his pure talent—made it impossible for them to refuse him. But Luca had never quite shaken off the feeling of not belonging among the other drivers—even when he'd won a championship his third year racing.

That was what had bothered him about losing his seat to a paid driver at the end of the last season—it had been like a confirmation that he shouldn't be there and had never deserved it. He'd been languishing in the backmarker team with a tiny budget, but he'd been clinging on just the same.

Even with the complications brought by being teammates with Ethan, he wasn't going to waste this opportunity.

He saw Heka Godwinson—his shock of blond hair and determined stride were hard to miss—and expected him to walk past, but the other driver stopped. Luca had always liked Heka. He was taciturn and grumpy about having to do anything but race the car, but he could always be trusted to be straightforward. Heka was a little bit older than him and Ethan, and they'd both looked up to him as they'd risen through the ranks.

Luca anticipated that the veteran driver would mumble a greeting and move on, but the Finnish former champion clapped him once on the shoulder. "I'm glad to see you back."

That was likely as close to saying, "I miss you," as Heka ever got. His usually flat mouth even turned up into something resembling a smile.

"Things turned out all right."

"If it makes you feel better, they didn't even come to me to fill the seat." Given that Heka had won two championships in a row and was always on the list when a team needed someone fast and aggressive, that made Luca feel a lot better. Lupo had wanted him and not just any warm body.

It didn't matter what the press release said or how the team principal spun the move, the team had egg on their face because their once-in-a-lifetime talented female driver had chosen to sign on with the American team.

Micaela Cartwright was supposed to bring the storied Scuderia Lupo into the future, and she'd jumped ship. It made the team look bad, and there would be questions about why she'd made that decision for years to come.

It would have made perfect sense for a team to go with a veteran driver—one who hadn't been fired. That Lupo had taken a chance on him without going that route made him feel better. Heka had a reputation for making people feel worse, even when he tried to comfort them, so this was different.

"I'm done racing after this year, anyway." There it was. He wasn't offered the job, because the team wanted experience *and* stability. Luca was still definitely not the top choice. Given that a driver was only as good as their last race, he probably wasn't even in their top ten choices. But he was the only guy available on short notice.

"I never thought you'd quit, Heka. If I'd had to hazard a guess, you'd be trying to race into your dotage."

The older man laughed, which was kind of a startling sound because it didn't happen very often. "I want to spend more time with my children." He didn't say anything about his wife, which figured. Jocelyn was kind of a bitch, and Luca had guessed that she was the only woman who would put up with Heka's brusque nature.

"Makes sense. It's good to see you." Luca moved on before it all became more awkward.

Since he was a last-minute addition to the team, he'd flown here a day early—straight from the factory car launch at Monza. Yesterday, he'd posed for all of the promotional photos he'd missed back in early February, when he'd still thought he was out of racing for good.

Today, when he walked into the team facility, Ethan would be there. They hadn't seen each other since the car launch, and the tense energy made him wonder how they were both going to survive the season.

Though his former friend was polished, Luca could sense the enmity underneath his responses to the press, which awakened Luca's competitive instinct. Maybe this would be a good thing.

He opened the door to Lupo's facility and ran right into Cece. Time slowed as he took her in. She was as flawless as she usually was in head-to-toe linen with nary a crease—a contrast to the way she'd appeared undone when she'd showed up at his door. She pasted a smile on her face but lost it after she looked around to see that there were no cameras. With a slight shake of her head, she moved around him, careful to avoid touching him at all.

—

In her brand-new trailer at her brand-new team, Micaela switched off the television. She felt sick to her stomach, but it wasn't because she was nervous about making her debut on the grid in testing this weekend. She felt sick because she had to wear a gown at a gala so that her new team could trot her out to sponsors.

Her new boss, Liam Sullivan, had sent a glam team to deal with her. He knew she'd spent her entire adolescence in a go-kart and then various single seaters, racing against mostly boys. And any signs or symptoms of girliness or softness had been browbeaten out of her by her father a long time ago.

Liam knew all of this intimately, because she'd dated his son for years—until a year ago. And his son was her new teammate.

She wasn't sure what had possessed her the day Liam had called and offered a seat at Panther. Part of it was because Lupo had been dicking her around for months; various members of the team had leaked name after name of other potential drivers for the open Lupo seat after she'd been announced as their new driver.

Everyone at Scuderia Lupo had assured her everything was fine. And she'd had a contract sitting in her dad's office at his estate in Kent. She'd been surrounded by all of the big game trophies he'd collected after his racing career had ended. They'd stared down at her—all eyes and antlers and fangs—as though they were waiting for her to become one of them. If she'd signed that contract, she would just be another one of her father's accomplishments. An object that he'd created out of his own violence. The impulse that she was signing away some essential part of her agency warred with her desire to prove herself to the world. She'd not only be the first female driver with a permanent spot on the grid in decades, but she'd be with one of the most storied teams in racing.

Ethan would retire in a couple of years, and then she'd be the number one driver on a top team if she was fast enough. And she knew she could. She had to have an even bigger ego than the guys she raced against. She was just "the girl" until she beat them by more than a mere nose, more than once. She had to spank them all, over and over again.

If she were a boy, it would have mattered that she was the progeny of Jack Cartwright, three-time world champion. The rest of the paddock would speak her name with quiet reverence if she were Michael instead of Micaela. Hell, her father probably would have revived his old team from the dead for her. But it seemed that she had more to prove because of her last name on top of her gender.

It wasn't fair, but she also didn't give a shit about fair. She showed up at the track ready to win, every time.

That was what made her pick up Liam's call when the ringtone shocked her out of signing the Lupo contract. She hadn't spent much time with Liam while she'd dated Brent. Liam was a team principal, which meant that he was a very busy and important man. And he and Brent had a weird relationship.

She and Brent had only started talking because their fathers were both legends in motorsports. They both had cute sob stories about how they started karting because that was the only way that their daddies would pay attention to them—winning was the only way any praise would fall from their lips.

It was clichéd, but Micaela had later learned that while her stories about her father's casual cruelty were completely accurate, Brent's were wildly exaggerated. Brent's little cousin had filled her in on that during the one family vacation she'd taken with them. Liam adored his child.

Liam was a compelling man. He'd have to be to start an American F1 team from scratch after dominating every racing series on the other side of the Atlantic—first as a racer, then as an owner. It didn't hurt that his family had oil money dating back to the early 1900s, but he didn't have to work that hard. He was just driven by something inside him that Micaela recognized and shared.

Brent, on the other hand, was your average rich little prick that was only motivated by money and attention. That's why he'd dated her in the first place. He wanted to siphon off some of her glow. He wanted the world to think that he was some great feminist because he was dating another driver, instead of an Instagram model. He wanted to prove that he wasn't threatened by a girl infiltrating their macho fiefdom at the pinnacle of motorsports.

She'd thought they were a friends-to-lovers story, but a few months ago, she'd learned it was bullshit. As soon as she'd started getting offers from teams for a permanent seat rather than just a reserve or test driver role, things had changed.

He'd started asking her whether she was sure she was ready—whether she could physically hold up to a full season of racing. He'd reminded her of the time she'd puked from heatstroke during an endurance race in Dubai. She'd almost let his words sink in until she'd remembered that her water bottle had malfunctioned in Dubai, and Brent himself had thrown up in his own helmet and had to be dragged out of his car by three mechanics after last year's race in Qatar.

At least she'd finished her race before needing medical attention in the desert.

She worked harder than Brent. She was actually physically stronger than him, because he was a lazy piece of shit who got into the sport because his father owned a team.

Her father, on the other hand, refused to pay for her to have a seat. She'd gotten some sponsorships because of her last name, but she'd hustled and pulled those together for herself.

And then, there were the pictures of Brent on a yacht with a supermodel. On the weekend of her former stepmother's funeral. Those had been the last straw. She might have believed his excuse—that he'd lost track of the days during summer break—if it hadn't been her favorite ex-stepmother. But she was really sad that Sylvie had passed away during her ill-advised third facelift.

She wasn't sure why Liam had offered her the seat. They'd had a perfectly competent driver paired with Brent who had scored most of the points for the team the previous season. It didn't make sense to have a total newbie paired with her ex-boyfriend, instead. But Micaela hadn't seen that angle—she'd only seen the potential for revenge.

After she'd done it, her father had a fit. *I should have made you take up a sport for girls—like tennis. You're too much like me and not enough like your mother, God rest her soul. Of course, you'd go and fuck up your whole career over a piece of tail. You'll never win the world championship now. You know you're nothing but a publicity stunt for that team, don't you?*

A few hours later, wearing a stupid gown that the team press officer, Paola Rodriguez, had forced her into, standing at the back of a ballroom instead of holing up in her room and preparing like any other rookie, she wasn't sure that her father was wrong.

Maybe the team didn't care as much about winning as they did about having her as a token girl. No one outside the paddock really knew about Brent and Micaela's previous relationship—they'd never gone Instagram official. It had seemed like a conflict of interest, given that she'd been a reserve driver at the time. So, maybe they just wanted the feminist shine of having a girl as a driver.

Micaela snagged a glass of champagne off a passing waiter's tray. She needed to be sharp tomorrow, but she clocked three other drivers having a drink. She was actually jealous of Danny's beer. But that wouldn't really go with the fucking pink tulle in her dress.

She had to get a stylist of her own. If she had her druthers, she'd be in something black and maybe leather. She could look feminine while also looking dangerous.

Like Cece Ramos, Ethan Harrow's wife, did. She wasn't wearing black or leather, but there was definitely danger to the way the sides of her breasts were perched in a white halter Valentino gown. She always looked badass, though. Even the pearls cascading from her ears—culturally relevant given Bahrain's role in the global pearl trade—made her look a little bit cool and untouchable.

But tonight, she looked badass and unhappy. Micaela hesitated for a second about walking over to her. Just because she had confidence in the car didn't mean she didn't have the same worries as any other twenty-two-year-old woman—that everyone hated her all the time.

Her job probably made that even worse. The boys just had more options for dealing with it. They could cry or punch walls. Someone would ask her if she was on her period if she did either of those things.

But Cece had always been nice to her—she'd even told a mechanic to shut his fucking face when he'd called Micaela an "entitled bitch" once after a support race. Hell, she'd come to the support race to cheer her on. Maybe she was upset that her husband's ex-best friend was the new driver for Lupo, but she wouldn't take that out on Micaela.

She just walked over. Cece smiled when she saw Micaela, but there was something weird about the look on her face. Now that she was closer, Micaela could see that Cece was gripping her glass so tightly it looked like it would break.

"Are you okay?" That was probably the wrong thing to ask. Cece was kind to her, but they were not close. She wasn't sure if she could even call the woman a friend. *There are no actual friends in the paddock, my girl. You'd do well to remember that. And keep your legs closed!* She should really maybe start taking her father's advice much more seriously.

"Not really." Okay, so they were doing honesty? Cool. "How are you doing? A lot has happened since the Christmas party."

"Yeah." Micaela took a sip of champagne. "Everybody's mad at me, aren't they?"

Cece threw her head back and laughed. Even her guffaws were sort of elegant. Micaela knew that she hadn't come from money, but she'd adapted to the world she'd married into seamlessly. Maybe she should take some sort of lesson from her. "Honestly, you caused some chaos, but I kind of admire it." She looked at Micaela and put a hand on her shoulder. “No one hates you.” Then, she scrunched up her nose. “Except for probably Brent right now. And he deserves to have his feathers ruffled, doesn’t he?”

Brent wasn’t at the gala. It was required for drivers, but he’d refused to attend and thrown something at the guy who’d tried to wrestle him into a tux. Micaela hadn’t seen it, but it was hard not to hear within the temporary structures at the paddock.

“You’re going to beat him so soundly.” Cece seemed sure about that. They both lifted their glasses, but Micaela noticed that Cece only took a sip. Cece loved champagne, which could only mean—

“No. No. I just—bad things happen when I drink too much champagne.” Okay, there was definitely a story there, but Cece didn’t seem to want to divulge details. Everyone had started speculating that she and Ethan would try for a baby if he won the championship last year. When that hadn’t happened—the final race had been highly controversial due to a safety car incident—everyone thought he might retire.

“I get the timing is bad.” Micaela had an IUD for precisely that reason. She enjoyed sex, but she’d been absolutely opposed to any tiny Brent-lets after dealing with the full-size version.

Cece saw that Micaela’s glass was empty and swapped with her. “You have absolutely no idea.”

“If you need to talk . . .” Micaela recognized the value of the gossip she’d just stumbled on, but she felt like she owed Cece for being cool with her. Some WAGs might have looked right through her or said nasty shit about her, just because she was another woman who spent so much time with her husband. But Cece was a good one.

There was definitely something going on. And Micaela would cover for her—whatever her secret was—by having a second glass of champagne.

But Cece didn’t give her anything. It was as though she had a mask that looked just like her face, and she put it on and became Public Cece. It didn’t bother Micaela—this sport could be a den of vipers—but she wished they were close enough friends that Cece could keep her mask off.

They made small talk for a few minutes, and then Cece wandered off to talk to Jocelyn Godwinson and some of the other WAGs. She didn't follow, because Jocelyn terrified her. She was mean and calculating and had said something about how she was fine with a female driver on the grid—as long as her husband wasn't paired with a girl.

Micaela turned and scanned the party for someone she should talk to. She was glad she had that second glass in her hand when she saw Liam in a tux. Of course, she'd seen everyone involved in the sport in a tux at one time or another, but it was different now that he was her boss instead of just her ex-boyfriend's nice and very good-looking dad.

Although he was a retired racing driver, Liam looked more like a swimmer—long-limbed and tall, with wide shoulders and a narrow waist. He had dark hair like Brent, but with a sprinkling of gray above his ears. He had a slightly crooked nose and a scar through his left eyebrow from a crash that had nearly ended his career—and his life.

Brent would never be as handsome as Liam. All of his injuries had been immediately set, healed, and erased completely. He'd be smooth and poreless until he died. Liam had distinguished lines around his eyes, because he'd driven in the early aughts, before men learned about sun protection. He had a slight hitch in his step from when he'd broken his ankle in the terrifying crash she'd seen over and over again in replays. He shouldn't have survived.

But he did. Liam seemed indestructible and immovable to her. People loved Liam. He was one of the boys and knew everyone on the team by name.

Brent, they tolerated.

Tolerated wasn't the word she would use for how she felt about Liam. When she'd dated Brent, he'd made sure to invite her to family dinners after the Grand Prix and on vacation with them during summer break.

He'd even invited her to Christmas once, when he'd heard her father was in the Maldives with prospective wife number six. But Micaela had been too embarrassed to take him up on the offer. He gave her a warm feeling inside that she couldn't quite trust. He made her feel special in a way that wasn't exactly paternal. So, she'd spent the holiday alone at her father's house with takeaway curry and some of Sir Jack's oldest and most expensive scotch.

Sometimes, she'd thought of Liam while she was with Brent. Just thinking about that now had her face heating, and that was when he walked right up to her.

Even though he was all dressed up and she could see where his hair was still damp in the back from a recent shower, he still smelled a little bit of motor oil. They didn't even use conventional motor oil in the cars, but it was like this close-to-raw petroleum scent had latched on to him in 2002 and never let go.

That was the year she was born. She shouldn't be thinking about the way he smelled. He was two decades older than her. He was her ex-boyfriend's dad. And, most importantly, he was her boss.

There was no way that he would have hired her if he felt anything but appreciation for her talent. There was no way that he felt heat creeping up his spine when he touched her upper arm in a totally innocent gesture and asked, "Ready for tomorrow?"

Her triceps twitched under his fingers. She had to have more upper body strength than most women so she could control the car, especially in the lower formulas where the handling wasn't as easy as it was in her current ride. But that didn't make it easy. And she didn't have fashionable, little-bird arms. Not like the women Liam probably dated—not that she'd ever seen him with anyone while she was with Brent. And not like the girl that Brent had cheated with.

But she liked her arms. *She liked her arms.* She had to like herself as much as she could because no one else would love her enough to make up for the things she didn't like about herself.

She missed his touch when he dropped his hand and took a sip of some amber liquid—probably fifty-year-old scotch. She licked her lips thinking about how smoky and rich his mouth would taste.

Micaela gathered up every scrap of ego she'd built over the years and said, "I was born ready."

He laughed, and she wished she didn't notice how much she liked it. It made her want to crack a joke when she wasn't funny at all. She hadn't had time to develop a sense of humor while proving that she was better than all of the boys.

"Have you seen Brent?" Micaela wasn't sure what Liam knew about the circumstances of their breakup. He'd obviously seen the pictures and knew they were no longer dating. But did he know that Micaela had called Brent a cowardly little toad who didn't deserve anything he had? Did he know that she'd told him he was only in the seat because his daddy owned the team? Did he know that she'd taken him up on his offer not because she was so completely fine with Brent a year after they'd broken up that they could work together, but partially out of pettiness and spite?

The way he looked at her, as though he could see right through her, made her think he knew all of those things and more.

She shook her head. "I don't think he's here yet."

Liam grimaced. She'd hate to have him angry at her—she still couldn't seem to break her habit of trying to please the most powerful man in the room—but he looked even better when he was peeved about something.

She didn't know what came over her, but she put her hand on his arm. His tuxedo was obviously made for him, but the heat of his skin seeped through all the layers of cloth, and she felt like it singed her skin. "I'm sorry." Why was she apologizing? She didn't apologize for herself—much less anyone else.

"He's my son. I know exactly how he operates." Liam sighed. Did he know what his son was like when they were together? Did he ever think of warning her? Did he offer her the seat in hopes that they would get back together, and she would straighten Brent's shit out?

"Liam, I'm so grateful for the opportunity—"

He looked at her then, and she didn't know what to say when he did that. "I didn't hire you because of my son. I hired you because you are quicker than any of the other drivers out of contract. I saw the numbers in the Lupo sim."

Micaela felt as though she could breathe again for the first time since he'd approached her. "I didn't want that kind of talent stymied by a machismo-driven Italian team that always would have put Ethan Harrow first."

"I'm still grateful."

Liam laughed, but it sounded as though he was tired. "That makes one of my drivers."

Chapter Five

Every time Liam saw Micaela Cartwright in the flesh, he cursed himself for hiring her. The glittering lights on the super yacht, the very fine scotch, and the hundred other women who were more appropriate for him to look at had all faded away when he'd looked at her. He'd spent plenty of time castigating himself for how much he liked looking at her when she'd dated his son, but apparently not enough.

She was too young for him. She'd dated his son. And now, she was his employee. There wasn't a universe—not even in motorsports—where a relationship between the two of them would be possible.

And it wasn't even a relationship he thought about. They were both in the same professional world, but he doubted they had anything in common beyond that. No, he was obsessed with her in a way that made him want to tear off his skin every time they were in the same room.

He'd had to work so hard to be nice to her at the gala the night before, because he felt like an angry bear woken from hibernation a few months too early when he'd seen the tasteful flashes of skin that showed in the dress that Paola had selected for her.

And then, he'd wanted to find his son to tear his head off. How could he be so stupid as to cheat on her? And it wasn't just the way she looked. Liam had dated some of the most beautiful—age-appropriate—women in the world after his first wife had left him for someone who wasn't obsessed with cars driving in fucked-up circles for most of the year. Someone who could give her more than four weeks in the summer and four weeks at the holidays.

Micaela hadn't even wanted that from Brent. She'd wanted to be part of the same world, and she'd clawed her way through the ranks, despite how opposed most of the old men in the paddock were to seeing her there.

And that was probably the issue. Brent knew that Micaela was faster than him. He'd seen the numbers from that test session in Silverstone. Didn't matter that they were top secret. Very little stayed secret among the teams that made up the grid.

Liam reminded himself of that as he watched Micaela zip up her racing suit. He had to fight not to turn his body toward her from the pit wall, and sweat dripped down the small of his back despite the temperate winter weather in the desert. She moved efficiently, pulled her balaclava and helmet on with determination. And then, she looked at him. He didn't grimace at her, and he didn't smile. Though he was tempted to do both.

She tempted him with her talent and excitement and passion. It didn't hurt that she had green eyes that seemed to see everything, down to his very soul. Her wavy, blond, surfer-girl hair was tucked into her fireproofs and completely covered, but he could still see the glint of the sun hitting it in the desert heat.

She was heaven to look at, and he was going to hell for looking at her. He barked a couple of orders at the head engineer, knowing he'd have to apologize later. He'd spend years atoning for his actions when it came to Micaela Cartwright at this pace.

He should talk to her, make sure she wasn't nervous about getting in the car for testing. It would be the first time she drove this year's car, and everyone in the factory was excited about where they were in development.

They'd secured an influx of funding from a financial firm that wanted to seem more cool and less monstrous, so they could spend all the way up to the cap this season. The numbers from the wind tunnel were excellent.

Although the team had shocked everyone by installing themselves in the midfield from their first season—even on a shoestring budget—this car should shoot them into the stratosphere. If the numbers were right.

And they could never be sure.

There was more to the lump in his throat than just her performance. He was nervous seeing Micaela get in the car that he built. Would it work for her driving style? Was every single part installed correctly? Would she be safe?

He should be worrying more about his son. Brent had shown up this morning at the track looking as though he hadn't slept. His trainer had assured him that he'd spent the night in the hotel room, but it's not like Adam couldn't be paid off or even fired if he didn't toe the line that Brent ordered him to.

But Liam didn't worry about Brent. He'd seen him drive a Hot Wheels Range Rover into a wall at its admittedly slow top speed, smash it to bits, and get out of the wreck giggling. He was resilient. And he'd learn to deal with his jealousy over Micaela having a seat and possibly becoming the team's number one driver as a rookie.

Liam saw great things for Micaela. As she slotted herself in the seat and looked at her engineer for last-minute instructions, he reminded himself that none of those great things included touching her.

Micaela vowed to herself, quietly, that she would never forget the feeling of dropping into her seat for the first time. In some of the lower series, the ones with spec cars, all of the seats were designed for boys—or people without meaningful curves. She'd had to wedge herself into a seat made for someone her size but narrower.

This seat, however, had been made specifically for her. The Panther engineers would listen to her feedback about the car, which they hadn't always done at Lupo when she was their reserve driver. She'd spent hours in the simulator, only to have some fifty-year-old man not believe her when she said that the balance of the car was wrong for a particular track.

That guy had gotten yelled at when Ethan spun into the gravel during practice, but Micaela had only been able to give the guy an "I told you so" look or two. She'd had no power within that team.

Technically, she didn't have much power in this team either. She was just a rookie, and still just a girl. But she didn't let that stop her from feeling a little bit special when her very own engineer did the radio check.

There was nothing like driving this particular car. She couldn't imagine a bigger rush than feeling all of that power around her body as she hurtled across the track. Maybe that's why they hadn't wanted girls to do it for so long—they were afraid they'd get a taste of this kind of wild autonomy and never be able to let it go.

She was aware of every breath, maybe even every pulse, as she took her first slow lap, weighed down with big, metal screens that served as sensors.

She knew this was more about the car than her in the car, but her heart leaped when her engineer, Frankie, said in a rolling Scottish accent, "Go ahead and take a fast lap."

As soon as she turned down the final straight, she changed the engine settings and went full throttle. The force of it seemed to move the organs in her body and she felt like she was seriously airborne for a moment. But she wasn't flying, and she was totally in control of her own body.

It didn't matter that she was hot, her neck ached as she fought to hold up her head against the g's going around the first corner, and everyone was watching for her to make a mistake. She was totally free at that moment.

Maybe she'd always been too focused on her goal of making it here that she'd never considered why drivers had a history of risky and reckless behavior off the track. But she knew it for sure now. They were monarchs in the car. Someone else might hand them the keys to this kingdom, but they were untethered by the regular rules of physics when they were behind the wheel. It was so heady that she couldn't imagine giving up that kind of power.

Maybe she could forgive Brent for behaving like an asshole when things in her life had gotten real. Who wanted real when you could have this make-believe world where everything happened at your whim? Where, as long as you focused, you were on top of the world.

Media Day
—
Bahrain

Chapter Six

Cameras clicked and flashes went off as Ethan sat on the couch at the front of the media room. Looking over at Brent Sullivan sitting on the other end, he sighed. The guy looked about as rough as he felt. He'd barely slept since seeing Luca Bendetto at the car launch. Hell, he'd barely slept since cheating on his wife on New Year's Eve. The constant threat of Cece slitting his throat in the middle of the night competed with thoughts about how he'd fucked up the only real friendship—the only real intimate relationship—he'd ever had before Cece in keeping him up at night.

He knew that 90 percent of the questions he faced this weekend would have to do with how he felt about having his former best friend and karting buddy as a teammate. He'd been happier when most of the questions were going to have to do with how he felt about having a girl as a teammate.

That he'd felt great about. Micaela Cartwright was a racing driver, through and through. He wasn't foolish enough to believe that she would be easier to beat, even with all of his experience. Her father had been a world champion, and he'd trained her from birth to be an assassin on the track. She was going to give every driver on the grid a run for their money.

He was glad to see that her team had put her in the pen for the first media day. Of course, everything she said today would end up broadcast all over the world. But she could answer questions to individuals, instead of sitting under blinding lights and being interrogated like she was a suspect or something.

Interrogation made him think of his wife, and a pit formed in the middle of his chest where his warm feelings for her used to be. She'd barely spoken to him since the New Year. He'd woken up alone and naked that morning, feeling like he'd been hit by a train. There'd been nothing but a huge blank spot from the night before. And then—after she walked in and hated him—pieces started coming back.

He remembered kissing her before people had shown up for the party. The way she'd trailed her fingers across his cheek and told him that he'd missed a spot shaving. That was the last time he'd gotten close enough to smell her.

Then, a bunch of friends he hadn't seen since secondary school brought some DJ from Ibiza to the party. There was champagne, and then he thought he did a line of coke—one line wouldn't hurt. And all the memories turned into flashes of him destroying his life as though he wasn't even the one in control of his body.

His wife was no longer in love with him. She could barely look at him as she passed the spare bedroom where she'd moved all of his things. She'd flown commercial to Bahrain last week for the gala he'd begged her to attend, and she wasn't showing back up at the track until tomorrow.

Their marriage hadn't been perfect before New Year's Eve. He'd been able to feel her pulling away from him as she got more involved in charity and influencing. It wasn't fair for him to expect her to sit around and wait for him whenever he could give her a few tidbits of time, but that's what he'd wanted. He didn't want her to be in London while he was at the car launch. He wanted her at the track with him.

His assistant had informed him that she'd booked two rooms for them. Cece had told him he needed his sleep, and she was too restless these days.

Ethan knew what was going to happen. She would stay with him until summer break to secure her future—maybe that's all she'd ever cared about—but she would leave him. He knew she would never be able to forgive him for cheating. But he didn't want to accept it. He loved his wife. He'd given up his best friend—and sometimes more—because he couldn't stand the idea of someone else touching her.

And he knew that she loved him too. Although he might have been the one to pursue her, she'd shown him how much she loved him every day since they'd met. Sometimes, he felt like she was the only person in his life who truly understood him. Who saw him.

The only other person who'd given him that feeling of—almost safety, but way more than that—wasn't in his life anymore because of Cece. Ethan was so greedy when it came to her. He could remember the night he'd spotted her in that club like it happened last night.

She'd woven her way through the crowd to the VIP area where he had a table with Luca. But she hadn't approached their table. They weren't in her section.

He still wasn't sure why he'd decided to approach her. Sure, she had the best ass he'd ever seen, and he'd wanted to run his fingers through her long, curly hair. But he'd seen a lot of fine asses in his lifetime.

It was probably the way she'd looked at him and rolled her eyes. She wasn't impressed with him, and that just made him want to impress her. It made him want her.

He'd never had to put too much energy into pursuing a woman before. He was good-looking, quick, and his family had loads of money. He was pretty sure that socialites were given his dossier every time he was scheduled to show up at a party.

Years later, he realized that this level of success and privilege had turned him into an asshole—truly, almost insufferable. But Cece had suffered the displeasure of his company for a drink. Probably because she'd enjoyed giving him a hard time. And getting teased and cajoled wasn't something he'd ever experienced before. Not even at boarding school—the aggression there was always more serious and violent.

Cece was a breath of fresh air. She was someone that he hadn't known he'd needed until she was in his life. And he fought to keep her there. He immediately noticed how Bendetto looked at her, and something made him territorial over this particular woman. He couldn't share her, like he had shared with his best friend before.

He didn't even tell her he and his best friend had shared women and sometimes hooked up when they were alone. He wasn't sure if he was ashamed of his sexuality or afraid that he'd lose her if Bendetto got anywhere near her.

It had been fine when they'd all been friends. It had even been okay when he'd had Cece all to himself. But he'd lost her, and he wasn't fine anymore.

"Ethan, you've been asked this question a million times—"

The commentators always started the same way. *Then why are you asking me again?*

"Can you give us any insight into how you and Luca Bendetto are working together now that you're reunited on the same team?"

Why did they always have to make it sound like they were getting the band back together, and that was a good thing? It was a terrible decision that he was half certain the team had made out of a desire for ratings that would come from the drama.

"Although, as you know, a driver's teammate is their biggest competitor, Luca and I have worked together before. We know how to behave like professionals." That was the answer his years of media training taught him to give. He sat back on the couch and held the microphone loosely in one hand, feigning a casual vibe that he didn't feel. He wanted to break the microphone in half and scream.

He was so glad that he could get in the car tomorrow. The team had given some of his test time to the new reserve driver, but he craved the focus he felt as soon as he strapped on the helmet. It was only a practice session, but it would be an hour without having to talk to the press or avoid the daggered glares from his wife.

Soon, someone was going to notice that something was off between the two of them. Since they'd started dating, and he'd convinced her to travel with him, they'd always held hands when entering the paddock every day. Today, he walked into the paddock alone, and he suspected that Cece wouldn't be touching him anytime soon. Not even to keep up appearances.

He got through the rest of the press conference without growling at any of the reporters, and he put on a good face to sign autographs and take pictures with fans in the paddock—until someone asked him where Cece was. He wasn't upset that she got almost as much attention as he did. She had the kind of beauty that radiated from the inside out. It made people wonder—including him—if she could possibly be as kind and funny as she seemed on TV.

When they'd met, she'd been living an ordinary life. She had a job that was never going to make her rich and famous, but everyone she worked with loved her. The short time he'd spent in her world had been a lesson in humility. He hadn't been the world-famous race car driver. He'd been the guy who was going to take everyone's favorite person away.

The idea that he was going to do that again, in public this time, made his chest ache. Sweat poured down the back of his neck, and he suspected his team kit would have sweat marks all over it by the time he got back to his room in the team motor home—the room right next to Luca.

Thinking about having to be in close proximity to his former best friend and occasional lover—while everything in his marriage was falling apart—was almost too much. He couldn't afford to lose focus, couldn't afford to let the mask slip. And yet, he wasn't sure how to stop it.

Once he got to the private team area, someplace air-conditioned, without press and fans taking a hundred pictures of him a second, he took a deep breath. He'd approach it like he did a race—sector by sector.

The first thing he'd try to solve would be the hardest—his marriage.

Cece stared at the door that joined her hotel suite to her husband's. She hadn't locked it, even though she'd promised herself she would. Her eyes were always irritated and raw from all the crying she'd done over the past two months.

The doorknob turned, and she regretted leaving it open. She couldn't deal with this now. None of this was fair or easy, and she'd gotten used to her life being both. But it was only a few months of difficulty, and then she'd be free.

She'd barely spoken to her husband. Their conversations had been brief and limited to logistics. Their agreement was that they'd stay married until the summer break, but that didn't require that they have much interaction at all. She turned her head to watch her husband walk into her room, still struck by how beautiful he was, even though she kind of hated him. People called him a "fallen angel" on social media all the time with his dimpled cheeks, square jaw, and soulful eyes. And he was always smiling, as though he had the best secrets in the world.

Before they'd let what they had die by getting married, he'd always had the best secrets for her—little gifts she didn't know she needed, romantic dates in between races, sometimes just the touch of his hand against the small of her back in a room he knew she wasn't comfortable in.

In that instant—remembering who they were before—she loved her husband. She missed him. She wondered what might have happened if she'd decided to stay that night and fight with him instead of waging a secret war by sleeping with his best friend.

"We have to talk," he said.

That was something they hadn't done much of lately. They hadn't much of a marriage for the past couple of years. It was like they'd become different people when they'd taken their vows. He didn't appreciate her in the same way anymore. Whenever he'd said he loved her, it was laced with duty rather than passion. She felt like a useful ornament rather than a trusted partner. Maybe that's just what marriage was—two people tied together, seeing how far they could push each other away before the ties broke.

Cece didn't sit up. It was like her body wouldn't let her move. She wasn't afraid of her husband, but that didn't mean that her fight, flight, or freeze reflex didn't kick on in that moment. She was afraid of what would happen to her. She was afraid that Luca had told him what happened, and that he would never forgive her. Even though it didn't matter, even though their marriage was over, she didn't want him to know exactly how she'd done her part in killing it.

"I know." She wanted to look away, but she couldn't do it. Not until he sat next to her. He didn't try to touch her.

"People are going to notice that you're acting like a bitch if you don't at least pretend to be in love with me." Of course, they didn't need to talk about the fact that he'd cheated on her, regardless of the fact that he'd been cross-faded on New Year's Eve. They had to talk about how her behavior while playing the role of his wife was inadequate.

Part of her wondered whether he'd let her catch him cheating—and then played dumb—just to get her to pull the trigger and leave him. It was almost a relief that she finally had a tangible reason to get angry at him. He might not have intended to drive her into Bendetto's bed, but he may have underestimated her need for catharsis.

The morning after, he might have made all the right sounds about how he needed her to stay with him until summer break but been desperate to get out of their marriage. This way, they could just put on a show for a few more months without ever needing to address the problems in their marriage. They could make a statement about growing apart and wishing each other the best, and she could disappear.

"When have I ever not acted like a perfect, loving wife to you?" *That he knew of.*

He sighed and looked at the ceiling. His hands flexed on the silk comforter. "Well, when you told that fan who said she was 'in love with Ethan' that she 'could have him if she wanted,' it sure seemed like you meant it."

Someone had caught that on video? "That was a joke." She'd been totally serious, but she'd kept her tone light. Hadn't she?

"She made a video on social media and now 'hashtag trouble in paradise' is trending with 'hashtag Ethan and Cece.'"

"I'm sorry." She might not like her husband very much, but this wasn't about her feelings anymore. This was about her future. If she didn't want to go back to modeling or move into her childhood bedroom, she needed to keep her game face on.

"Just try a little bit harder to pretend like you don't hate me." He looked at her and gave her the panty-melting half smile that she wouldn't have been able to resist even a few months ago. "Maybe I should fuck you until you're walking funny. You always remember why you're in love with me after you've come a few times."

She sat up then and scooted away from him until she faced him. Fuck him and his pretty face. "Maybe it'll just make me remember seeing some other woman bouncing on your dick in my bed."

"Watch your mouth, Cecelia." Sometimes, he had the worst habit of expecting her to act like a lady. If he'd wanted that, he should have listened to his mother. Ethan's mother had made it clear she wasn't suitable. Cece had been surprised that she'd said it over breakfast at the drafty, old estate their family had occupied in the English countryside for centuries. But she'd quickly learned that posh British people just said whatever the fuck they wanted.

But the old bat had been right. Cece didn't have the patience and fortitude to take a man like Ethan in hand. She was too impulsive and prone to temper. At the time, Cece had bristled at the woman stereotyping her because of the color of her skin and the fact that she was American.

Maybe it was time that Ethan knew exactly who he'd married. She leaned back on her hands and cocked her head to the side before saying, "Does it bother you that, after this is all over, every time you're inside a bitch, you're going to have to wonder if she's there because of you or if she wishes she was me?"

He bared his teeth at her, and something like a growl came out of his mouth. Before she knew what he was going to do, she was on her back, he was on top of her, and he had his hand cupping her throat. He didn't squeeze.

She wasn't afraid—she was desperately turned on.

She was truly sick.

They were sick together, and she was coming to believe that they never should have met. Something went very wrong somewhere to set off that series of events.

"I did fine before I met you. I'm one of the finest race car drivers in the world." He leaned down and ran his nose against her cheek. Then, he bit her earlobe. "I will do fine after you leave me."

"It doesn't count as leaving you when I found you fucking another woman in my bed." She pushed against his shoulders, but he didn't budge. Part of her didn't want him to. She wanted him to fight for her, even though she didn't deserve it. "*You* left *me* that night."

"I was fucked up, and I made a mistake." His grip on her softened. "You should forgive me."

"Why?" She didn't know why she asked. Maybe she wanted him to explain himself. Maybe she wanted to have a fight and put everything on the table.

But, knowing Ethan, neither of those things was going to happen. He was so buttoned up, so controlled, that he would give a logical explanation for all of the reasons why forgiving him would be advantageous for both of them.

"Why do you think?" He pushed his hips in between her thighs so she could feel him against her. "Because I want to fuck my wife again."

She tried to push him off her again, and this time she really meant it. It didn't matter that the smell of him and the feeling of him on top of her had her wet and achy. He didn't have to know that. She wanted him to leave her alone. "Have you been tested?"

She had. Didn't matter that she'd trusted Luca. She couldn't trust Ethan.

"You know I have." He did have to get a physical before the season started, but she didn't know they tested for STIs.

Cece bared her teeth at him this time. "I'm not forgiving you."

He had the audacity to laugh at her. And then he rubbed his cock against her center. "There hasn't been anybody since . . ."

"Why should I believe you? You'll say anything, do anything to get what you want. You're an absolute terrorist on the grid, but you promised never to play dirty with me. You lied."

"And I apologized." He thought that was enough. He seriously thought that was enough. He'd been around enough shitty, bloodless marriages growing up that he thought it was okay.

"You promised me that you wouldn't act like your father." When they'd met, Ethan's worst fear had been becoming his father. But now, he was a manipulative, cheating asshole, just like the generations of his forebearers.

She really didn't have a leg to stand on. She had it on authority that his mother had her share of extramarital shenanigans motivated by revenge in her day. Perhaps she'd been wrong, and Cece was perfectly suited to their family.

"My father hasn't tried to fuck my mother since I was conceived. He wouldn't let her out of their marriage, no matter what she promised him. He doesn't want her, and he won't let her go." He squeezed her throat a little, not enough to cut off her air. Just enough to establish his power. "I want you—quite desperately—and I've promised to let you go. Tell me again how I'm just like him."

He pulled up the bottom of her dress and pushed his fingers into her panties. He smiled when he felt how wet she was. She pushed into his fingers, unable to help herself. He rubbed her clit with one of his calloused fingertips, and she gasped. "You want me, and I know exactly how to get the best performance out of you."

His touch became harder and more insistent, and she squeezed her eyes closed against the avalanche of pleasure she was about to be buried in. But then he stopped.

She growled from frustration. And then she nipped at his stubble-covered chin with her teeth.

"Eyes on me, Cecelia." She opened her eyes to find him grinning down at her. "You need to think about how hard I make you come the next time someone asks you about your husband."

He speared her with two fingers and rubbed her clit with his thumb. She didn't know whether she was trying to get closer or get away from him. Her mind and the rest of her body wanted to tear itself in half. She should run from this kind of pleasure.

Her body won out, and she undid the fly on his pants, and pulled his cock out. She pulled on it how he liked it when he touched himself until he stopped her and pulled his fingers away. "If I can't fuck my wife, I want to fuck myself with you on me."

She hesitated as she watched him masturbate with her wetness. "Need you to come." Sure, he was buttoned up, but he was also filthy. She'd been so angry at him that she'd forgotten how much he turned her on. "Touch yourself."

She couldn't decide whether to look at his face or his hand on his cock. And she couldn't focus on the way her core tightened with every stroke of her fingers or his hot breath against her face. He looked agonized. He stroked himself angrily. And that turned her on. She'd been so close but seeing him like this pushed her over in no time. "Ethan!" She didn't mean to call out his name. That was too intimate, but they were way too intertwined for this not to be.

And then he came all over her, his come splashed all over her panties, sticky and hot.

He fell to his back at her side, and they both stared at the ceiling. Neither of them moved for long moments. Only their deep breaths and the whir of the air conditioner filled the room.

He had to go. She would fall into him and forgive him if he stayed. She was weak and lustful and greedy. She had to get used to not having this.

But he beat her to the punch. He looked over at her, and she met his gaze. "Are you going to behave?"

If this was her punishment? "Probably not."

Race Day

—

Bahrain

Chapter Seven

Somehow, in the crush of humanity, a sense of calm settled over Luca on race day. He lived for it. He could ignore the reporters trying to get a glimpse into the team, the celebrities trying to be seen, and the engineers and mechanics just trying to do their job.

Since he'd joined the team so late, he didn't have a physio assigned to him. Just a glorified body man who made sure he had water when he wanted it or various pieces of team kit that he could put on or shed, depending on where he was in the paddock, and whether the race was going forward or stopped under a red flag.

He wasn't used to wearing Lupo's fiery red, though. It felt as though he was wearing a beacon that said, *Here I am. Come watch me fail again.*

But he wasn't going to fail. He knew he wasn't going to fail so much that he'd put himself on pole position yesterday. He hadn't started the race from the front during his final three years on his former team. It hadn't taken long for commentators to declare his career over. And he'd believed them.

Until the team principal at Lupo had called. They were one of the most storied teams in the series—they'd been there from the beginning. Sure, they'd only wanted him because he was the only high-caliber, experienced driver available when their golden girl, Micaela Cartwright, had unexpectedly spurned them on 4 January. But he would take it.

It was almost like that night with Cece had broken a curse. It had initiated a whole bunch of other bad omens, but it was a few hours of feeling like he'd won something—like he could beat Ethan at something.

It seemed like she'd gone back to him and either pretended as though she hadn't seen what she'd seen, or they'd ironed things out. Although they hadn't been doing their usual tourist-documented date nights in Monte Carlo, they'd walked into the paddock today holding hands and bumping arms as they made their way to the facility.

So, maybe he couldn't get the girl. But he could beat the shit out of the guy who'd taken her from him. The burning in his gut every time he thought about Ethan being able to touch her had driven him in qualifying. It was dumb—they were fucking married—but he swore his jealousy gave him a few extra thousandths on that last lap in the third qualifying session.

Ethan was starting in P3, right behind him. He hadn't looked at him all day—not even in the mandatory briefings with the engineering team. His former friend wasn't giving anything away. He hadn't even grimaced when they'd been informed that the strategy was favoring Luca.

That didn't mean that Luca trusted Ethan to listen. He knew him too well. Out of the corner of his eye, he let himself look at his teammate. Everyone thought that he was cold. His face was all brutal lines and frigid glares. He held himself like the descendant of aristocrats he was.

But Luca had been around before all of that facade had hardened into the carefully curated exterior the world saw now. If he looked hard enough, which he wouldn't do right now, he would see the years fall away. He'd see the eight-year-old boy that he'd met at a dusty track in the middle of Sussex. He'd been choking back tears because his father had slapped him across the face for taking second to an Italian immigrant kid who'd grown up in a council estate in Brixton.

Luca didn't let himself fall for the aristocratic veneer. He'd seen enough from the inside to know how fake it all was. It might all look smooth and curated, but every bit of cold Ethan projected had been built from rage and pain.

And Luca wouldn't think about the times that his friend had shown him what was underneath. That would make him feel things he didn't get to feel anymore. It would interfere with the objective—winning. That's what he had left now, and he'd take it.

Micaela Cartwright was starting in P2. A lot of people in the paddock thought she was a novelty. Most of them were raging misogynists who wanted to see her fail—they thought women were meant to be ornaments on drivers' arms, not racers.

Some female pundit—a former racer in another series herself—had said that women lacked the killer instinct to make it in this series. So, the sexism ran deep. But Cartwright didn't seem to care. She was a pure racing driver.

Sure, it didn't hurt that she was the daughter of a former world champion and a total smoke show. She had hair that belonged in a shampoo commercial and looked as though she stepped straight off a runway and into some fireproofs.

Scuderia Lupo had wanted to sign her because of her skill, her name, and the sponsorships that poured in when she was one of their junior drivers. She was the total package, and Luca guessed a lot of the guys were jealous that they couldn't pull half the endorsements that Micaela had before she was even in the series.

He wanted to win, but he kind of hoped she kicked everyone else's ass.

Liam stood next to her car in a crisp, light-blue shirt peppered in sponsor logos. He looked grumpy, but then he always looked like that before a race. She knew because she'd always watched him, even before she was associated with his team.

Earlier, when a commentator was doing a grid walk, she'd heard him speculate as to why Liam was next to her car instead of his son's. If Brent heard that, it certainly wasn't going to help the mood in the team.

He'd rolled into the paddock on Thursday angry, giving terse responses to the press and refusing to do videos with the social media admin. Paola, the team's press officer, freaked out on him. That hadn't helped his attitude either.

Liam hadn't done anything. Yet. But his gaze tracked his son all over the garage, and she had a feeling he was standing near her to keep him away.

Her breath had caught when Liam approached her, and she nearly choked on her own tongue now as he put his hand on her shoulder. She could tell herself it was just nerves, but she didn't make a habit of telling bald-faced lies to herself.

"Are you ready?" Liam asked.

He is only concerned about the team's performance. He is only concerned about the team's performance. He is only concerned about the team's performance.

With his dark eyes searching her face, she had a hard time believing that. But she was simply a racing driver to him. Probably a tool he was using to drive his son to get faster. He didn't look at her like she wanted him to look at her. That could never happen.

So, she nodded. "I've been ready my whole life."

He smiled at her as though he believed in her. No one had ever looked at her like that.

Race Night
—
Saudi Arabia

Chapter Eight

Jeddah didn't have as many celebrities as the other Middle Eastern races—not even as many fans—but the floodlights along the streets of an ancient city along the Red Sea made it magical—glinting off the glass windows of the luxury hotels and highlighting an ancient mosque at 250 kilometers per hour. It even got to someone as jaded as Brent. When he thought about giving up racing, his heart clenched at the prospect of giving up night races. But soon, giving up racing would be out of his hands. He could feel Micaela pushing him out of the team with his dad's hand at her back. It made him feel helpless and angry, and it made him make mistakes.

He'd crashed out at the first turn in Bahrain. He'd started in the middle of the pack, farther back than usual. He'd had a shit qualifying. What did he expect when he'd gone to bed with a bottle of tequila the night before? This wasn't the seventies—he couldn't show up to the paddock smelling like a distillery—and this wasn't how top-caliber drivers operated anymore.

But he couldn't help it. Deep down, he knew he was being a baby about his father hiring his ex-girlfriend. But the knowledge that she was better—she'd placed second in the race—ate at him.

Anyhow, the other rookie driver who'd started behind him had tried to make a move in the first turn and made contact with Brent's car, and they'd both spun and hit the wall. The other driver had flipped his car over, but he was okay. One of the things that made Brent glad it wasn't the seventies anymore was that the rookie would have died for sure back then. Last week, he was merely sore and embarrassed by a DNF (did not finish) in his first race.

Brent probably wouldn't have gotten hit if he'd been focused on driving instead of being petty, so he'd vowed to show up for training fresh and ready to go this week. His sulking had still left him trailing behind in fitness, but he could catch up. He knew he could catch up.

The Scuderia Lupo drivers had placed first and third, and he could imagine how Ethan was taking his former best friend doing better than him on the first outing.

He hadn't shown up to watch her on the podium. He'd been sitting on his dad's jet, waiting for everyone else to board. But he'd seen it on TV. First race, first podium. It had taken Brent two years and significant media speculation that his dad should replace him before he'd gotten his first podium. And he'd only placed third.

He hated himself for being jealous of Micaela. She was an awesome girl—that's why he'd dated her. It was also why he'd sabotaged their relationship—didn't take a shrink to figure that out. He'd known all along she would eventually outshine him, and he couldn't deal with that.

Because he was a spoiled brat. Why did he hear those last two words in Paola's voice?

Maybe because she was always on his ass. She was next to his car right now, fending off the press, because he could no longer be trusted to talk to them without an intermediary.

Lately, she was his shadow—a very fine-looking shadow. He smiled at her as he put on his balaclava and tightened his gloves. If she knew he thought she was hot, she'd yell at him. Her hands would end up pulling at the end of her thick, dark hair in its perfect ponytail, and her nearly black eyes would throw off sparks of rage.

She'd slap him across the face if she knew how often he thought about wrapping that same ponytail around his hand and feeding her his dick. Before meeting Paola, he hadn't had intrusive thoughts about getting a blow job since he was about sixteen. And he'd always been able to control them. It was shocking how frequently thoughts about his dick and Paola showed up without his bidding. He didn't have the willpower to push them away.

But he needed to get control over his own mind. Because he loved racing. He reminded himself of that feeling of crashing out last week as he lowered himself into the cockpit. His engineer leaned in and gave him last-minute tire instructions.

Micaela would be favored this week because she had qualified ahead of him again—this time in P1. But this week, he was in P4. Only the two Scuderia Lupo drivers separated him from his teammate. He tried not to think about beating her. He hadn't even been able to go race distance in a car this season. He tried to focus on a clean race.

But then, as the crews were leaving the grid, he saw Paola walk past him, a little switch in her step that made her hips sway. He thought about the way she'd given him a rare smile when he'd showed up to the paddock on media day in a pressed team kit and a decent attitude. The way she'd given him another when he did a stupid TikTok dance for the admin.

Would she smile at him if he got up on the podium? Would she even care? Or did she only think about him when it directly pertained to her job? He pushed those questions out of his mind as the formation lap started. He had to get his head in the game, and getting involved with someone else connected to racing was a sure way not to do that.

Watching races was Paola's least favorite part of her job. It was ironic, given that thousands of people would trade places with her, but she hated the feeling of impotence that came along with the drivers and engineers doing their thing. She crafted the story of the team—both for the team and for the press. But a crash or a sound bite from the radio could tear down everything she'd built over the days leading to the race.

In other words, after media day, her whole week went downhill.

She put her headphones on so she could listen to the radio communication between the pit wall and the drivers. She ignored the private communiqués about telemetry and tire degradation, keeping her ears tuned for smart-ass remarks from Brent. She didn't have to worry about that from Micaela. She was golden in the press, never putting a foot wrong.

Micaela was only a couple of years younger than Paola, but she felt like a proud parent whenever the new driver gave the perfect answer to the increasingly stupid queries from commentators. They kept trying to provoke her to say something about the situation with Brent, but she was too much of a professional for that.

Paola, on the other hand, was on the verge of losing her cool with Brent. This morning, a commentator had walked right into the team motor home and approached Brent while he was eating breakfast. And the idiot had actually snarled at the man, as though he had forgotten that he was a part of a society.

"Brent." Paola was proud that she'd kept herself from hissing at him. "What was that about?"

He'd shrugged. "I haven't had my coffee." And then he'd smiled at her as though moving his facial muscles out of their perpetual scowl would get him out of trouble with her. The thing was, in another time, it might have worked. Paola had a crush on Brent when she'd joined the team. But everyone had a crush on Brent Sullivan. He looked like a surfer boy who'd just hung his board on the wall of the team motor home to hop in a race car instead and see if he could make it go fast.

And when he was in good form, he could. But he also had this air of not really caring about anyone or anything. Paola suspected it was a facade, though lately she'd come to realize that he might not just be empty inside. It made sense that he would be hurt by his father—the one who had never denied him anything—going behind his back and betraying him. But he had to see the opportunity this was for the team. He was a brat, but he wasn't stupid.

“You can’t act like that in front of the press, Brent.” Paola tried to be gentle in her reminder, but she really wanted to smack him. His hazel eyes twinkled at her in response. He wasn’t taking her seriously at all.

He popped a grape into his mouth and bit down on it. She shouldn’t look at his mouth. He was trying to flirt with her to get her off his back. He’d done it before, and it had worked when she was the deputy press officer. But she was in charge now, and she couldn’t be charmed out of making him fall in line.

“What are you going to do to punish me, Paola?” He leaned closer to her, and she should have shoved him away and filed a complaint with HR. But he was the boss’s son. Liam might be losing his patience with Brent, but he wasn’t going to let him get fired for being too fresh.

Like it or not, part of her job was to flirt and cajole. That mostly happened with the old-school guys who would die in their commentary chairs, and it never went anywhere. She had to be nicer to them because she was a girl. But there were boundaries—they couldn’t touch her.

And trying to manipulate Brent into acting right was different in that—deep down—she wouldn’t mind if he touched her. She thought about it—a lot.

“Can you at least not growl at them when they ask you about—”

“Don’t say her name. All I ever hear is that girl’s name.” Paola’s back went up when people called Micaela a “girl.” It was this minor sign of disrespect that she would not stand for. Her job was to make the whole team look good, but she felt the need to protect Micaela a little bit extra.

“She’s a woman.” Paola put her hand up. “But I understand. This is all going to blow over in a few weeks. They’ll realize that she’s just a racing driver, and the focus won’t fall so heavily on her.”

He looked across the cafeteria, and Paola knew he was looking at his teammate. There was something hurt in his gaze. It wasn’t that he didn’t care, it’s that he knew he’d screwed up. And it was the one thing his father’s money couldn’t fix.

Paola felt a pang of jealousy. No one had ever regretted her leaving them. All of her breakups had been neat, clean, and mostly mutual.

She had a habit of coming into a man's life, fixing everything, and then moving on. Her exes had all gone on to bigger and better things than what they'd been doing when they'd met.

She'd always been kind of proud that her relationships were so grown up. But, just once, she'd like to break someone's heart. She'd like to know she'd meant enough to a man that the thought of her pained him.

Brent's usual careless demeanor slipped back into place. The flirtatious grin was less compelling to her now because it wasn't genuine. It was a defense tactic. "Okay, Ms. Rodriguez, I promise I'll behave." He put two fingers up when he said that.

"You were never a Boy Scout," Paola reminded him that she knew everything about his past.

He winked at her, and she tried her hardest not to react. "Nope."

But he kept his promise. He didn't wreck his car, drove a nearly perfect race, and made it to the podium. He didn't even pitch a bitch fit that Micaela was a step higher as the winner.

Chapter Nine

A lot of the WAGs didn't attend the race in Jeddah, including Cece and Jocelyn Godwinson, who was probably the only person Cece would call a friend in the paddock. Jocelyn was *friends* with everyone and was an ideal WAG. She was invited to all the right dinner parties, and she knew every tidbit of gossip in the whole of the motorsports world. Cece was a bit surprised they'd formed a genuine connection. She'd even been at New Year's Eve, though she'd thankfully disappeared before Cece had found her drugged-out husband fucking another woman.

Even though she and Ethan had settled into a very tense stalemate, Cece couldn't wrap her mind around what he'd done. He'd chosen to do cocaine, and he'd chosen to take another woman to her bed. Even though he'd been under the influence, she couldn't completely absolve him in her mind. He claimed he would never cheat on her sober, but a part of him must have wanted to. That didn't just come from nowhere.

She inhaled the sea breeze as she navigated the narrow streets of Monte Carlo, focusing on arriving at her destination in one piece. She would never get used to European drivers, even after learning to drive among the many Miami drivers that seemed to have a death wish every time they got behind the wheel.

She still wasn't sure whether she would be divorcing Ethan at the end of the season, and no amount of ruminating seemed to solve that. Their estrangement laid bare a lot of the preexisting problems in their marriage—all the things she'd ignored when she'd thought they were blissfully happy. And him cheating had woken a passion for Ethan—in the form of jealousy—that was hard to ignore.

Right now wasn't the time for deep thoughts about marriage. She and Jocelyn had arranged to have lunch in Monte Carlo the Tuesday after Jeddah and before Melbourne. She parked her restored 1967 Lupo convertible in front of the valet stand at the Metropole and handed them the keys. A few tourists held up their phones and snapped pictures or took videos of her as she entered the hotel. She was sure they would show up on social media in the next few minutes, and the details of her outfit would be public knowledge a half hour after that.

She walked in to find her friend sitting at a table in the restaurant, near the window. So, she wanted to be seen today?

Jocelyn was married to a Finnish driver, notorious for loathing the press. Like a lot of the WAGs, she'd been a model and met Heka at a party on a yacht. Jocelyn had immediately become the head-WAG-in-charge, and she was loath to give up that moniker.

Honestly, if Cece had known that modeling and going to parties would likely end with her married to a race car driver, she might have reconsidered some of the decisions she'd made at twenty-one.

Anyhow, the way Jocelyn told it, she'd informed Heka they would end up married that first night, and he'd just smiled and said, "We'll see."

Six months later, Jocelyn's prophecy had come true after the British Grand Prix. Cece sometimes thought Jocelyn had probably just presented Heka with a tuxedo and a license as he got out of the shower, and he'd walked into the suit and posed for pictures. Heka seemed relieved to be in the presence of someone who loved the spotlight as much as he hated it. She and Heka made a good team. Every time Heka had so many points on his license he got suspended for a race, Jocelyn got pregnant, and everyone forgot that he sometimes drove like they were in a game of bumper cars.

They had four children, and Heka still had a racing seat.

Most of this was before Cece's time. Heka was in the twilight of his career—each season, rumors flew about his retirement. But he still put in performances that kept his team in the midfield, with the occasional brilliant race. So, teams kept him on.

Jocelyn's shiny blond hair looked effortless, which she ruthlessly maintained with eight-hour-long hair appointments in luxury hotels around the world. She had a wide smile with a slight gap between her two front teeth, which told everyone they were real and not veneers.

She was just as lean as she had been while modeling, and Cece wasn't sure if she'd seen her consume anything other than a green vegetable when she wasn't pregnant. Jocelyn might have baby-smooth skin underneath her fake tan, but she was old enough that she'd missed the boat on body positivity.

But in Cece's experience, body positivity just meant that you couldn't talk about what you hated about your appearance in public without pushback. Everybody still hated how they looked and employed any means necessary to adhere to intractable beauty standards. It was just a secret wrapped up in platitudes about wellness now.

Jocelyn stood up and hugged Cece. She smelled like her husband's cologne. She wore it to mark her territory. What Cece appreciated about Jocelyn was that she would admit outright that's what she was doing. There might be artifice with Jocelyn, but there had never been a lie.

Her friend pulled back and looked Cece up and down. "I missed you at my Jeddah watch party this weekend, and I also need a drink. Lola is suspended from kindergarten for biting another student."

Lola was their oldest. She took after her father. "What did he do? Cut her off on the way to the crayons?"

Jocelyn threw her head back and laughed, steering Cece to a chair. "No, he told her that her father was going to get fired after Sunday's race."

Heka had DNF'd after defying team orders to let his teammate pass him. It was typical driver behavior, but team principals tended to get pissed about that. And they had a long memory for that kind of thing when it came time to renegotiate contracts.

"She's so protective of her father," Jocelyn said, her voice laced with admiration for her daughter's naughty behavior. Lola seemed to take after both her parents. Jocelyn also had a little bit of bite when her back was against the wall.

Then again, when photographers had crushed her outside her kids' school, she'd told them, "I wish we just gave kids little go-karts and their own lane to take themselves to and from school. Taking them myself limits how long my colorist can keep foils in."

When one of the photographers asked, "You mean, give them bikes?" she'd smashed his camera.

"Speaking of fathers, is Ethan going to be one anytime soon?" Cece's skin heated at the question, and her stomach sank. Even before the cheating, she'd felt like she had a sign over her head, saying "Inadequate Woman" in lights when she was questioned about having a baby.

She trusted Jocelyn, to a point, but she didn't want to get into anything heavy with her. They didn't have that kind of range in their friendship. "Not yet." She poured herself a glass of champagne to bring the point home and took a long sip.

"You're not getting any younger," Jocelyn said, a tinge of censure in her voice. Cece was already aware enough that she didn't have the rest of her life to have children. And not that she would share this with the woman sitting across from her, but she wasn't sure if she even wanted to have children with her current husband.

"I'm aware of that." Cece lifted up her glass in a toast. "At least I'm getting smarter."

"It would be smart to bolster Ethan's image as a family man." Cece almost snorted champagne out of her nose at Jocelyn's ridiculous statement. "And it would get you some great press coverage."

"Oh, I'm sure that @WAGsandSLAGs will cover my hypothetical pregnancy breathlessly."

"You make jokes now, but it's a big contract year. No one's seat is safe." Cece had the feeling that Jocelyn was projecting her own anxiety. "And @WAGsandSLAGs has been very kind to me over the years."

"Yes. They barely ever photograph you when you're overdue for Botox." Cece bared her teeth with her smile. She realized that it was currently a nonnegotiable part of her life, but she resented that there were Instagram accounts and Substacks devoted to picking apart drivers' wives, girlfriends, and dates.

Jocelyn rolled her eyes, and Cece wasn't sure whether to be offended. Usually, she found her fellow WAG charming, but she was grating on her already rough nerves right now.

"Is there something wrong between you and Ethan?"

Nope. Cece wasn't going to give out any information about what had happened on New Year's Eve and what she and Ethan were going through at the moment. That was not for public consumption, and Jocelyn didn't deserve her confidence today.

"Ethan is at a crossroads in his career, right now. Just like Heka." Jocelyn choked a little on her champagne. "It's tough having Luca with the team, given that they are no longer friends."

"Did you ever get answers about what happened between them?" Cece had told Jocelyn that she didn't know why Ethan and Luca had fallen out, and Jocelyn had suggested it was because Luca was in love with her. She'd dismissed her completely at the time, but maybe Jocelyn had been right.

"I have no idea." Cece looked down at the menu, even though she ate here almost weekly. Monte Carlo was such a small town. She couldn't wait to leave for Melbourne next week.

Media Day
—
Melbourne

Chapter Ten

She was going to crawl out of her skin.

Micaela had gotten plenty of attention as a junior driver—because of her name and because she was the most talented of her crop—but the way the media felt entitled to every moment, every facial expression, would drive her completely mad.

Right now, she was sitting in makeup for the driver press conference instead of going over data with her engineer. Only a few of the guy drivers ever bothered with any makeup at all, and that was only the fashion boys.

Now, Micaela wasn't opposed to becoming a fashion girl, but that had a time and a place. And it wasn't at a racetrack.

She grunted when the makeup artist told her to blot, growing more restless with every passing second. And then, Paola walked in. She'd orchestrated this whole charade.

Micaela stood up with mascara on one eye. "I'm done."

"No you're not. Sit down." She could see why Paola had been put in charge of wrangling Brent of late. She could be terrifying when she wanted to be. "One more eye of mascara, and then you're done."

Micaela sat down. "I'm not doing this for every press conference."

"It's part of your job."

She wondered if Paola recognized how sexist that was. "Brent doesn't have to slather a pound of makeup on every time he sits down for an interview."

"He does have to sober up, though. And that takes longer than a glam squad." Paola said that without any indication that she was joking, but Micaela laughed.

After a beat, Paola joined in. "I can teach you how to do it yourself in half the time. How's that?"

Micaela sighed. "Perfect." She looked at her colleague for a second. Her mouth was tight, and she looked tired. "Is everything going okay with Brent?"

Her ex-boyfriend actually hadn't been quite as much of a dick when they'd both been at the factory the previous week. She wasn't sure if it was because Paola had threatened to tase him in the nethers if he said anything sexist or dumb or whether being in front of his father had made him behave.

"I don't know how you dated him for years." This was the most Paola had ever said about Micaela's personal life. She'd always appreciated her for being professional, but she started to wonder how much that cost her.

"I mostly never saw him," Micaela said. And that was the truth. She didn't tell anyone, because it might hurt her image as a tough, take-no-prisoners kind of girl, but she loved reading romance novels. And her relationship with Brent had always sort of felt like the prelude instead of the main event.

She was definitely never going to tell anyone she had started reading a lot of romance novels where the female protagonist fell into a relationship with her ex-boyfriend's dad or her much-older boss. Those she would definitely keep in the vault where she stored her ever-intensifying fantasies about her ex-boyfriend's dad and much-older boss.

"Not ever seeing him would be helpful." The makeup artist powdered over the cream blush and concealer she'd used. Paola looked at her and said, "Thank you." Although the other woman opened her mouth to say something, she realized she'd been dismissed before anything came out.

Micaela sort of wished she could do that with the press. "I need more time with the engineers."

"Seems you're driving pretty well to me." Yes, but she could always be better. That's what growing up with a father like Jack Cartwright had taught her. No matter what she did, he always had a story about someone doing it better—from finger painting to ballet class. She'd never finger paint like the avant-garde artist he'd shacked up with in New York for three months when Micaela was six—leaving her with the nanny. And she'd never dance like the Russian ballerina that he'd moved in with while she was in boarding school.

And driving was the one thing her father was best at. Beating all of his records could be the only thing that made him proud of her. Or it would destroy his source of power and make his massive ego crumble into dust.

Either way. "I want to be the best."

Paola smiled at her. "You will be. That's why teams fought over you. I think Liam called you a 'generational talent.' We believe in you."

At the mention of Liam's name, Micaela's insides heated up. What kind of fucked-up daddy issues did she have that she was feeling this way just because he'd praised her. Of course he'd praised her. He'd hired her.

"Thank you for offering to teach me how to do the makeup. It will really save some time."

Paola winked and led her out to the press room.

Cece had been very careful to avoid being alone with Luca since New Year's Eve. He'd thrown her glances laced with both anger and longing over the past three months that made her a little weak. But someone was bound to notice him staring sooner or later, and they couldn't have that.

For all the world knew, Cece was still very happily married to Luca's teammate and rival. She had to look like she was on Ethan's side. That was part of the deal between them. Their actual romantic relationship might be murky right now, but that had to stay behind closed doors.

And financially, she *was* on Ethan's side. He had to beat Luca to secure her future comfort. She was thawing toward her husband, but she wouldn't let her support of him be about her feelings. It had to be about logic.

She'd held Ethan's hand earlier as they walked into the paddock in Melbourne for media duties. There were fans surrounding them on all sides. Ethan had signed autographs with the hand that wasn't entwined with hers as they walked along. Cece stayed slightly behind him so people wouldn't reach out and grab her. Most people were cool, but some fans got excited to see Ethan and wanted a piece of him. They forgot boundaries sometimes.

It was harder now when everyone had a little paparazzi machine in their hands. Part of the reason her feelings for Ethan had cooled from red-hot anger was that she had to look as though she was still in love with him. For a few hours, almost every weekend, she had to look like New Year's Eve had never happened. It was almost too easy to pretend.

This was only the third race of the year, and she'd skipped the second, but that was all it took for the memory of seeing her husband fuck someone else to fade away.

Maybe she was feeling vulnerable, but her edges around Ethan had softened even before Bahrain. She'd started listening to podcasts and books about how to heal after cheating. It would apparently require a lot of talking, which was still difficult for her.

Sooner or later, she was going to run into Luca. They lived blocks apart in Fontvieille, and he was part of the same team. Close quarters for over twenty weekends a year, traveling together sometimes. It was going to happen eventually.

Walking to her hotel suite later, Cece thought she was braced for the moment they came face-to-face. But being close to him wasn't something you could prepare for. He was so full on at every moment that it almost took her down. But especially since they were both rounding the same corner on their floor of the hotel from different directions.

He reached out and grabbed her upper arms, probably not realizing who he was touching. "Are you oka—"

His question stopped, and so did her heart for a split second. He dropped his hands like she'd burned him. In a way, she had. "I'm sorry, Luca."

He shook his head, and his mouth twisted. He probably thought she was a feckless pushover. He definitely had to regret touching her. He likely wished Ethan had never existed. "I'm not okay, Luca. Despite how things look, I'm not okay."

"You're still with him." The pain in his voice was tangible, and Cece wanted to tell him the whole story. But they were in public.

"I don't have a choice."

"I gave you a choice."

Cece shook her head. She didn't know if she wanted to deny that it was true or if she just wanted to shake thoughts about how much better things would be if she'd chosen Luca in the first place out of her head. "You don't understand."

She wrapped her arms around her waist. Luca said, "Make me understand."

He took her by the arm and turned her, marching her to his door. "What if someone sees?"

She hated that she cared so much—hated that she had to think about what other people thought of her. She wished she could have both of these men all to herself. That thought blanked out her brain long enough that Luca maneuvered her into his suite.

It was empty—thank God. Luca had never traveled with a huge entourage. He liked it that way. He'd always said it reminded him of when he was a kid, and it had just been him and his dad. He had a team, but they were mostly in their offices in London and New York, making sure his life ran smoothly from afar.

"No one is going to come in. I'm the only one with a key to this room. Other than the hotel staff." He turned and put the Do Not Disturb sign on the outside of the door.

Cece's breath caught. They were alone for the first time since New Year's Eve, and it didn't feel like that long ago, even though everything had changed.

"It was only supposed to be once—"

He took a step toward her. She wasn't looking at his face, couldn't really bear it. Her muscles and bones were trying to crawl out of her skin. She wanted to touch him, and she needed to run far away. She wanted to spill every thought in her head, like she had the night they'd spent together. She wanted him as her friend, and the man who made her forget anything outside of them.

Ethan knew almost everything about her, but she'd always tried to hold back on the ugly parts with him. When they'd first met, she'd thought he didn't have any experience with the difficult parts of life. He'd never lived paycheck-to-paycheck. His family had gone generations without having to work.

But she'd eventually realized that kind of wealth came with a different set of ugly things. And they were somehow darker because they couldn't buy themselves out of them with money. Because the money and the way the family had gotten the money—through the blood and suffering of thousands of people over hundreds of years—held bad energy. It was almost a curse.

Centuries of excess rotted something inside the core of a family. Ethan had always seemed salvageable. He seemed eager to separate himself from his family's debauchery.

But standing here with Luca made her think it was more about who her husband had chosen as a best friend. With Luca, everything felt cleaner and more direct. She never felt as though she had to hide who she was and how she felt with him.

"I want more."

"We can't have more." Tears pricked the corners of her eyes when his face fell. She shouldn't feel as sad about this as she did.

"Why not?" Luca asked, and she honestly didn't know how to answer that. "Why couldn't we be together?"

"I don't think it would work out at all. I think we'd be fucked, and not in the fun way."

He didn't talk for a beat, didn't try to fill the space with platitudes. "I'm sorry. We shouldn't have—"

Her eyes filled with tears, and so did his. They just looked at each other. She wasn't sure whether they were sorry for what they'd done or how things had turned out.

He pulled her into his arms, and she burrowed into his chest. She wasn't going to question this right now. It was different than Ethan touching her. There always seemed to be a strategy around his affection. But there were no reservations with Luca. His touch was sure. For the first time in a long time, she felt held. She felt safe.

Her feelings at this moment weren't facts, though. She would definitely regret this—and probably sooner than later. But she was desperate for something that made her feel tethered to the ground. She was resigned to the fact that he would always give her that feeling.

"I really want to kiss you right now." His words were muffled against her hair.

She turned her face up and brushed his neck with her lips. He smelled freshly showered with just a hint of the cologne he'd been in an ad for. Being held by him felt almost as much like home as Ethan had. That was the only thing that kept her from completely surrendering.

His arms tightened around her, and her hesitation proved temporary. She pressed her mouth against his neck again, and he took that as an invitation, shifting her in his arms and pressing his mouth against hers.

—

Cece Ramos drove him crazy. He'd been thinking about her almost constantly for months, looking at her every chance he got, and now he was kissing her.

Fuck.

They would have to figure something out. Either they would have to be more assiduous about avoiding each other, or there was going to be a next time. He pulled her closer so she could feel how hard he was for her. She stiffened for a brief moment, and he was prepared to let her go. He didn't want to make things weirder than they already were.

But then she wrapped her arms around his neck and deepened the kiss. He let her be the aggressor. He was the one comforting her. If she wanted to tear him apart, he would let her.

She could do whatever she wanted to him—having her once and then having her walk away had already taken the heart from his chest.

"I haven't been able to stop thinking about you," he said when her mouth trailed down his jaw.

"Shut up. Shut up. Shut up."

She didn't want to hear about how she'd ripped him to shreds in one night. Fine.

He picked her up and tossed her on the bed. She made a little squeaking noise as she landed. She might be fierce, but she was still incredibly cute.

"I'll shut up, if you give me a reason to shut up."

She bit her lip. "I can't do the feelings."

"Hmm." He didn't want to tell her they were doing the feelings by being in the same room together—hell, by being on the same planet.

"This has to be just what it is, and it can't happen again."

He wouldn't agree to that. But he also needed her. He could convince her again. She wouldn't be able to stay away. That might sound arrogant, but she felt it too. "If you say so." If she needed to pretend she wasn't as caught up as he was, he would let her think that. For now.

But his ego was big enough, and the way he felt about her was unique enough that he knew this wasn't going to be the last time. And both of them felt more than they would say out loud.

Part of him wanted to make her admit this wasn't just sex and comfort; this was real, and she was going to leave Ethan. They'd find a way to be together.

Before he'd signed with Scuderia, he'd been at peace with leaving this series. He'd made his mark, and the business had decided to spit him out. He knew he'd survive without racing at the pinnacle of motorsport. But he couldn't say the same thing about living without Cece. That would haunt him to the end of his days.

Maybe he'd just replaced his obsession with racing with his renewed infatuation with her. He wouldn't tell her that his competition with her husband wasn't just about beating his teammate anymore. It wasn't about how she'd chosen him way back when or that Ethan had beaten him in a few karting races when they were kids. It was about showing Cece that he was the better man—or that both Cece's and Ethan's lives were better with him in them.

But now he had the opportunity to seduce her directly, and he wasn't going to waste it.

"If this is just about fucking me, take off your clothes." Luca had guessed she wanted him a little mean, and he'd guessed correctly. She slipped off her shoes and rushed to shimmy out of her white T-shirt and matching linen pants.

She wore a nude bra and panties that he normally wouldn't find very sexy, but this was *Cece* almost naked in front of him. She could be wearing a bra with the Welsh flag on it—heresy for an English rugby fan—and he'd still want to fuck her.

"Everything." He walked slowly toward the bed, reaching her in time to unfasten the front of her bra while she took off her panties. "Every time I think I've forgotten about New Year's, an image of your tits jogs across my brain."

Cece laughed. "I'm sorry about that."

"I'm not." He pulled off his shirt and leaned on the bed, dipping down and taking one of her nipples in his mouth. They didn't have much time, but he wasn't going to rush this, not when both of them had been waiting so long for a second go.

It almost made it better that it had to be a secret. He'd have won something on Ethan before the weekend even really started. Cece moaned and pulled his head closer, her little nails digging into his skull as her fingers tangled in his hair.

He crawled over her and released her nipple, needing to kiss her again. Her naturally tan skin was like silk against his, which he cataloged for later. He didn't know when she'd let him have her again, and he only wanted her. And maybe Ethan, if he could share.

Once Luca decided he wanted something, he went after it with a singular focus. He didn't allow any treats or goodies on the side of the road to distract him. He'd let Cece go once, hoping it would save his friendship with Ethan, and instead, he'd lost both of them.

He'd learned his lesson.

She tried to undo his belt, but he stopped her with his hand, stretching both of her arms over her head. "Not yet."

She groaned in protest but gasped as he kissed his way down her torso and spread her legs. He wanted an entire week in Bali where they'd have nothing to do but sun themselves and fuck, but that was out of the question at the moment. But he wouldn't leave this room without tasting her again.

Given that they didn't have much time, and he wanted her to come all over his face, he latched on to her clit. Her thighs squeezed his face, and he couldn't really breathe. But he didn't care. He'd die this way.

She came so fast that he was almost disappointed. He didn't pull away immediately, and she squirmed away from him, pulling his head away by his hair. When he lifted his gaze to hers, she had a lazy smile on her face. "I think that was pole position, Bandit."

She used his old nickname. He closed his eyes and smiled back at her. The silken sound of her voice wrapped around his dick and squeezed. "I aim to please."

He crawled up her body and allowed her to push down his pants as he reached to the bedside table for the box of condoms he'd found there when he'd checked in.

There was something to be said for luxury hotels. He didn't need most of the trappings of the wealth that came along with his profession, but they did make things a whole lot easier.

He didn't bother to push his pants all the way off. They had to leave this room soon, and he needed to be inside her now. Even though she'd just come, she wiggled desperately beneath him, stroking his cock and bringing him close to the edge.

He barely managed to bite his tongue to stem the tide of everything he wanted to say. *He doesn't do it for you like I do. That stuffy, posh boy will only lose control when he's really desperate for it. Do you have to goad him into sucking you off like I used to? Or does he do it out of duty? What has to happen for him to lose control with you? Has he ever?*

Ethan's appeal was the fact that he was a buttoned-up private school boy with money as old as the realm. His family line hadn't survived since the Plantagenet kings for no reason. They were always upright and stayed out of the mess. But Ethan could be coaxed into murky waters under the right circumstances.

Apparently, the right circumstances included cocaine and women other than his wife.

And yet, she was still with him.

He pushed that thought away as he sank into all of her soft heat. They both groaned, and he kept still for a split second, never wanting the feeling of being inside her to end. He wished she was his.

And he would make that wish come true, if only for a few stolen minutes. "You're mine, Cece."

"Yes." He didn't know if she knew what she was agreeing to, and he kind of wished she didn't. "I'm yours."

Shit. Hearing that, he slammed into her over and over, unable to get deep enough inside her. "Only me. You only do this with me now."

She scraped her fingernails down his back, declaring her ownership. "Only you. Only me."

He took that as seriously as some people did marriage vows. He'd always shied away from commitment before. Sex was great, and he wanted all the different flavors of it he could find. But there wasn't anyone else he could have his favorite flavor with but Cece.

"Only you, baby." She grabbed his butt and pulled him deeper, grinding against him until she choked off his blood flow with her second orgasm. He came right after, talking pure nonsense. "You're so good. So good. Such a good girl."

"Fuck, Luca."

He wanted to stay inside her forever, but he had to get rid of the condom, and the phone rang.

He was late.

Qualifying — Melbourne

Chapter Eleven

Something was off with Cece. She might think Ethan didn't pay attention to her moods, but she would be wrong. Growing up how he had, he'd been required to take care with everyone in his house. He had to know when his mother had gotten into the fifty-year-old scotch, when his grandmother's doctor had dropped off a new batch of pills, and when his father had a new girl in the office.

The memory of the way the rooms of the dusty, old manor where generations of his family had pickled their livers and ruined their souls changed when his father had been home and on one of his tirades still tightened his gut to this day. The fact that he'd taken after his philandering father after years of trying not to made him a bit sick.

Even though the fresh lake air around the Albert Park Circuit was eons away from the English countryside, he felt a similar sensation when Cece kissed his cheek for the cameras before qualifying. The feeling that she was pulling even further away from him had been growing all day, but he'd confirmed it when she looked at Luca.

Maybe it wasn't just the promise of a healthy divorce settlement that kept her with Ethan. Maybe she was staying with him out of a desire for revenge? If that was the case, there would be no better revenge than to sleep with his best friend.

The idea of Cece with Luca had crossed his mind under much more pleasant circumstances before. There was only so much debauchery you could engage in with one other person. With two, there were more options.

It had always remained clear that they wouldn't have a threesome with Cece. But Ethan had thought about it. Sometimes when he'd been with his wife, he'd craved it. And it wasn't as though there hadn't been looks between the two of them at the very beginning—hell, the very first night.

When Cece left him, it wouldn't be a huge surprise if she went with Luca. The shocking part to him was that he wouldn't be that pissed off about them being together. He'd be more hurt that he couldn't be with them both.

But he was the one who'd cheated on her, and he still didn't think there was a way to fix that. Had he even really tried?

Before he left her in the back of the garage, he leaned close. "When this session is over, let's have dinner."

For a second, he thought she would say no. He couldn't read her for a split second, and he wasn't sure if he'd played his hand right. He hated having to be this careful with what he said and how he operated around his wife. "Sure."

He smiled at her, and that made her even more nervous. She pulled away and made a show of putting on her headphones. The smile she returned was wary.

He wasn't sure if it was jealousy that made him need to earn his wife back, and he didn't think it really mattered. But, if the competition was Luca, he was going to win.

Nothing good could come from Ethan wanting to talk. He'd seen her looking at Luca. She knew she had to stay away from her husband's teammate, but she couldn't train her gaze to not find his long, lean body as he pulled his race suit over his fireproofs. His profile caught her eye every time. He had a strong face. As she'd kissed her husband's cheek, she'd wanted to be back in that hotel room with Luca.

And Ethan had noticed. He may have thought he had the whole careless aristocrat thing down, but that just meant he'd grown up in a nest of vipers and learned to be attuned to predators for his own survival.

And now he wanted to talk. How much did he know? Had someone seen her and Luca together that day? Did someone catch them leaving his room a few minutes apart? Was someone watching the hotel security tapes?

She didn't know, but she was sure they couldn't do that again. Not during a race weekend with everyone associated with the sport—journalists included—crawling all over the same few miles of Melbourne.

Cece sniffed and leaned on the barrier between the back of the garage where family watched the sessions and the area where mechanics and engineers worked on the cars. She adjusted the headset she wore to dampen the ambient noise. Maybe she'd still smelled like Luca. Ethan would know that smell, maybe? She should have showered after returning to her hotel room, but there hadn't been time.

And she felt cleaner with Luca all over her, for some reason. With Luca, she wasn't a money-grubbing soon-to-be-ex-wife. She was wanted and desired. And she hadn't felt really desired by Ethan for a long time before she'd caught him cheating.

Both Lupo drivers were expected to do well in this qualifying session. It was way too early to pick winners for the season yet; teams were still developing their cars. Panther Motors was bringing a new package to the next race in Japan, which would allegedly blow everyone else out of the water.

But Ethan and Luca were currently the first and third on points, and the team wanted them to be first and second. The mood between the two sides of the garage was frosty, which was acceptable as long as the drivers didn't crash into one another.

As soon as the green light went on at the end of the pit lane, Ethan pulled out, followed a few seconds later by Luca. They wanted to bank a lap before the other cars, even though they would have a better chance for a faster time once the track rubbered in.

Each took a slow lap to warm their tires, and then Ethan tarted his fast lap. She usually tuned into his radio, but not today. She didn't want to listen to her husband's calculated, almost cold tone when he talked to his race engineer.

At Bahrain, she'd noticed he'd spoken to her that way. That's the way it had been for months. Maybe that was why she'd agreed to have dinner with him after qualifying? There'd been a hint of warmth in the way he'd asked.

He used to be so gentle with her. He'd checked in with her all the time. But somewhere along the line, his care for her had disappeared. She'd become nothing more than an accessory he carried around the world with him.

Ethan's fast lap wasn't anything to write home about. He'd had some understeer into the last turn and lost a few hundredths of a second. He would have to come in and get fresh boots to do another lap.

Luca, on the other hand, was in first by a whole second and a half after all of the drivers finished their bank laps. He'd probably keep the same tires for his second lap in Q1, which would give him extra later in the session.

For the first time this season, Cece didn't know who she wanted to win. She'd had to cheer for her husband for years, but she'd actively wanted him to lose this season. Except for the part where his winning might make her wealthy.

Ethan finished that session P5, and Luca kept his P1 until the end. In the second qualifying session, Luca hit traffic during his fast lap, and their places were reversed going into the final ten minutes of qualifying.

In the end, Ethan finished first and Luca second. And Cece had longer to wait before the sword dropped at dinner.

Chapter Twelve

"I'm not sure why you picked such a romantic spot." Cece said as she looked around the dining room of the slick, Michelin-star restaurant he'd snagged a last-minute reservation at. Ethan's girl was prickly tonight. And she would be his girl again. After he'd gotten pole position for tomorrow's race, the whole team had celebrated. And then they'd been delayed by strategy meetings. Ethan usually didn't mind staying at the track until midnight before a race, but he was eager to leave tonight.

Before he'd cheated—it felt like another era entirely, like an ice age—she'd always pushed to the front and kissed him through his helmet when he'd gotten pole. Today, she was at the back of the garage with her arms around her waist. The cameras couldn't have picked it up, but he knew she wasn't excited. She was nervous.

Ethan shrugged. "The food is good here." The server filled his glass with sparkling water and hers with red wine. "We always come here after qualifying in Melbourne."

She bit her bottom lip, and he wondered if it was a mistake to remind her of the traditions in their relationship. He wanted to move forward, not dwell in the past. She didn't speak and took a long sip of her wine.

"I wanted to talk because I've changed my mind." She gave him a sharp look when he said that, and ice crystals seemed to form in the air between them. "I don't want a divorce. I want to try to give our marriage a chance."

If she could have moved away from him, she would have. She looked at the table, not at him, when she said, "I don't know, Ethan. I think it's too late for that. Nothing that happened in Bahrain changed—anything."

"I will give you whatever you need." He grabbed her hand, needing her to feel what he was telling her, even though he couldn't quite get the words out. "Whatever you need."

Even Luca. If she couldn't stay married to him without Luca being a part of her life, or a part of their life, he would give her that. He had no idea whether he and Luca could become friends again—whether they could share her as friends, or maybe more, again. But he would try. It ripped him up to look at him looking at her. He wouldn't be able to be in the sport if Cece divorced him and got together with Luca. He would be torn apart by jealousy coming from both directions.

He would do almost anything to keep that from happening.

"I thought you were going to give me the divorce if I made things look good." She leaned close to him, lowering her voice. "The way you were with me—I thought you hated me. I thought you wanted out too."

He tried to ignore the knife in his gut that came along with her admitting she wanted out. "I don't. I never did. I just acted like I did."

It didn't matter if she was already cheating on him with Luca. He'd cheated first, and this was his fault. But they were going to have to get a lot better at communicating if they were going to make their marriage work.

"That's the problem with our whole marriage, Ethan." Cece snatched her hand away. "You decide you want something and then it happens. I never get a say over my own life. You decide that it's boring being married, so you do some blow and fuck another woman—and I don't give a shit that you're foggy on the details. You made the decision to invite your degenerate friends into our home and do drugs with them."

He looked down. She was right, but she was vibrating with anger right now. "We should have talked about this at the hotel."

If her eyes could have ejected fire, they would have. "You wanted to do it here, at a restaurant I love and would like to be able to return to, so that I wouldn't blow up at you. Because you know that what you're asking for is selfish."

"I saw you looking at him." Her head snapped back as though he'd hit her. He wanted to take it back. He sounded ridiculous. He'd cheated, but now he was jealous. Maybe she was right, and he was a jealous asshole who didn't deserve her. Actually, she was definitely correct in that assessment. But couldn't she give him credit for trying?

"Looking at who?" She'd decided to play innocent? Fuck that.

"Luca." The name dropped like a stone in the middle of the table. "Do you want to fuck Luca to get back at me?"

She snorted out a laugh. "I don't know what you're talking about."

Bloody hell. This was a mistake. If she wasn't admitting to wanting him, then something was definitely going on. Right underneath his nose. "You're going to get caught." He leaned closer and took her hand again. "Neither of you can hide your emotions for shit, and you're going to get caught. I'm the one with the strategy, remember? That's how I won you in the first place."

"I'm not a fucking trophy."

He wanted to hurt her, so he cocked his head to the side and said, "Aren't you?"

"I guess that's why you put me in a dusty case and forgot about me after *winning* me." Part of him was thrilled at her anger. It wasn't exactly what he craved, but it was more passion than she'd shown for him in ages. "Fuck you, Ethan. If anything was going on with Luca—and there *isn't*—it's your fault. You started this."

It was true. He was the one who treated her like a prize instead of the treasure that she was. But that didn't dissipate his agitation. "I might not have started this if you'd actually paid attention to our marriage in the past six months."

Her pupils were blown wide on pure adrenaline. He'd seen it in other drivers—in himself—more than once after a crash or an incident during the race. He knew she felt out of control at that moment, and that's why he'd said what he'd said. He wanted her out of control with him.

Before she said anything, though, she looked around the dining room. People were paying attention to their meals, but they would probably take notice if she threw a plate at him or emptied her glass of wine in his lap.

He was disappointed. "You kind of like your dusty case right now?" He knew he was goading her, but he couldn't stop. "You don't want anyone to see how angry you are at me because they'll know that you're not perfect."

"No one thinks I'm perfect, Ethan." She leaned back in her chair, crossing her arms over her chest. He looked down at her tits. "Those are, but that's not what we're talking about right now."

"What are we talking about?" He might have been the one who arranged this dinner—to talk—but then she got mad at him, it turned him on, and he forgot about everything but how much he wanted her.

"We're discussing how much I hate you." And that made his dick hard.

He drained his water and wished there was something stronger in his glass, but he had to stay sharp for the race tomorrow. He stared Cece down, and she narrowed her gaze at him. He looked down at her chest, and her nipples were hard. She shifted in her seat. This was making her hot for him too.

"Do you hate me enough to meet in that single-stall bathroom in two minutes?"

She bit the inside of her cheek for a long moment, and he was afraid she really might slap him across the face.

But she nodded, and he let out a breath he'd been holding unconsciously.

On her way to go fuck her husband, Cece recounted to herself all the reasons that fucking her husband was a really dumb thing to do. She didn't know precisely why she was doing this, but she couldn't seem to stop herself once he'd propositioned her.

Ethan hadn't looked at her like that in ages. When they'd first met, she'd thought he was an arrogant prick, and that was half his appeal to her. She liked his cocky walk and the way he seemed to pose and preen for his adoring fans—chiefly her—sometimes.

But then, they'd gotten into an actual relationship, and she realized he was damaged and scared that no one liked him. Just like everyone else. It had given her the ick, but she'd told herself it was a good thing. He was opening up and being vulnerable. They were in a real relationship. She had to mean something to him if he was letting her in to see the side of himself that wasn't so macho and toxic.

There was something fucked up about her, though. She needed the toxic arrogance to get off with him. She'd started to miss it and think about it when they had sex.

The way he'd told her she was nothing but a trophy to him should not have made her wet, but it had. And she might have had sex with his former best friend—earlier that day, and it was over, so she hadn't lied—but he was her husband. They were allowed to do this.

She opened the door to the WC he'd indicated, and he pulled her inside immediately, slamming her against the door and ravaging her with his mouth. His hands were everywhere.

After qualifying, she'd changed out of her linen set and into an archival Hervé Léger black bandage dress. As he touched her exactly where he knew she liked to be touched, she felt like she couldn't get enough breath in her body. His mouth trailed down her neck, over the tendon there, and he bit down into her shoulder, almost so hard she yelped.

"Ow," she said, but then he laved the welt he'd made with his tongue. Just like in the hotel room a few weeks ago, he was feral. She loved it.

She grabbed the back of his neck and pulled his mouth to hers, rubbing up against his body and feeling his hard length press into her stomach. They were the same height because she was wearing heels. So, when she pulled away to get a breath, they were looking into each other's eyes.

"I still hate you." She hated that she still wanted him—or maybe that she wanted him again. And she hated that she wanted him for all the wrong reasons.

He yanked her dress up over her hips so hard she jerked and dug her fingers into his shoulders. Then, he pushed aside her panties and opened her up with his fingers. She squirmed against his rough touch, even though she wanted more of it. "I still make you so wet that you can't think straight."

He gave her his crooked little grin, the one the cameras had immortalized earlier when he'd put his car on the front row for tomorrow's race, the smile that told the world he was winning. The smile that told her he thought he deserved this, that he'd done something to earn it.

She lunged at him and bit his bottom lip. A big part of her wanted to rip his face off. But he groaned as though he liked her rage. "Hurt me all you want, Cece." But instead of letting her sink her claws into him like she wanted to, he put one of his hands around both of her wrists and pinned them above her head. He pressed against her, the hard of him making her ache. She arched into his body.

"Please." God, two minutes of him touching her and she was begging. It had never, ever been like this between them before—not even at the beginning. It was so twisted.

He pressed inside her with one finger, then two. She was still sore from Luca there, and that made her smile. In that moment, she almost wanted to tell him. But that would end this completely, and she needed to come. If she was his trophy, she was going to get something out of it.

She smiled at him, and he took that as a sign to rub her clit with his thumb. It was like she'd stuck her finger into a socket.

"Ethan." She didn't decide to say his name, didn't want him to hear how he affected her. But he'd stripped her down to a needy mess, just by pissing her off.

He took his fingers away, and she knew she wasn't going to be able to just take one orgasm from him and leave him hanging. That's what a vengeful wife in a movie would do. But, despite the fact that she was on magazine covers, she was just a regular girl in a body that needed to be touched.

He leaned his forehead against hers and put the fingers that had been inside her in his mouth. He was still holding her hands up over her head. She was at his mercy. "You taste like you're still mine."

She didn't want to melt at his words, but she liked them too much. Those words made her wish she could rewind time and suggest that they go on vacation for New Year's, that she could intercept the friend who brought the drugs and the girl who had fucked her husband in her bed.

Even though she didn't even really have the right to be all that mad about it anymore, it still twisted in her gut.

"Don't go there." He must have felt her pull away from him. "It's just the two of us in this room, and I know you need another one."

When he said that, she noticed she was rubbing against him, pressing to get closer. It was kind of humiliating, how well he knew her. "Then, what are you waiting for?"

He released her wrists and turned her to face the door. If she looked to the side, she could see them together in the mirror over the sink. It was one of those bathrooms in a nice restaurant that some people would call a lounge—the only thing that saved this from being totally sleazy.

Also, she was fucking her *husband* in the bathroom. So, it was almost classy. Or that was what she told herself as Ethan smoothed over her ass with his big hand before undoing his pants. Her fingernails might have gouged holes into the door as he pulled his cock out and entered her. She didn't look at where they were connected, but at the lock of dark hair that fell into his face as he slammed into her.

His hands twined around her waist and jerked her closer to him on every stroke. A drop of sweat from his face hit the middle of her back and caressed its way down her spine. "Fuck, Ethan. Don't stop."

She shouldn't be the one begging him for anything. It felt pathetic, even when she was this turned on. But there was a primal part of her brain that needed him to lose control for her. It didn't matter that her conscious mind had decided their marriage was already over, she needed to know he still belonged to her.

"So greedy," he whispered against the back of her neck as he fucked her. And it was true. He didn't even know the extent of it. She wanted Ethan, and she wanted Luca too.

She wanted the one thing she was sure she couldn't have—both of these men to call her their very own.

Thinking about what it would be like if Luca was there, leaning on the sink, telling Ethan to reach down and press on her clit so she would come harder, sent her over the edge. She started babbling, not sure what she was saying, until Ethan covered her mouth with his hand and came inside her.

He kissed the back of her damp neck, almost like he saw her as someone to be treasured instead of something to be won. "I've missed you."

She felt the same way, but she couldn't return the words. She hadn't missed him all that much until tonight. Her guilt had made it almost impossible for her to feel anything else.

And now that guilt was subsumed by shameless fantasies of having her husband, and Luca too.

She would never tell either of them how she felt. They could barely stand to be together in the same room, and Ethan didn't know what had happened with Luca—twice—but she could keep the thoughts for herself. She'd take them out of the back of her mind and play with them once neither of them knew her anymore.

Race Day
—
Melbourne

Chapter Thirteen

Paola closed her eyes and imagined herself in Liam's avocado green 1976 Dodge Charger with pin-thin racing stripes. She thought about how the leather steering wheel would soften under the heat of her hands and how the engine would vibrate through her whole body as it revved. She could almost feel the breeze coming across the lake against her skin.

Mostly, she settled into the imaginary bucket seats and saw Brent standing about twenty feet in front of the bumper as she pressed down on the gas pedal, and the car sprung forward. And then, the climax of her fantasy, the clunk-clunk sound as she mowed him down where he stood. She'd probably have to back up and hit him again, but those cars were designed to take a beating.

Brent hadn't shown up—again—for required PR duties. And when he'd arrived at the track, he'd had an unexplained black eye. As in, he couldn't explain how it happened to anyone, including himself.

Liam had held Paola responsible. Of course, he hadn't said that, but his disappointment was etched in the lines between his brows. Paola had tried to flatten her elevens, but that would take some mighty Botox at this point. And that would have to wait until summer break.

When Brent had finally shown up, she'd cornered him in the team motor home, not wanting any fans or photographers to see her yelling at him. She leaned against the thin wall of Brent's room as he said, "I think I must have done it in my sleep."

"*Deuxmoi* had pictures of you at a club opening last night, and @ WAGsandSLAGs has already found the girl who was pictured grabbing your ass." She was jealous. She hoped she didn't sound it.

He stood up and came closer to her. If she could have backed up, she would; he didn't smell like a bar. Maybe he was partially telling the truth. "It would be more believable if you told me that someone saw you at the club and punched you in the face because of your performance this season."

Brent laughed, which wasn't a sound anyone in the paddock heard very often. "You're funny, but that's not true. I've really been working on not being an asshole lately. Getting a stranger arrested for not punching me would be an asshole move, don't you think?"

She released her face and looked up into his green eyes. His messy hair fell over his forehead, and she needed him to let her find him a hairstylist. It was too long.

"If you weren't drinking, why are you late?" That was probably too loud and too sharp.

His smile disappeared. Yelling at this asshole did not help, but it was nearly impossible not to do at times like this.

"I told you that my alarm didn't go off."

"This is not helping your reputation." He was somehow even closer to her, and she didn't realize when that had happened.

"But you'll forgive me?"

"Not if I lose my job. Then, I'm going to find the bruja who lives down the street from my mother in Santo Domingo and get her to curse you."

"I'm already cursed, Paola." He winked at her. "The girl I'm interested in is never going to give me a chance if I make her lose her job."

Where was this coming from? How could he be interested in her? She'd just fantasized about committing vehicular manslaughter.

"Don't do this, Brent."

He backed off then, holding up his hands, palms out. "Do what?"

"Flirt with me."

He laughed again, and she hated how much she liked it. "If I were flirting with you, you'd know it."

She pressed her lips together and paused. "The pictures didn't get much traction because Ethan and his wife were snapped by a fan leaving a restaurant bathroom together last night."

"So, I can't flirt with you, but you can gossip with me like one of your girlfriends?" He was teasing, but she wasn't in the mood.

"No, I was strategizing with you like one of my colleagues." She shook her head and moved toward the door. "In the future, I'll direct you like one of my minions."

"Is that what it's going to take for you to give me a break?" She hated that he didn't see she could actually help him. He could get out from under the narrative of him as a scorned lover, destroying his career and getting beaten by a girl. He could grow up and change how the motorsports world perceived him.

He just had to listen to her.

"No, I'll give you a break if you'll do what you're told until summer break. And then, you'll come back and do what you're told until winter break. After that, if I'm still employed with your father's team, and you're still my problem, you'll do what you're told from the car launch until I say so."

He sat on his chair and looked up at her with a mischievous grin. She needed that grin captured on camera, so he could charm the world. "I'm going to need proper motivation for that kind of focus."

Paola threw up her hands. He was completely impossible. "You can focus on driving. This is part of your job, which is driving. You can't do the driving if you aren't going to do the other stuff."

That was only partially true. His seat was almost guaranteed, and she wasn't sure what it would take for his father to fire him. But part of having a profitable team was garnering sponsorships with popular drivers. Brent could be a popular driver if he channeled some of his flirtation away from swimsuit models—and her—and toward the cameras.

She was about to explode or say all of that to him when he shocked the shit out of her. "If I cooperate until summer break, will you go out with me?"

That would be totally unethical. She would probably—definitely—get fired if she dated Brent. But no one had to know it was a date, did they? They could just be colleagues getting dinner.

Sure, that's all it would be.

"If you cooperate until summer break, we can go out to dinner. As friends."

Race Day

—

Suzuka

Chapter Fourteen

The Japanese Grand Prix was one of Cece's favorite races of the season. The paddock was lush and thoughtfully designed to highlight the area's vegetation, and the fans were incredibly friendly and enthusiastic about the drivers. Cece and Jocelyn walked through the fan zone. A few people stopped Cece and asked for her autograph or a selfie, and Jocelyn scoffed. "You shouldn't do that."

"Why not?" Cece smiled and tried her few words in Japanese. The girl asking for her signature corrected her politely. "If I don't do it, that makes me a bitch."

"It's better to be a bitch than to steal the spotlight."

Jocelyn probably thought it was better to be a bitch than it was to be a lot of things. She was also probably jealous because Cece was almost as popular as she was at this point. Although she was frequently featured on @WAGsandSLAGs, it seemed clear that a lot of those stories were planted—by her.

She'd married Heka when he was already a world champion, and he wasn't super interested in playing the press game. And now he was on the downswing of his career and would probably announce his retirement at summer break—especially if his season kept going the way it was. He hadn't been in the third qualifying session since Bahrain. And he had only scored three points all season long. Maybe Jocelyn felt her crown slipping. And she could only stave the end of his career off with a pregnancy so many times.

Ethan and Luca, however, were in a tight race for first place with Micaela and Brent. Brent had taken P1 after starting in fifth in Australia, with Luca and Ethan in the other podium places.

Cece had been pushed up next to Micaela watching the podium. She was surprised to see the younger woman there; usually drivers who didn't place went off to sulk after they got weighed and before they were required to talk to the press.

"If I don't show up to support my teammate, everyone will think I'm a spoiled brat," she said.

Cece winked at her. "And you did great. You're still ahead of him in the championship, so you can afford to be magnanimous."

"Thank you." Micaela squeezed her arm. "I'm glad you get me. How are you?"

Cece wished she hadn't allowed the younger woman to see her vulnerable at the gala. They were friendly but not really friends. "Everything's fine."

Micaela got the message—that Cece didn't want to get into anything deep—but she didn't let it show on her face. She'd grown up in the world and understood the need for discretion more than anything. "I'm here, if you need to talk."

"Thank you." Cece had changed her mind and decided, in that moment, that she and Micaela were going to be friends. The press had gotten a hold of photos during their exchange and asked about them. It was odd to them that Cece would reach out to a young woman who was trying to beat her husband on the track.

"Girls in this world have to stick together," Cece had responded. "She's a gifted, young driver, and I fully expect her to beat all the guys, including mine."

Ethan hadn't been happy with that, but he'd also been pissed when their bathroom hate fuck hadn't turned into a full-on reconciliation. His response to the idea of any friendship with Micaela demonstrated that it wasn't just his infidelity they needed to work on.

Her husband had been the one who'd suggested she hang out with Jocelyn this week in Tokyo before heading to Suzuka on the train. It had been a long week. Ethan knew Jocelyn was a "small doses" friend, and he'd suggested they hang out all week to punish her.

Cece loved Japan—with the people, the food, the contrast between the bright lights and endless novelty of Tokyo and the green and quiet countryside—it was so different from where she'd grown up. She never missed this trip. But having Jocelyn along had been a drag. It was difficult to fathom how someone who'd been traveling all of the world for a decade could still find so much to complain about.

The first day, she complained about the food. "I don't want omakase. I want to eat a burger." Which was how Cece found herself asking their driver to find them a burger joint when she'd had reservations at a four-seater, Michelin three-star restaurant.

"None of the clothes are in my size," Jocelyn had said, as Cece's face heated with embarrassment at an atelier Cece had arranged to visit back in November, when they were in Japan last year.

And now she was bitching about Cece signing a few autographs. "I'm in commercials here, Jocelyn." Cece needed to extract as much out of her public profile as she could, while she could. That meant hawking everything from Korean sunscreen to Cuban sandwich–flavored potato chips.

"I can't believe you still work." Jocelyn couldn't believe anything in Japan. And she'd always indicated she was above influencing as a profession. "Is that because you and Ethan are having marital problems?"

Her "friend" had also been fishing for information about her marriage all week. Although she and Ethan had been caught by paparazzi in Melbourne leaving a restaurant bathroom together, he'd mentioned to Heka that things weren't great at home. Cece wouldn't have expected the taciturn Finn to gossip, but he must have said something to Jocelyn.

"Our marriage is fine." Cece had tried her hardest not to snap at Jocelyn all week, but she was at her wit's end. "I was just pissed about the pictures. It's not the 'family image' that Lupo likes to portray."

A few decades ago, Ethan might have been summarily fired. But he was a huge personality in the sport today, and even the Italians really couldn't fault him for banging his own wife. They would definitely find fault with Luca for fucking Ethan's wife. And Ethan's wife for fucking Luca.

But they would never need to know about that.

Cece didn't usually disturb Ethan while he was prepping for a race—especially not this season. He was so wound up about competing with Luca that he was monstrous to be around. But he'd told her to pop her head in when she got to the track. And he was trying to be nice to her. He hadn't cheated on her again, for starters.

She knew because he was constantly sharing his location with her. But she didn't know how to tell him she needed more than just fidelity by the letter of the law. She wasn't sure they could fix what was broken between the two of them before he'd cheated.

But before she got to Ethan's room, Luca grabbed her and pulled her into him, just inside the door to his room. His mouth was on hers before she could push him away. And the way he kissed her made it impossible for her to pull back for a few long seconds. She only broke their kiss, her breath ragged from just a taste of him, because she had to.

"What the fuck are you doing?" she yell-whispered, well aware of how thin the walls were between the drivers' rooms.

He didn't speak for a second, maybe two. It didn't make any sense, but he seemed just as lost and confused as she was. "Cece, I—"

She shoved his chest away, and this time he backed up. "We can't do this. We can't."

Luca backed up all the way and dropped to the cot. Cece cringed at the creaking sound it made moving a little across the floor. "I'm sorry. I saw the pictures, and I lost it."

Cece could imagine how that felt for him. He probably felt used and discarded. That was the last thing she wanted him to feel, but how could she explain? Things between her and Ethan were still unimaginably complicated. But the thing between her and Luca was supposed to be simple. And over.

It didn't feel like it was either of those things.

"It's what you think it was." She wasn't going to lie to him. "But that doesn't mean that I'm not still fucked up over you."

He looked up at her, and the raw emotion that had coated him from head to toe when he'd pulled her in that room was gone now. Iced over. That's how he could drive at unspeakable speeds without thinking about death. She couldn't freeze him out that way.

"I have to go." She shook her head and looked away from him. "I'm sorry."

She was sorry she'd hurt him, but hopefully he could move on now. But then, he surprised her by standing up and crowding her against the wall again. She still wouldn't look at him, so he waited.

He might have iced over any feelings he had for her, but his body heat singed her from head to toe.

"Look at me." His words were deadly and quiet, and she felt like she had no choice but to do what he told her. "I'm going to win."

"The race?" She hated how her broken whisper felt small. She was not afraid of this man. But barely being able to get words out meant she was afraid of her feelings for him.

"Everything." He dropped his head and ran his nose along the side of her neck, like he was a predator scenting his prey. There was nothing about this situation that should have her turning into a boneless puddle on the floor, yet here she was.

Before she knew exactly what was going on, she was in the hallway, facing her husband.

Luca stood behind her, and she could feel he had some sort of shit-eating grin on his face. Ethan's gaze dipped to her swollen lips, and it took everything in her not to touch them. He'd know she'd kissed Luca for sure if she did.

Shockingly, her normally loquacious husband had nothing to say. But the same energy that had possessed him to fuck her in that bathroom clearly came over him now as well. The vibes were extremely volatile, and Cece wanted nothing more than to escape. Or see what would happen if everything exploded.

She was saved when Lydia, the team's press officer, came walking down the hall in a cloud of musky perfume. "Good, both of you are here. You need to come to the team brief, so you're prepared to answer questions about the upgrades on the car."

Cece took the opportunity to slip behind Luca and out to the garage. She waved her hand behind her head and said, "Good luck."

"Stay the fuck away from my wife." Ethan bit the words out.

Luca snarled at him. "Keep your dick out of other women."

They walked behind Lydia in the paddock, and they both had smiles on their face, even though they wanted to murder each other right there. There wouldn't be time before the race for Ethan to try to kick his ass.

"She went to see you that night, didn't she?" Ethan might be a real douchebag sometimes, but he wasn't stupid.

"She's my friend. She was always my friend. And I'm glad I could be there for her when you fumbled the bag."

Ethan stopped for a second, but then he must have remembered where he was. "We don't share her."

Luca sighed. This was the most they'd spoken to each other when it wasn't for socials or about the car since he'd joined the team. And Ethan was making it about marking his territory.

"She's not a possession, and *she* gets to decide who she shares herself with." They'd both slowed down, so they were out of Lydia's earshot, and they walked with purpose, only briefly pausing for selfies well behind fans. Still, this wasn't the best place to be talking about who had the right to decide who Ethan's wife fucked.

"I know that." Ethan's tone was sharp, and Luca was pretty sure a reporter had heard that. Tomorrow, there would be rumors about strife in the team. The speculation about how the teammates and former friends were getting along was already brutal, and Luca resented Ethan adding to that now. "But I'm not going to let you have her."

Luca barely stopped himself from rolling his eyes. The last thing they needed was that photo. He was also going to have to watch his six during the race. Ethan would run him off the track at any opportunity, and they were starting on the same row. He wasn't going to follow team orders either. This was going to be a long race.

Chapter Fifteen

Micaela didn't love rainy races. Didn't love driving them. And she hadn't loved watching her dad in them as a kid. Rain at Suzuka made her even more uneasy. People had died when it rained at this track.

But it was a lot of drivers' favorite track in the wet. The grid got out of order when it rained. People who shouldn't win races made gambles that paid off. Or didn't.

It was the precisely wrong race for her to have a chance of being out of position. The track had started out dry. About five laps in, it had started to mist. And five laps after that, it had started to rain hard enough that her tires were slipping. It was too early for a pit stop in the carefully calculated race strategy, but it didn't matter. If she wanted to finish this race with her car and body intact, she'd have to stop and put on wets.

She also hated the pit lane during the beginning of a bout of rain. Everything was chaotic and everyone was a little on edge. Rain might have been in the forecast, but the sky had been clear all day. And they'd moved the race from October to April to avoid conditions like this.

Fortunately, no one hit her as she pulled into the pits. Brent had stopped on the lap before her, so she had a lot of time to make up. Her tires came off without a problem, and the whole stop lasted 1.7 seconds of stationary time. But it felt like a billion heartbeats between when she stopped and when she got going again.

"Perfect pit stop, Micaela." She was surprised to hear Liam's voice over the radio. She usually only heard from her engineer, Frankie.

"Thank you." She didn't smile, even though praise from Liam was really nice to hear. In any other context, she'd probably melt a little. But her heart was still in her stomach thinking about where she would rejoin the race.

"Almost everyone has pitted in front of you, Micaela," Frankie said in her light Scottish accent. When they'd started together in the first open-wheel series after graduating from karting, Frankie had been nearly impossible for Micaela to understand. But her engineer had worked on her enunciation for "Mikey's delicate and fragile ears," and Micaela had started listening to a series of audiobooks narrated by a Scot. They'd come together. "But that means that they'll have to pit before you again. The rain is supposed to last another thirty minutes. Just hold tight, and you'll be able to push until the end."

Frankie was talking too much. Micaela slotted in between two other drivers from backmarker teams. Shit.

"Where am I?"

Again, she was surprised when Liam spoke. "You're in P14. On the current strategy, you're projected to finish P4."

Most of the time during races, she liked to pretend Liam couldn't see her. She knew she wouldn't perform at her best if she thought he was always watching everything she did. Well, she got a sick thrill from thinking about him watching certain things she did, but she couldn't think about that now.

And she hated that the highest she could finish on the current strategy was P4. She needed to get on the podium again. She needed to be on the top of the podium. But this was not the kind of race that was going to let her hunt for glory. It was the kind of race she just had to survive.

She felt like she was on her own for several laps. Frankie knew how nervous the rain made her, and her engineer knew she needed more silence when she was nervous. She wondered if Frankie had told Liam about her not loving the rain, and that's why he'd spoken over her radio during the race.

The rain started to let up. She would be able to strap on slick tires in a few more laps. "Frankie, I want to get in before Brent to put on mediums. I know I can beat him." She kind of hoped that Liam was listening. It was very odd to compete for her boss's approval with his own son. But she didn't even think about Brent in that context anymore. She didn't even think of him as her ex. She thought of him as competition that needed to be vanquished. And, when she was behind the wheel of this beast of a car, she felt completely invincible.

Frankie didn't respond right away, and Micaela started to wonder what was going on. "Bendetto and Harrow crashed at the front." Micaela saw the yellow flag and safety car lights come on immediately and she slowed down.

"Are they okay?" That was always the first concern when there was a crash. It didn't matter at all how much she hated another driver. If there was a crash, she wanted them to walk away from it unscathed. Even though acceptance of death was a requirement in this sport, it didn't mean you wanted it.

"They both walked away, but they're both out of the race." That was the best kind of crash. "We're just strategizing."

Micaela hated waiting for them to strategize, but she tried to suppress her impatience. It was one of her best and worst qualities. But the team needed a few moments to revise their plan for the rest of the race.

"Okay, it's going to take them several minutes to clear the chicane. We want to double stack the stops and strap on hards." So, they'd crashed on the Casio Chicane right before the pit lane—a wild and desperate place to make a move.

"What?" Micaela didn't question Frankie often, but hard tires were probably the worst choice for her.

"We're going to keep you out until the end of the race."

Micaela didn't know how to feel. She knew Frankie had to believe there was a good chance of her winning if she was willing to try something this risky—if the strategist agreed with her. There was every chance her tires could fall off a cliff at the last moment. If there was another safety car, then all this might be for nothing.

"You're sure?" She hoped she didn't sound as scared as she felt.

"We know you can do this, Micaela. You take good care of the tires, and you're smarter than everyone on that track," Liam said. So, he was on board with this plan too. And he thought she was smart. Most girls wouldn't have pants feelings about their tire management, but Micaela wasn't most girls.

"Head down, Micaela." Frankie knew she was spiraling.

"Got it."

Micaela stood on top of the podium, next to her teammate, and raised the trophy above her head. She had no idea what she'd said to the former driver that had interviewed the top three after the race. In her head, all she heard was the rush of blood and adrenaline from winning.

She'd won tons of races before just to get here, but this was special. Only the best won races in this series. It didn't matter that two of the top contenders had crashed to make this happen. She was the winner.

Liam stood behind her on the dais to collect the prize for the top constructor. She'd been expecting to see Frankie in the cooldown room and was surprised to see him instead. He had a reputation for shining the spotlight on other team members out of some faux-egalitarian, American thing, but he was there.

She looked over her shoulder at him, and they locked eyes. Something danced in the atmosphere between them that she would name as attraction if he were anyone else.

They started playing "God Save the King," so she turned around and put the trophy down. Then, they played the "Star-Spangled

Banner," which people didn't get to hear very often before Panther Motors had signed her. Before she'd won this race today.

She was vibrating with excitement, and the cork from the bottle of champagne they gave them to spray almost hit her in the chin. Liam frowned at her and looked like he was about to tell her to be careful, but she started laughing.

Brent smirked at her and sprayed sticky, fizzy wine right in her face.

Chapter Sixteen

After the podium, they had to rush to the private airport. Her assistant had packed everything from her hotel room after she'd left that morning. It was weird how she still wasn't used to having all of these things done for her. Micaela'd had to manage her own self for so many years. Her father could have hired help for her, but he'd chosen not to. Anything he could do to show her he might want to be painted as the good guy enough to appear to support her career. But he wouldn't do the actual work.

Brent was stopping at the factory in Lincolnshire before the next race, so Micaela got on Liam's private plane. When she boarded, she was surprised to find him alone, drinking a scotch.

"Where's everyone else?" She kept looking around, like the technical director would pop out of the bathroom at any moment.

"Almost everyone else is headed back to Lincolnshire."

"So, Brent got to be on the crowded plane?" She wasn't quite sure what to say. She had never been completely alone with Liam, and it made her want to shift around on her feet. As it was, she couldn't look directly at him. Even with the win, it made her wonder if she'd made the right choice.

She hadn't known how she would start to feel about him after working with him. Hell, she wasn't sure how she did feel about him.

She didn't know where to sit, so she took the seat across the aisle from Liam. Her trophy took the spot next to her. She belted it in.

Liam chuckled and motioned for the flight attendant. Then, he handed the woman his phone without noticing the way she looked him up and down. A spike of jealousy hit Micaela out of nowhere. She didn't think Liam was interested in sleeping with her, but she wished she was allowed to look at him like that.

"Can you take a picture?" Liam asked.

The flight attendant looked a little shocked he wasn't asking her to enter her phone number, but she covered it with a smile. "Of course, sir."

Then, she aimed the camera at Micaela and the trophy. "Wait," Liam said.

"Did you want her to fix her hair first?" The flight attendant made it sound innocuous, but Micaela's face heated and she reached up to touch her hair.

Liam grimaced. "No, she's perfect." He didn't look at her, and she knew she didn't look perfect. She'd had time for a quick shower, but her hair washing was going to have to wait until they were back in Monaco. Still, his words made her heat up inside for a different reason than the flight attendant.

And then Liam squatted next to her chair, wrapping his arm around her shoulders. He smiled at the camera, but she was stunned he was touching her. He'd hugged her after the race, but she hadn't been in the headspace to catalog the way the heat of his hands set her on fire.

But they were—almost—alone right now.

And when Micaela looked down, she saw he was hard. She froze in place. She didn't know what this meant. Maybe the way the flight attendant was so obviously hot for him was doing it. Maybe they were sleeping together, and they were just holding off until Micaela fell asleep in her seat before going back to the bedroom and having wild, monkey sex.

"Look at the camera." Liam's voice was soft, and it felt like he was stroking her with it. She complied and posed for the picture. She hoped her eyes weren't closed, because the flight attendant seemed to be rushed about getting the shot. "Good girl."

Fuck.

Chapter Seventeen

Liam should have gotten someone else to join them on his plane. He could have made up a reason for one of his three assistants to fly back with them. It was a bad idea to be alone with her. She probably thought he was a lecherous old man with the way he looked at her.

But he couldn't stop his gaze from dipping down to her lips, wondering if they tasted like candy or just looked like they did.

He was so attuned to the way her expression changed with every emotion that he noticed the way her eyelids dipped when he'd called her a "good girl." He hated himself for the thoughts he had after that. But he wanted to spoil her, give her everything. He wanted her in ways that would be wrong, even if she didn't drive for the team he owned and ran.

Some people in the sport would say this was why they didn't have women drivers for decades. They were a distraction, but Liam had no one to blame but himself. He'd noticed her when his son was dating her. He'd been thinking about her and the way she would feel against him since she was nineteen years old.

The plane was way too quiet, because he could hear her tossing and turning in the bed in the back. He should put his headphones on and crank them all the way up, but he didn't. He thought about her lean curves rolling around in his sheets and clenched his fist on the armrest to keep from grabbing his dick. The flight attendant wouldn't bother him until mealtime, and she'd probably enjoy the show. He hadn't given her any reason to flirt, because he didn't sleep with his employees, no matter how much he wanted to.

He should have been reading emails from the team, reviewing technical information and telemetry from the race so he could give them cogent directions on how to develop the car in Micaela's direction.

She was the future of his team, and she shouldn't be the future of his erotic fantasies.

He flipped on his phone and looked through the contacts. He needed a list of women he could contact when he landed, women who might help him forget about the one on his private plane.

He heard her moving again, and he barely kept himself from opening the door and telling her to go to sleep immediately. Being alone with her was going to drive him crazy, and he could never let it happen again.

And then he heard her make a sound. *She's asleep. Probably just dreaming.* It sounded like a moan, but it couldn't be. Maybe it was just a sound in the engine, and he was simply imagining things. But then he heard the sound again. And his seat belt was off. He was standing, and then his hand was on the doorknob.

He was in the bedroom at the back of the plane before he could think about it too deeply. Maybe if he just looked at her while she was asleep, he could remember how young she was. How innocent. How she was his employee and his son's ex-girlfriend.

But her eyes fluttered, opened, widened to the size of saucers. He opened his mouth to say something, but what the fuck could he actually say? That he'd heard her moaning and came to check that she didn't need him to make her come so she could go to sleep. Because that's what the feral part of him had wanted to do.

Liam had always been in control on the track. He'd always had a cool head. A smooth operator that some assumed didn't act on his emotions. He'd had them, but they'd been locked down.

He'd been a twenty-five-year-old race car driver, raising a toddler son alone. The money had helped, but there was no amount of money in the world that could alleviate the awesome responsibility of being solely responsible for the health and well-being of a little boy. He'd never been young because he'd never been allowed to be. He'd been totally focused on giving his son everything he needed. He'd turned everything else in his life off in favor of his responsibilities.

And now, he was standing here, thinking about throwing it all away to touch a woman that was too young for him, and off-limits in every way he could imagine.

He couldn't even speak his son's name inside his mind right now because of the way he was thinking about fucking his ex-girlfriend, his teammate, his rival. Where the fuck was Liam's loyalty?

It had been extinguished with a lust he couldn't get ahold of. He gripped the doorframe as though it was a lifeline, but he was drowning.

"Is everything okay?" She was breathy, and her voice was sleepy. Her lips a little swollen and a crease on the side of her face from the pillow. She was totally rumpled and imperfect, and she wasn't wearing a bra. He should not be seeing this.

"Why aren't you asleep?" His mouth was dry, and his voice sounded strained and raspy to him.

Her low laugh gripped him by the balls and tugged. He nearly groaned from the pleasure of it. "Because my boss is in the room staring at me like a weirdo. Seriously, what's wrong? Did I get a penalty and lose P1?"

Of course she was worried about the race. Why else would he come barging into the room where she was sleeping? Something had to be wrong.

He shook his head. "No. Nothing like that. I just—"

Her gaze dipped to his crotch again. At this point, he was so used to having a hard-on around her, he didn't even think about it. He willed it to subside but being in the same room with her aged that part of his body down to his twenties at the very least.

"You just what?" She licked her bottom lip, and he let out a sound that was a cross between a moan and a growl. She smiled at him, as though she knew every thought in his head and wasn't turned off at all by how perverted they were.

He didn't say anything. He didn't dare. He was holding on by the very thinnest of silk threads. He was a few milliseconds away from losing all control, and they both knew a few milliseconds could mean everything.

But it was clear to him, as she got out from under the duvet and crawled toward the end of the bed, toward him, that she was going to press her luck. She was going for the gap in his self-control. She stood up on her knees, and he allowed himself to look—just look—at her. Her pajamas consisted of a flimsy tank top that made her nipples seem almost lewd. And a pair of panties that might have seemed modest on anyone without the same hard-won muscle tone. There was a muscle in her hip he wanted to bite down on before he licked between her thighs.

He could smell her arousal now that she was this close. He'd memorized the way she smelled, sweaty and full of adrenaline, after the race. It was almost the same now, except different.

She ran her fingers through her messy hair and bit her lip again. "I feel the same way, Liam."

"You couldn't—"

"Shut up." She paused, seeming shocked she'd said that to her boss, but then she continued. "I can't get to sleep at night without touching myself and thinking about you. Whatever sounds you thought I was making back here were for you."

"You did that on purpose? To see if you could lure me back here?" Such a naughty fucking girl. He really ought to take her over his knee. He wondered if she would like that. "What did you think was going to happen if you did that?"

Micaela shook her head and took a deep, quivering breath. "I didn't know, but I had to try."

"Why?" He wanted to know why she'd decided to seduce him now. Was she not that into him and trying to use his attraction to her to get a leg up in the team? Or did she really feel the same clawing ache he felt whenever he was anywhere near her? Whenever he thought of her?

He couldn't move, because he didn't trust himself not to reach between her legs and test out whether she was wet and desperate for him. "Why do I think about you every time I touch myself?"

He nodded. His mouth completely dry.

"I have no idea. I know it's not because you're my ex's dad." She stepped off the bed and her body was just inches from his. "I know it's not because you're my boss. Both of those things would lead me to run far away."

"I don't want to hurt you." He did want to hurt her, but only in ways they'd both like. And only if she begged. He had the distinct feeling she was the kind of person who needed to push through some pain to feel any pleasure. He'd seen her smile on the Instagram she'd posted after doing a VO2 max test. He'd thought about it later, in the shower. He'd wondered if she would smile like that after taking his cock down her throat.

"I don't want to hurt you either. And I know this is messy."

It was his turn to laugh. "This is more than messy. This is a disaster waiting to happen."

"It is." She looked down and pressed a hand against his chest. It burned him through his shirt. He closed his eyes. "But I feel like when you didn't make sure that we had a chaperone on this plane, you committed to the move. There's no pulling out now. We're fully spinning towards the wall."

"But—" He could argue all he wanted that he'd thought he had more self-control, but that would be him lying to himself. And though he might be questioning his own integrity right now—really whether he controlled his own fate at all—he wouldn't do that.

"If I kiss you, you're going to kiss me back." She was right. "And I want to make sure that you know it was my choice. I want this just as much as you do. And I want you to promise me that you won't hate yourself for it."

"I won't just kiss you back, Micaela." He shouldn't have said her name. It made this dream of a moment more real. "I won't be able to stop touching you unless you want me to, and you won't want me to."

She cocked her head to the side and trailed a finger of the hand that was on his chest across the skin right above the collar of his shirt. He had to lock his knees. "I won't want you to? Why not?"

"Because one kiss will be all it takes to tear you apart if you feel the same way about me that I do about you. You'll need more, thinking it will put you back together. And then, we'll fuck. We'll tell ourselves that it will only be once, but we'll know that's not true. Both of us are drivers. We'll always push the limit."

She grabbed the lapels of his shirt and pulled his face close to hers. "I don't see a problem with that."

He could see a million, but he didn't pull away when she kissed him.

Chapter Eighteen

Micaela would never have to wonder what it would be like to blow up in a car crash again. The way Liam kissed was like a supernova happening in her own body. She felt as though she was floating through space instead of trying to join the mile-high club with her boss. And, at that moment, he wasn't her boss—he was the only person she ever wanted to kiss again.

In her mind, when she'd imagined this, his kiss had been hard and uncompromising. Her fantasies had him plundering her mouth and taking what he wanted from her. This was far different. Instead of a marauder, he was an explorer, using his mouth on hers and his hands on her body to discover everything he could. And it may have felt like she was floating, because he held her several inches above the ground, his hand holding her ass. Their pelvises were aligned, and she now knew his hard-on had definitely been about her and not the flight attendant.

She never wanted this moment to end, but there would come a point—probably at about the time clothes would start coming off—where one or both of them would become very conscious that they were making a decision. He would think about how he was betraying his son—she didn't agree with that assessment, but Liam was honorable to a fault.

And she was absolutely sure he'd never tasted any of his employees' mouths the way he was tasting hers. No one would have ever left his team, for one thing. She didn't care what flavor of person someone usually liked to kiss; everyone and their dad would like to kiss Liam. That's why men spoke about him with such hushed reverence—they all respected his career in motorsports and secretly wanted to make out with him.

She giggled into his ear when he moved his mouth down to her neck. She was drunk on him.

"Are you laughing at me?" he growled. People made fun of growling heroes in particularly salacious books, but the way her pussy clenched when he spoke in a low warning tone made her a believer.

"No." She hoped he would just accept that as an answer and keep kissing her, but he stopped.

"What are you laughing about?" He pulled back and looked at her. She was almost grateful she was getting a moment to memorize him like this—debauched puffy lips and disheveled hair. There might have been a wrinkle or a bit of her lip gloss on his usually perfect shirt.

"I was thinking about how every straight guy I know wouldn't think twice about making out with you—kind of like the Ryan Reynolds of motorsports."

His brow furrowed, but he grinned at her. "If you can think about something as silly as all that, then I must not be doing a very good job at kissing you witless."

"Why do you think I'm having such silly thoughts?" His grasp on her body tightened with the tension creeping into the conversation.

"Because we shouldn't be doing this." A statement and not a question. And they shouldn't be doing this. But now that she'd kissed him, she couldn't imagine not doing it again and again and again.

"And yet, I don't really care. I'm having silly thoughts because I'm under the influence of your mouth. The bad news is that I'm already addicted."

He didn't return her light smile and seemed to grow even more stern. Too bad that turned her on even more and she squirmed in his arms. "You know, I'm not part of the mile-high club."

She didn't tell him the only other person she'd dated with access to a private plane was his son, and yet Liam would be the one to defile her on a plane. And she wanted him to do that right now.

He dropped his head onto her shoulder, and he seemed to be curled around her body. "I want you, Micaela. I just know I shouldn't have you."

"Maybe if you did have me, you wouldn't want me so badly anymore." She hoped that wasn't true, but she'd say anything to convince him to move this party over to her bed. Maybe her father was right, and she was careless with her life. This could end in disaster for both of them. But part of her thought maybe it wouldn't end. She felt completely right in Liam's arms. She wanted to stay there. "I wouldn't be forbidden fruit anymore. The thrill would be completely gone."

He looked down at her, incredulous. He knew that was a lie. Them fucking on this plane wouldn't end the fascination they held for each other. It would unleash something neither of them could control. Someone would find out, and then people who shouldn't find out would find out. There would be scandal and controversy.

"I don't want anyone to question why you're where you are. I don't want anyone to be able to take your success away from you—"

"Shut the fuck up, Liam." She doubted any of his other employees could get away with talking to him like that, but he said nothing. "I'm fast because I'm fast. My results on track speak for themselves. This is completely separate from the fact that I drive for you."

He paused before he started talking again, probably afraid she'd slap him if he spoke out of turn. But then he said the other thing standing between her and an orgasm. "And this isn't about Brent?"

"Listen, I know you love him, but I don't give a shit about Brent anymore. He's a teammate. A rival. A colleague who I don't like very much. But it's not about the fact that we used to date or that he cheated on me. If I wanted to get revenge for that, I'd tell the press any number of embarrassing things he did when we were together."

Liam's brows rose. In another context, he'd probably want to know more about the embarrassing things. Unlike her, he cared about his son, and doing this right now probably made him feel like a shitty parent. But she'd just told him what he needed to hear. Must have, because some of the tension left his body, and he nuzzled the side of her neck with the tip of his nose.

She shivered. "Yes. Yes. More of this."

He chuckled and slipped his fingers inside her tank top, seeking out her nipple. When he found it, she sighed. He acted like they had all the time in the world, and she knew they had a few hours, if that.

"When do we land?" she asked.

"You're worried about plane schedules, now?" He didn't stop touching her, though.

"You're just going so slow." She didn't mean for that to sound like a whine, but it sounded like a whine.

"So, you like everything to go fast?" He didn't sound like he was judging her. He sounded like he did during briefings—as though he was filing away every bit of information shared for a later date.

"Not fast, but faster than this." She didn't have a lot of practice in telling men what she wanted during sex. Outside of her relationship with Brent, she hadn't had a lot of experience with relationships. But Liam would demand to know what she wanted and needed—and what she didn't want—at every turn. He wouldn't let her just tell him what he needed to hear so he could get his rocks off.

He demonstrated this by moving faster. He tossed her on the bed. She bounced a little, but she didn't fall off. And then, he was hovering over her, so close she could feel the heat of his body through his clothes. "Tell me what else you want. What else you like."

He was staring at her face, and she wasn't quite sure what to tell him. At the moment, she liked that he was close to her. But they were both wearing too many clothes. "I want to feel your skin against me."

He sat up, kneeling between her thighs, and started to unbutton his shirt. "Take yours off, too, Micaela." He said her name like he was reminding her that he was fully aware of who he was doing this with.

She pulled off her top without sitting up, and his breath caught. Now, she knew he'd been with models and actresses—some of the most beautiful women in the world. But the way he ate her with his gaze told her that he wasn't thinking about anyone else right now. He was as wrapped up in her as she was in him.

Liam spent a lot of time in the gym. The Panther social media team made sure to document his time there for team thirst traps. But seeing the results of all that hard work up close was entirely different from scrolling through and seeing a video of him doing biceps curls.

He was all sharp angles and power. Without his shirt, he felt even bigger than he normally did. He was still wearing his pants, but she could see his thighs flexing through the fabric. "Take off your pants."

He shook his head. "You first." She pulled off her panties, flinging them against the wall of the cabin with one foot. "Now, what do you want?"

Her mouth went dry, but she still managed to say, "Your mouth."

"Where?" He leaned close to her again, and then they were skin on skin. She opened her legs and wrapped them around his thighs, almost embarrassed by the wetness between her legs. But Liam groaned, so she was pretty sure he didn't mind.

Liam kissed her again, before she could tell him she wanted his mouth everywhere. He was more urgent with her this time. She dug her fingers into the hair at the nape of his neck and he growled into her mouth, satisfied. His erection dragged across her clit as they pressed together. She wanted more, but she could come like this.

"More. I need more," she said when he finally broke their kiss. And he didn't make her tell him what "more" meant. He methodically moved down her body until he was between her legs.

He kissed the inside of her thighs as though he was committing the flavor of her skin to memory. And then, she realized why he'd been going slow. He didn't think this would happen again. He believed the lie he'd told both of them when he'd said they could only do this once.

But he didn't know her well enough to know she wasn't going to give up something she wanted—and she very much wanted him—so easily. Sure, she understood his reasons, but he was licking the tendons between her pelvis and thigh when her pussy was right there for the taking. He somehow knew touching her there would make her desperate for his mouth on her clit, for his fingers inside of her.

"Please, Liam." His responding laugh was darkly sexy. But he heeded her plea and kissed her clit, sending electric desire coursing through her veins. She found her fingers gripping his hair and her thighs shaking as she pressed them against his skull.

He made feral sounds as he ate her out, but he was perfectly in control as he caressed her opening with one finger until she was pressing herself around him. She wanted to be filled up with him. She wanted him to take every part of her and make it his own. Tears formed in her eyes—the pleasure was so intense.

She felt like she was bracing for some kind of sudden impact, like she might die if it didn't come and might explode when it did. Every part of her was taut with a delicious tension that she wasn't sure she could survive much longer. "Liam, it's so good."

He made an agreeing sound into her body and added another finger. Fuck. Fuck. Fuck. She didn't know if she was chanting that in her head or screaming so loud the pilot could hear her. But it didn't matter.

She came so hard it was like the g-force of a sharp turn. Her whole body jerked and braced, and all the blood rushed through her veins and vessels. He kept touching her until it stopped.

It was like the first few seconds after hitting the wall, where she didn't know if all of her parts were in good working order. The tears leaked from her eyes.

When she looked down at Liam, he was sitting on his haunches, his face drenched in her, with an expression of concern.

Until she started laughing and sat up to unfasten his belt.

"More?" he asked, as though he had come instead of her.

She nodded her head. "More."

Media Day

—

Miami

Chapter Nineteen

"How do you feel about your girl driver winning the last two races, Liam?" First, he wanted to punch the reporter who called Micaela his "girl driver" until he passed out because he'd swallowed all of his teeth and choked on them. And then, he didn't want to say how he felt every time she passed him in the garage—how he wanted to bury his face in her hair and snort her like a drug.

"We're extremely proud as a team with what she's been able to do in the car so soon into her career. We made the right choice in picking her as a driver." He'd made a ton of wrong choices ever since, like having sex with her at every opportunity since the plane trip from Japan to Beijing.

She'd spent most of the short two-week break since the Chinese Grand Prix practically living at his house in Lincolnshire, near the British factory. One morning, after an event for sponsors at the facility, they'd been eating breakfast in the sunroom. She was sitting there in his T-shirt, half a croissant hanging out of her mouth and a cup of coffee dangling from her fingers. She looked like an old photograph of a sixties film star, with some of her makeup from the night before still around her eyes.

They hadn't had time to wash their faces when they'd returned to his house. The way the dress she'd worn made him insane with hunger meant the garment had been above her waist as soon as the door had closed. He'd been inside her seconds later.

Thinking about it now, weeks later, made him hard. He adjusted his stance, so it wouldn't be obvious. He already felt like enough of a pervert; he didn't need the media knowing the mere thought of his "girl driver" made him hard enough to split wood.

"And your son hasn't been performing as well? He wasn't on the podium in the last race."

That was enough to get rid of his erection.

"Brent's been meeting the targets we projected with the car, often exceeding them. We're very happy with our driver lineup. They are both outperforming the car."

Micaela had been halfway through her croissant when they'd both heard the front door opening. A Sunday morning, it wasn't the gardener or the housekeeper—he'd been keeping them away as much as he could with Micaela there. He trusted them, but everyone had a price when it came to the British tabloids.

And then he'd heard Brent yell, "Dad!" from the front hall.

Micaela had looked at him, frozen in panic. Half of him wanted to tell her to stay put, that he'd get rid of Brent so he could have her after breakfast. But he knew she didn't want their affair to get in the way of his relationship with Brent. He didn't want that either. At first, he'd been surprised she was worried about his son at all—but then he'd realized she only cared about how Liam felt about his relationship with his son. She didn't want Brent to find out because it would ultimately hurt Liam.

So, he stood up and gently took Micaela's arm, making sure she didn't spill her coffee. There was a pantry to the side of the sunroom where she could hang out unnoticed until Brent went up to his room. Then, he moved the plates around, so it looked like it was just him for breakfast.

Brent hadn't noticed a thing. He hadn't stayed long. Something about meeting Paola for some styling advice. Liam had wondered if his son had moved on with the team's PR manager.

Luckily, after the one question about Brent, the reporter turned to Alessandro Rossi, the team principal for Lupo. "How frustrated are you that your drivers aren't beating the Panther cars?"

"We've been very impressed with their results so far this season." He ought to be. Ethan and Luca in the same driver lineup was like putting two stray tomcats in a bag and expecting them to cooperate their way out instead of tearing each other to pieces. "They are getting along quite well, and we see this as a long-term indicator of our success."

The Italian was full of shit, but they were media-trained up the ass at Lupo. The storied Italian brand had been in every single season of the series, and they were the most winning team of all time. Recently, they hadn't been as successful, but they'd been giving Panther a run for their money the past few years.

But, the past two races, Micaela had won. Liam smiled at that.

"Liam, do you have any comments about the competition Lupo has been bringing?"

Caught. At least it wasn't the hard-on. He searched for something quasi-intelligent to say that didn't include the fact that he thought he might be falling for the last woman he should have ever touched. "I think it's admirable that their internal driver rivalry is pushing both of their guys forward. It was a gamble that seems to be paying off for the team."

The reporter went back to Alessandro. "The internal driver rivalry pushed both of your drivers right off the track in Suzuka, didn't it?"

Qualifying Day

—

Miami

Chapter Twenty

"Mami, I don't know why we're not just staying at your house." Ethan had paid off Cece's mother's mortgage during the first year of his marriage with one paycheck. But every time they visited Miami, Graciela wanted to stay at the hotel too.

Cece's mother made a dismissive motion in her direction and poured another glass of champagne while the makeup artist touched up Cece's foundation. "If I wanted to stay at home, I would stay at home and not even watch this stupid race."

Graciela liked that Cece had found a man with money, but she also thought motorsports were stupid. She'd once told her daughter she would have been better off tying herself to a race car driver with dinero viejo in the seventies, when they routinely died. That way, she would have had money and wouldn't have had to deal with a man.

On New Year's Eve, Cece might have agreed. But things were different now. Ethan had been different since Japan. Maybe the ugly crash with Luca had made him see how precious life was. The collision had mixed all of the feelings she had for both of them and turned them upside down. It was like an amusement park ride she couldn't seem to stop.

But Cece didn't know how Ethan felt because he didn't talk about any of it with her. They hadn't really had time. During the break, she'd been asked to pose for a *Vogue Italia* photo shoot with some of the other WAGs. Although Jocelyn had seemed ecstatic to escape her husband

and children for five days on the Amalfi Coast, Cece had wanted to be with her husband for a change.

Neither he nor Luca had been severely injured in the crash, but Ethan had been bruised up. He'd seemed vulnerable and sad when she'd told him she was leaving for her trip. It was the first time he'd shown her anything other than asshole mode in ages, and she'd wanted to stick around for it.

While she'd been away, he'd called her every night. But he hadn't talked about any of the hard stuff, he'd asked about her day and actually seemed to listen to her. After the first night, she'd sent his favorite physio over, one who'd left the race circuit and started their own business, to check him over. He'd thanked her for it—which was rare given how he'd always just expected her to take care of him—that night on the phone.

Today, he'd sent over a hairstylist and makeup artist to do up both Cece and her mother. The moment her husband had met her mother, he'd clocked that a British accent, money, and charm were going to dazzle her. Cece had been more difficult to pin down. She didn't trust he was for real. And she still wasn't sure she could trust that Ethan was for real.

"How's it going with Luca?" Cece sat, stunned for a second, by her mother's question. Did she know that Cece had an affair with Luca? Was it written all over her face? Had she seen the way Luca had stared her down during the team dinner on Wednesday night? Cece's heart was beating so fast she almost didn't hear her mother add, "You know? On the team?"

"Well, they crashed during Japan, but they both took the podium in China." Cece narrowed her gaze. "Ethan's racing pays for your whole life, and you don't even bother to check the results?"

Graciela shrugged again and looked into Cece's closet for something to wear. They were the same size, and Cece always brought extra clothes for her mother to steal when they visited. Cece had been so upset when they'd added Miami to the race calendar permanently because she wouldn't have an excuse not to go home and see Graciela. Before that, she could have gone two years without seeing her mother face-to-face.

It wasn't that she didn't love the woman who'd given birth to her. She just didn't want to look into her future if she made all the wrong choices. She didn't want to stay tied to a man who didn't love her or a string of men who didn't love her just to survive.

But Ethan was trying. And that was promising. "Could you get me some champagne?" she asked Graciela. "And tell me about the plastic surgeon you've been dating."

Graciela was after a deep-plane facelift, and she could talk about her new beau's qualifications for hours.

Luca watched Ethan pass his door, and he hesitated for a few seconds. He knew they had to talk. Mostly ignoring each other during the China weekend had worked, because Cece had been in Milan modeling. He didn't follow her on his official Instagram account, but he'd made a fake one for a dog he didn't have so he could see what she was doing. Along with the Google alert, he knew it was creepy and obsessive, but he couldn't seem to help himself.

But Cece was here this weekend. This was her hometown. And the tension during the team dinner had been so thick it had made the humidity seem non-oppressive. A feat.

They couldn't have another crash like Suzuka. He was only a few races into his second chance at a career, and he wasn't going to let Ethan or his own misguided feelings for Ethan's wife ruin it.

So, he stood up and walked next door to Ethan's room. He didn't bother to knock, which was a mistake. Ethan was changing into his fireproofs and was standing there without a shirt on.

Luca shouldn't let himself look, just like he shouldn't have let himself look at Cece during dinner the other night. And he didn't know why he was having any sort of feelings about Ethan. He'd made it clear that neither he nor his wife was available for that kind of looking.

"Am I late for some stupid social media shit?" Ethan was annoyed. Of course he was. There was no reason for them to clear the air between them. They'd made it through a race without crashing into each other.

They were colleagues. Not best friends. Not even friendly acquaintances. Luca didn't know why that bothered him so much.

"No, I—um—wanted to talk." Ethan's brow furrowed, and he put on his fireproofs.

"About what?" His question was harsh, but he didn't slam the door in his face. He backed up and sat on the cot provided to the drivers for naps or relaxing before races.

Luca stepped into the room and closed the door. The walls in this temporary structure were thin, but it would give them some privacy. At least, the social media admin wouldn't think they were entitled to capture and post this conversation.

"I don't want it to be like this." Luca didn't know what else to say. He just knew he didn't want to feel this tension with Ethan anymore. There was nothing he could do to go back and not sleep with his wife. He definitely couldn't travel back in time and not fall in love with her. And he wouldn't do that to himself. He might never be able to be with her publicly, but he knew he'd never feel like that about anyone else. He wouldn't take that away from himself, even if he could.

He'd never tell Ethan how he felt, though. He'd go back and find some way to hide his feelings from a man who knew him better than almost anybody else.

"You don't want us to race?" Ethan chuckled. "That's literally our jobs."

"I love racing you, Ethan." That was the truth. There was no one he loved matching up his skills against more. "Last week, I knew you were going to make that move at turn five. How do you think I knew?"

Ethan shrugged. "Because I made that same move on a similar turn at that karting track in Cologne."

"Exactly. It's like second nature to race you. When I'm in that car, and you're in my mirrors or just ahead of me, I feel like I can think seconds into the future. I know what you're going to do next, and yet you sometimes surprise me." It delighted him, really. Before this season, he'd been done with racing. Or it had been done with him. He wasn't sure which was truer.

His body had been tired, and he couldn't have imagined dealing with the kind of pressure that came along with driving millions of euros' worth of machinery and the hopes of thousands of people in a team. When it wasn't working out, like it hadn't worked out the past two seasons, everything felt awful all the time. That, along with the fans and the press and the drama, had left him empty.

Now, the racing part felt good. It felt like home. Except for that crash with Ethan, he felt like nothing could touch him when he was in the car. When he was wheel-to-wheel racing with his teammate, he could only think of a handful of times when he'd ever felt more alive.

But he couldn't say all that to Ethan. They weren't even friends, and the man knew that Luca was in love with his wife.

"I promise, I won't touch her." Luca knew that promise would strain every fiber of integrity he had. But she didn't want him. Couldn't want him. And he didn't want the media circus that would come along with them trying to be together. So, he could let it lie for the good of everyone involved. It would hurt, but he could do it. It would make the situation easier if he could repair his relationship—his working relationship—with Ethan, though. "I just want to race you like we did when we were kids. I want us to win the championship and be able to celebrate together as more than rivals."

Ethan leaned back on his hands and looked Luca up and down, as though any lies he'd told might be written all over his body. "Why now?"

Because Luca couldn't do this anymore. It would break him. And that would be tragic. They might never be able to capture what they'd had when they were fifteen—something that had transcended friendship and even brotherhood. But maybe they could have something richer. At the very least, they could have closure.

Neither of them knew how long they had in this sport. The clock moved in only one direction. But they could have an ending that fit the bond they'd had when they were young.

"I might only have the rest of this season." Luca motioned to a photo of Ethan hoisting a trophy during his first victory with the team above his head. "You might only have the rest of this contract before they pull one of their junior drivers up and try to convince the fans that he's better than either of us."

Ethan grunted in acknowledgment. "Yeah, so? The media loves the narrative that we hate each other. We might last longer if we keep it up."

"But do you want that?" The idea of Ethan wanting that made his chest ache. "I don't."

Ethan shook his head. "I don't know, mate. I don't know if I can put everything behind me. Me thinking that you are going to try something with Cece when my back is turned is going to eat me up inside. I know you. I know you don't give up when you want something. Is this all just so that you can get close and try to steal her?"

It truly wasn't, but Ethan thinking that revealed a lot about the current state of their marriage. He'd fucked up, but he still loved her. And he couldn't say for sure that—deep in his subconscious—he wasn't trying to make it okay to be close to Cece again. He craved her almost as much as he craved a win in tomorrow's race.

"If you weren't worried that I could take her, you wouldn't hesitate to put our past in the past." It was really a question, but they both knew it was true. If Ethan felt like his marriage was safe, he would be able to put his big-boy pants on and move forward.

"We can work together." Ethan looked away from him. "Maybe we can all have dinner back home and see what's what."

That was likely all he was going to get from his friend right now. "No more crashes."

Ethan pinned him with his gaze. “No more looking at my wife as though you know what she tastes like.”

Just him mentioning her taste had memories of her rushing over his tongue. He tried not to lick his lips thinking about it. He nodded and refrained from saying he knew what they both tasted like.

An image of all of them together clouded his brain for a split second, but he pushed it away. That wasn’t even close to what was on offer—a tentative peace between the two of them as long as he stayed away from Cece.

“Dinner in Monte Carlo would be great.”

Free Practice Friday — Imola

Chapter Twenty-One

Brent looked away from the camera for a second and smiled at Paola. She rolled her eyes at him. She did that a lot. He would never say a word, but he loved it. It made him even hotter for her every time she did it. And he was already so hot for her that he was about to burn up.

"Good, good. Now, look at the camera." The photographer was taking new promotional pictures of him and Micaela. This probably should have happened yesterday, but there was some sort of snafu with the lighting, so they were doing it before the first practice session. Brent looked at the camera and attempted to smolder.

He glanced over at Micaela and saw her smiling at her phone. She used to smile at him like that over FaceTime. Had she met someone new? Where had she found the time?

Brent didn't have the capacity to date during the season. That's why he'd found it so easy to cheat on Micaela—a lack of object permanence when it came to his girlfriends. He was starting to realize that he fell in love with whatever was in front of his face most of the time.

Before the season, he'd been wondering if he'd only started racing because he was exposed to it all the time. But he did love it. Maybe not as much as Micaela or some of the other drivers, but he did love the rush of putting in a really good qualifying lap as much as anyone else.

He just wondered how his father had managed to build a life for himself that worked around racing.

Brent admired that his father hadn't just stuck him with a nanny or his grandparents to race. He'd wanted to tuck his son in almost every night. They'd traveled the world together with a tutor and a babysitter, who sometimes doubled as an assistant for his dad.

His father might be the only person he truly loved, in a way that wasn't dictated by convenience. And his father was definitely the only person he could really trust. Everyone else was just out to see what they could get from him half the time.

"Stop furrowing your brow like that, Brent," Paola said from behind the photographer. "It might be distinguished for a man to have wrinkles, but not at twenty-three."

He couldn't help but grin. She'd loosened up considerably since the beginning of the season. The more he showed up on time and ready to fulfill his professional obligations, the more she loosened up. He didn't know if she knew she was incentivizing him this way, but it worked.

The photographer straightened up and lowered their camera. "I think we have enough here."

Paola looked at him. "Are you sure? We can make him stand there and look pretty as long as you need." She thought he looked pretty. He tried not to react and had to bite his lip to keep from making a crass comment, but she'd never admitted she found him pretty before. He knew he was good looking, but she'd never said that before. He liked it. He liked her.

He stepped off the set, probably standing closer to Paola than he should. "Are you hungry?"

She looked up at him with a quizzical look on her face. "Hungry? What?"

"Do you need to eat some food?" He gave her his most charming smile, reveling a little that she seemed to be off balance. "I'm going to grab an espresso and something small before practice, and I was wondering if you wanted something."

She looked down, and he could swear she was blushing. "I'm fine." She cleared her throat. "I have to stay while they get shots of Micaela."

He nodded and caught a whiff of Paola's scent. It was light and floral, but with a bit of spicy musk. Just like Paola. Lovely, underneath all the fierce bite.

Brent stepped back. "I'll see you later, then."

"Brent was acting—strangely." Paola sat down in the makeup chair next to Micaela, startling her.

Micaela lifted her head and turned her phone over. Paola did not know about her and Liam, and they needed to keep it that way. Micaela didn't even know what they were *doing*. Well, she knew the mechanics and anatomy of what they were doing, but she had no earthly idea of what to do with all the emotions of what was happening between them.

She craved Liam's presence like it was a drug. Part of her knew it was probably just lust that would fade and/or blow up in her face eventually. But a larger part of her knew she'd never felt this way before and probably never would again.

She was falling in love with her boss. The way he respected her—considered her—was more than she'd ever hoped for. Which was a sad thing all wrapped up in a good thing.

But if Brent was being weird, maybe he knew something was up. Maybe he was starting to suspect that Liam and Micaela were sneaking around?

She shook her head to dislodge the thought. He couldn't know. They were being so careful. They weren't even visiting each other's rooms over race weekends. She was starting to look forward to the end of the weekend—when they could be together—more than the races themselves.

It was so dangerous, and she was so lost in it at the same time.

"You shook your head. Do you not think he's acting weird?" Micaela needed to pay attention to what was going on in front of her, or she would let something slip. That was unacceptable.

"I mean, I guess he's acting like his normal asshole self with me. He mostly ignores my presence unless we're forced to interact." That was fine with Micaela. It was better than what would happen if he found out what she was doing with his father. "What did he do? Is he harassing you?"

Paola blushed a little, and that piqued Micaela's curiosity. Then, she shook her head. "He's not doing anything bad. But he just asked me to go eat with him. Most of the drivers I've worked with want to spend less time with the team press officer, not more."

"Do you have a crush on him?" She didn't add that Brent had never—not once—checked in to see if she was hungry or needed anything unless she'd been standing next to him. Not even after he'd literally been inside her.

Once, he'd actually rolled off her and then ordered takeout for himself. It was a bonus if there had been any left for her.

"No, absolutely not." Paola shook her head and gave a dramatic, fake shiver—as though the thought of having a crush on Brent was disgusting to her. It was telling. "He's rude, ungrateful, and spoiled. Definitely not my type."

Micaela laughed at that. "Say what you will about Brent Sullivan, but he is almost everyone's type. He might be an asshole, but he's charismatic and beautiful to look at."

Paola snorted. "You're right."

"It's okay to like him. There aren't any team rules against it." Micaela knew. She'd looked at the handbook as soon as she'd gotten off that private plane with Liam.

"But it's messy." Paola shook her head again and stood up. "Too complicated."

Micaela made a noncommittal sound, stood, and moved over to the soundstage. She knew about complicated better than anyone right now.

Race Day

—

Imola

Chapter Twenty-Two

Cece watched as Jocelyn ginned up fake tears for the camera. To be fair, they could also be real tears. Her husband had just announced his retirement, and she would be devastated to leave the paddock. She doubted he would return as a broadcaster—he might be a huge personality, but none of the networks would risk him dropping a hundred f-bombs a minute during a race.

Unlike Jocelyn, who never met a photo lens she wouldn't flirt heavily with.

"We're just so grateful for all the opportunities this has given us as a family." She was grateful for all the brand deals that kept her in designer clothes and high-end skin care. "But it's time for us to really put down roots back in Finland as a family." Cece tried really hard not to laugh—especially given that she faced a somewhat uncertain future—but she just couldn't picture Jocelyn chilling in a hunting lodge while Heka snowshoed across the Finnish steppe all winter long.

Ethan approached her and put his arm around her shoulders. They had a few hours before the race, and the drivers parade would start in a few minutes. Because Imola was one of two home races for Scuderia Lupo, which was headquartered in Italy, he'd been mobbed since they'd landed here on Tuesday. There were photographers everywhere, and fans where the photographers couldn't go.

Racing was religion in Italy, and Emiliano Lupo—the founder of the team—was a minor god. If Cece had to guess, he ranked somewhere between the Virgin Mary and Jesus himself. He was definitely above the pope.

Cece's mother had crossed herself and walked straight into a church when Cece had shown her a prayer card with Ethan fashioned as a beneficent saint on it. Her mother wasn't even religious—she was just wary of people using religious imagery in a mocking way. Cece didn't tell her that she and Ethan had sometimes played "confession" after that.

It was starting to feel normal to have Ethan touching her casually again. It had only been five months since he'd cheated on her, but she was starting to think they could put their marital problems behind them.

"She's really putting on a show." Ethan didn't know Jocelyn well. He'd always said he didn't need to know her individually; he knew the type. At first, Cece had been offended at the idea that Ethan was stereotyping a certain type of woman, but she kind of got it after knowing Jocelyn for half a decade. She *was* a type, and Cece had never felt entirely at home with her.

"I mean, I sort of get where she's coming from. She's going to miss this." Cece was very much like all the other girls, but her motivations were different than Jocelyn's. Her erstwhile friend had grown up in privilege, but Cece had known struggle. Maybe it made her more grateful and more aware of how fake all of this was at the same time. Or maybe it just made her more wary.

"Do you have money on how long the marriage will last into retirement?" Cece looked up at Ethan. His mouth was twisted in amusement, but there was something in his eyes that told her he wasn't just asking about Jocelyn and Heka's chances. Was he thinking of retiring? Or was he just wondering about the chances of their marriage lasting if they didn't have this lifestyle to keep them together anymore?

"I think she loves him." She honestly didn't know if Jocelyn actually loved Heka. But she was speaking for herself at that point. "But who knows if they even fit together anymore."

He squeezed her shoulders and moved so they were pressed together, side by side, as another reporter pushed past them in the crowd. "I think they fit together in ways only they understand."

When he said that, something clicked inside Cece. She didn't know if she and Ethan could make this work forever, but they'd always fit together in ways only the two of them could understand. That's why it had been so difficult to explain to Luca why she'd chosen Ethan in the first place. But he'd always offered her a kind of security that only came with generational wealth. Although that security had been rocked by his cheating and then hers, it was still there.

They'd both made mistakes, but mistakes could always be confessed and forgiven. Maybe they needed to play confession for real this time.

Tuesday Before the Grand Prix

—

Monte Carlo

Chapter Twenty-Three

If someone were to frame one of the thousands of photos being taken of the three of them in this moment and hang it in a gallery, it would be very tempting to entitle the piece, "The Most Awkward Dinner Ever."

The artist and gallerist would not be wrong in their interpretation of the image, and Cece was tempted to turn her phone camera on all of the people recording them from the plaza.

Cece was seated next to Ethan and across from Luca on the patio of a very well-known restaurant in Monte Carlo. The photos from tourists had started as soon as she and Ethan had pulled up in his Ferrari F430—she should have known he was going for spectacle when he chose to take out the only car he owned with gullwing doors. There was something about the sight of doors opening upward, even in the principality, that was like a homing beacon for every gossip and amateur paparazzo in town.

She'd dressed carefully—in a vintage Diane von Furstenberg wrap dress, wedge heels, and giant gold hoops—something she felt comfortable and looked rich in. It didn't work. She couldn't calibrate her physical response to seeing Luca up close again.

He wore a white linen shirt. It was unbuttoned down to the bottom of his pecs. Had he worn a chain, he would have looked like a minor mafioso. As it was, he should have looked like any other man in the restaurant. But he stood out wherever he went as long as she was the one looking.

He couldn't be more different than Ethan, who looked like he'd just stepped off his yacht for a bite. It was the kind of careless, good-natured aristocrat who doesn't even know he's hotter than the sun vibe that had people wanting to consume him.

At this point, after years of marriage, Cece should not be crawling out of her skin having a meal with her husband and his teammate. And Luca and Ethan didn't seem to be ill at ease with each other at all, which was weird. They'd even exchanged a cursory bro hug before sitting down. Maybe it was all for the cameras. She just needed to know what they were all doing here before her head exploded into a million tiny pieces.

Instead of standing up and going to the bathroom, she sat and picked at her fish. She was completely zoned out of the conversation between Ethan and Luca. They were casually chatting about a karting race in Hockenheim they'd competed in at fourteen or something.

She was spiraling a little bit until Ethan put his hand on her upper back and said, "What's wrong?" Then, she felt as though she was in a free fall.

She couldn't yell. Someone would hear. And she couldn't let her riot of emotions show on her face. Someone would take a picture, and then she'd be on the blogs and WAGs Instagram accounts with a flurry of speculation about the state of her marriage. She'd done everything possible—well, everything but refrain from fucking her husband's teammate—to avoid that.

Instead, she smiled widely, angling her face as far away from the cameras as she could, and said, "This is so fucking weird, you guys."

Ethan smiled back at her. "Yeah, it's definitely weird that you've been with both of us."

Ethan thought saying that to both of them would be more satisfying. He'd had some ideas about confronting them, but he'd ultimately decided on the route that would be least likely to have his wife in hysterics and Luca flipping a table and beating him until he couldn't race on Sunday—public place, lots of onlookers.

At that moment, Luca looked as though he didn't care about the surroundings and would beat him regardless. Cece looked as though her stomach had dropped to the ground and her heart was ground meat. So, he'd been right. They had been together.

"Doing that here is dirty business." Luca was right. This was awful of him, but Ethan was a little bit terrible. They both knew that, and they were the ones who had an affair.

"How many times did you fuck my wife?"

Cece's voice was so small, even though they were all speaking in hushed tones to avoid any other diners hearing. "Twice. It was twice."

"You're the one who cheated with a random girl your tosser schoolmates brought over on New Year's Eve." Luca was trying to defend her, but he sounded petulant. Ethan refused to look at him right now.

Ethan had tried not to think about that night after Cece had told him she was willing to move forward with him. She didn't throw it in his face every time they disagreed about something. He'd thought she was being mature about his cheating when she was really just acting out of guilt. She'd done something wrong too.

"I'm sorry," Cece said.

"No, you're not." Ethan thought she felt guilty because of how not sorry she was about fucking Luca. "You're sorry you got caught."

"I'd planned to tell you the truth at some point." Cece was starting to look distressed, and that wouldn't work to keep the rumors about trouble in their marriage at bay. "But there's never a right time. We're never home. We're never just the two of us. There's always—always—someone lurking who could hear something that they shouldn't."

She was right, but she'd chosen this life with him. She'd known she would sacrifice her privacy. But she hadn't anticipated cheating in their marriage. He'd promised her, and she'd promised him. The fidelity that had seemed so important when he was looking at her and not wanting to become his parents had slipped away. He'd allowed it first.

"I actually didn't ask to make you feel guilty." He cleared his throat and then looked at Luca, who glared at him. "I asked because I wanted to have an honest discussion."

Luca looked around and gave an offhand smile to the camera pointed right in his face. Ethan was surprised not to find a boom mic over the table. This had been a terrible idea. "Not really the right venue."

"I know." Ethan scrambled for a second, and he squeezed Cece's shoulder again. "I'm not angry at either of you. At least not—that's not the whole picture. Can we go back to our place? Alone?"

Luca stared at him for a long moment and nodded. "I'll park at home and come in the service entrance to the building." They'd done that when they were younger and didn't want a bunch of tourists to know how much time they were actually spending together.

Chapter Twenty-Four

Luca had an inkling of what Ethan wanted, and he was filled with a kind of hesitance that he'd never felt before. He wasn't even sure he understood the way his stomach clenched. It was bigger than any nerves he felt before any race, even the one the prior season he'd thought would be his last. Even his first.

He felt as though he was standing on the edge of a cliff, thinking about taking a dive into the clear blue azure of the sea. Making the leap might give him just enough of the adrenaline he needed.

Or it might end in him crashing on the rocks.

Anything worth having in life was worth getting hurt for. And, in the past few weeks, he'd been thinking about Cece every waking minute. Ever since she'd cut him off. After Imola—when there was a moment with Ethan in his room—he'd been thinking about Ethan too.

He parked his car, but he didn't get out right away. If he walked into Ethan and Cece's home, if Ethan suggested what Luca thought he would, and if Cece agreed, there would be no turning back. It was a lot of ifs, but his instincts were rarely wrong about the next three steps or the next five.

If he thought about all the ways this could go wrong, he'd never do it. If he thought about how many things could go wrong every time his wheels made contact with the track, he'd never drive a race car again.

He'd never feel the thrill of moving so fast that his organs had to catch up. He'd never feel the way he did when he was totally hooked up in the car and on the edge for the perfect qualifying lap. He'd never feel the disappointment of losing power and seeing smoke stream from the engine box as he had to retire the car, but that was worth the winning—every single time.

Cece—and Ethan—would be worth the price. He got out of the car and exited his building from the back door. The alleyway was quiet, and his steps echoed over the old cobblestones. Cece must have walked this way in the rain on New Year's Eve. She'd been lonely and angry. She'd needed him.

Just like she'd needed him while she was sitting at the table tonight. He'd wanted nothing more than to reach out to her—to have as much right to touch her as Ethan did. He wasn't going to kid himself into thinking he would be able to do that if they were all together. As long as they were in this sport, with all of its machismo, there was no way that two queer drivers could be in a throuple with one of their wives and have any sense of peace and privacy. It would be a complete and utter frenzy.

Cece hated the invasion of the press as things stood. She would absolutely not be able to tolerate the level of attention that a public relationship between the three of them would bring. So, it would have to be quiet. It would probably be temporary. Things would get complicated, and they would fall away from each other. But it would still kill him to not be able to touch her out in the open.

Ethan had texted him the code to the service entrance. As the door clicked open, he realized any pain would be worth having just a little bit of what he craved.

Cece paced the floor in the foyer of their flat. Ethan sat on the couch in the living room, flipping through a magazine as though he hadn't dropped a bomb at dinner. He hadn't spoken at all on their way home in the car. And he hadn't said anything except remarking on how the restaurant wasn't as good as it used to be on the way upstairs.

Finally, she'd snapped. "What are you planning?"

"To talk." He'd just smiled at her. "Don't worry so much."

Of course, that had made her worry more. He'd put his hand on the small of her back in that possessive way, and it had been oddly comforting. Maybe she didn't have anything to worry about, and maybe she had a whole new host of problems scratching and biting at her door.

But she was saved from spiraling further when someone knocked on the door softly. Her heart almost leaped from her chest. He was here.

She must have stood still for too long because Ethan walked to the door and opened it. Cece didn't want to speak. She wanted to wait for them to say something. The tension—the energy—in the room was a thick, syrupy thing that had its own momentum. Its own timing.

Luca nodded at Ethan and crossed the threshold, walking straight to her. "Are you okay?"

He grabbed her upper arms and looked her up and down, as though he was inspecting her for damage. The only damage she felt was to her nerves.

"I'm fine. Just—"

Ethan came close to both of them, and that didn't help the anxious boulder in her gut at all. "Confused. And I wish I could say I was sorry about ambushing the both of you. I'm man enough to admit it was petty."

Cece could protest that it wasn't fair he'd put them both on the spot in public. But it made sense—unlike wanting to talk later in private. "Are you ever going to just say what you want to say? Or are you going to extract your revenge in perpetuity?"

This was torture. Ethan knew that when he smiled at them both. "Drinks?"

Cece would throw up if she had a single drop of alcohol right now. "Nothing for me."

"Whatever you're having." Luca might be confused, but he wasn't a mess quite like her. He even let go of her arms as they walked into the living room. But she could feel his fingers brushing against the base of her spine. It was a small, nothing touch. Just knowing it was there gave her some fortitude.

Ethan went over to the wet bar and poured two scotches from a bottle that was older than all three of them put together. Despite her not wanting anything, he poured her a fizzy water with a twist of lime.

Luca sat on the other couch, across from her.

"Drink this," Ethan said as he put it down in front of her. She looked up at him, and his gaze was soft and loving, but he took a seat on the chair perpendicular to both chaise sofas. He took a long sip of his drink before looking at both of them in turn. "I want to watch you."

Cece's breath stopped. He wanted to *what*?

Luca, for his part, was way cooler about this than her. "You've never wanted to watch before. You've always liked to be an active participant."

"You've had—um—threesomes? Like together?" Cece didn't mean to sound angry. She was angry, but it wasn't about the fact that her husband and her lover had fucked the same person together before. She was mad the other person hadn't been her. But first, she needed to clarify what had actually gone down.

Ethan had the courtesy to blush. Of course he did. Luca looked her straight in the eyes and said, "Before you. But he refused to share you. He was extremely possessive, which is why I'm questioning this change of heart years later."

Cece motioned between the two of them. "And you two?"

One side of Luca's mouth turned up. "Yes." He took a sip of his drink.

Images flooded her brain. She knew how both of their mouths felt against hers, and it didn't take anything for her to imagine them kissing each other. They would be rougher with one another than they were with her. They were both sort of dominant, in their own ways.

For Luca, it was like breathing. He was just in charge in any room he walked into.

Ethan was more Machiavellian than dominant. He was like a chess player. It was reflected in his racing style as much as the way he'd orchestrated them into position this evening.

She took a sip of her water and suddenly wished it was scotch. Her blood was rushing through her, flooding every part of her body but her brain. She could feel the air touching her skin. Or was it the way that Luca and Ethan both looked at her with expectation in their gazes?

"You expect me to respond to that?" She still sounded angry. "I'm not pissed that you two have had threesomes. I'm not pissed that you've fucked each other. I'm not even pissed that you both lied to me about both for years. After all, I've lied to both of you."

Ethan grinned, and she wanted to punch him. He'd guessed all of this, and nothing was more satisfying to the man than being right.

Luca leaned forward. "What did you lie to me about?"

"Not wanting more of you."

Despite this utterly wild situation, a weight came off Luca's chest when Cece admitted she'd been lying. He'd known it deep inside, but it helped to hear her admit it. He supposed he understood why Ethan had done all this. It helped to see the people who'd wronged you admit what they'd done. It helped to see them squirm.

But demanding to watch him and Cece together was a bridge too far. Ethan would be able to keep himself at an emotional distance. His clothes would be on, and he wouldn't be vulnerable. This was not how it had been before. He was turning their friendship—or what was left of it—into something sordid and wrong.

It was never that.

"Why do you want to watch?" Knowing that was key to what would happen next. Cece's skin was flushed, and her eyes darted between the two of them. Her pupils were blown, and she shifted in her seat as though she needed one or both of them between her legs. He wanted to give her all of that and more, but Ethan had to use his words.

"I've always thought about it, and I think the two of you owe me."

Sometimes his entitlement was so pernicious that it made Luca want to scream. He wanted to strip away the smug demeanor Ethan wore at this moment.

"Yes." He didn't agree they owed him any damned thing, but he wasn't going to argue that point right now. "But you always enjoyed being part of the action before, and I'm wondering why that's changed."

He glanced over at Cece, who was looking between the two men in her living room as though they were all strangers. "I'm sorry I didn't tell you. I didn't think it was my place, and I wanted you too much the night you showed up dripping in my apartment."

Cece said, "Apology accepted." He didn't know he'd been expecting her not to forgive him until then.

"See how easy that was, Ethan. I apologize, and she accepts and moves on." Ethan's grip tightened on the arms of the chair he was pretending to relax in. "And my apology even involved a minor betrayal. It seems to me that you two are even on points when it comes to lying and adultery, and the only reason that you want to watch me fuck her is because it's going to get you off. But I'm going to need you to articulate your reasoning."

"I—"

It was rare that Ethan was at a loss for words. He was quotable and meme-able, but he didn't seem to have anything right at this moment. Cece filled in for him. "You want to watch so that you won't feel anything."

Luca had to remind himself that Cece knew a lot more about Ethan than he did. At least, at this point in his life she did. A hint of jealousy hit him. He used to be the person who knew Ethan best, and Cece had taken his place.

"And I'm not going to give you that." If Cece was going to play hardball, then he was going to let it play out. "Maybe Luca and I will agree to letting you watch—the first time."

Luca was instantly hard. He'd walked in thinking this probably wouldn't happen. Even if this wasn't about some petty bullshit from Ethan—just like dinner had been—there was no way Cece would agree. She was the most sensible out of all of them. After all, she'd gotten Ethan to avoid cocaine and his bad friends for years before the cheating.

This whole scene was out of Ethan's control, and he couldn't get it back. He'd half expected them to balk at his ask, but for some reason, he hadn't thought of them turning things around on him. "This is not about me. This is about me wanting to see what you're like together, so I can decide if I still want to be with her."

"That's a load of bullshit and you know it," Luca said right back. Cece didn't even look horrified. She looked as if she expected him to lash out when he was in a corner. "In fact, I think *you* should let *me* watch the two of you. You never let me do it before, and now you bring me here like some kind of hired stud."

Now Luca was trying to be funny. He always made a joke out of serious topics. Sometimes, like when reporters were digging where they shouldn't, it was an asset. But it was getting on Ethan's nerves at the moment.

Unfortunately, Cece found his humor appropriate at the moment. She threw her head back and laughed. When she did that, she threw her entire body into it. Her whole body shook with it. God, he loved his wife. He didn't just need her sitting on a shelf at home like a trophy. He needed her laughing in their living room and sleeping next to him. He needed to hear how she sighed when she was done laughing, the way she curled into herself as though he'd just made her come when he'd only told a half-decent joke.

Luca had always made her laugh. His best friend had always brought him to life too. He'd missed his friend. He'd missed how Cece was when they were all friends.

"Maybe I made a mistake all of those years ago when I said that I couldn't share her with you. It's just that I didn't see how we could make it more than a one-night stand, and Cece has always been more to me than that." Ethan turned to Cece, who had stopped laughing and looked at him with watery eyes. "I know that I don't deserve trust from either of you. I know that it seems like we're falling apart. But I thought that seeing you two together would finally put my doubts to rest."

"But you're not thinking those silly thoughts anymore, are you?" Luca narrowed his gaze at him. "You truly think we should all try being together?"

Ethan wasn't going to deny them. He could tell by the look in his oldest friend's eyes. Ethan nodded, and then he and Luca both looked to Cece. This was all up to her. She was the deciding vote.

Chapter Twenty-Five

Cece shook as they walked to the bedroom. She was pretty sure they didn't touch her because they were afraid she would change her mind. And she probably should change her mind about all of this. This could ruin her marriage. Or her life. Maybe both.

It could also save them. When they were all talking about whether and why they could or should fuck each other—other than the moment the ridiculousness of this situation hit her, and she started laughing uncontrollably—it had felt like it did when she'd met them. They'd communicated with each other, and it wasn't just through words. She'd been able to see they still cared for one another. They were still friends.

The fact that they'd sometimes been more than friends didn't bother her. It made this feel right. She hadn't even been angry when Ethan had said he hadn't wanted to share her back then. It might have saved them all a lot of heartache, but she might have discounted an encounter with the two of them as an adventure she'd had one time.

She might never have married Ethan. Despite how he'd acted at dinner and directly after, despite him cheating, she didn't regret being married to him. He'd promised her the world, and he'd delivered.

But now she wanted more. She wanted the deepest, most intimate parts of his soul. And to have that, they both needed Luca.

She got to the bedroom first and then froze. Her back was to the door, the light from the hall spilled over into the room, until she felt the heat and smell of her husband as he approached her from behind.

"Are you sure you're okay with this?"

Cece wasn't sure how to answer that question. She was sure about very little at the moment. "I'm sure that I want you."

He kissed her neck where it met her shoulder and trailed his fingertips along her collarbone. "And him."

He didn't sound as though the idea that she wanted Luca bothered him. Come to think of it, he'd seemed resigned to the fact that they'd been together at dinner. "You're not mad."

He shook his head, and she felt the disturbance his movement caused in the air behind her. "He was always attracted to you, and I thought you were always attracted to him. I was upset that you went behind my back, but I couldn't be too angry. I'm not a hypocrite."

Luca entered the room then and walked around them until he stood facing them. He had his hands in his pockets and cocked his head. "Were you serious about wanting to watch?"

"Hmmm." Ethan didn't make words because his mouth was on the back of her neck. He'd gathered her hair up in one hand, and the other hand was about to undo the tie on her dress.

A frisson of panic made its way through her, but it was overpowered by the lust that drugged her and made her limbs heavy. Luca watched Ethan's hands. It was as though he was looking at a car he'd been thinking about buying. She could see him cataloging the cadence of her breath as her husband undressed her.

"That's not an answer."

Ethan lifted his head. "That was an affirmative moan."

Luca took a step forward and said, "You know that's not how it works. I need verbal answers." Cece gasped as Luca grabbed Ethan's chin. Although they'd had an affectionate friendship before they'd fallen out, she'd never seen them touch like this. It was as though Luca was claiming Ethan too. And it took Cece's breath away. She wanted to see them kiss—wondered if they would. But then, Ethan stepped back, and she lost his heat.

"Yes, Luca. I was serious about wanting to watch you fuck my wife." The tension between these two men was incendiary—more intense than the on-track rivalry they played out for fans at every race. This was base and animal. It made her a little bit dizzy.

She thought her knees would give out when Luca placed his attention and his hands on her. He finished untying the dress and opened it, just so he could look at her. Gooseflesh formed all over her body.

"Go sit in that chair. Turn on the lamp first."

Fuck. She liked it when Luca took charge. And Ethan must not hate it, since he followed instructions. It was sort of strange, given her husband's general attitude of defiance. But it also made sense. He thrived on boundaries until he transgressed them and didn't want to live with the consequences.

But the result that ultimately came from his cheating—the three of them in this room together—wasn't entirely negative. Cece couldn't recall ever being more aroused. She was surprised that her whole body wasn't shaking with the need she couldn't contain.

Luca pushed the dress off her shoulders as she saw Ethan settle into the leather armchair that faced their bed. She liked to read in that chair, and now her husband would watch her fuck his best friend. It could have felt sordid and wrong. They probably should have discussed this more. Any expert on polyamory would probably want them to communicate a lot more before jumping into this.

But if she thought about this too deeply, she would put a stop to it.

"I need—"

Luca met her gaze then. "Tell me."

"I need you to touch me." She heard Ethan's clothes brush against the upholstery as he shifted in the chair. She didn't know whether he was settling in or about to bolt. She believed he would kick Luca out and deal with the consequences if she said she was uncomfortable. But

Cece didn't want that to happen. She wanted the three of them to happen. "Kiss me."

Luca didn't hesitate further. He leaned down, cupped her face between his palms, and touched her mouth with his. She wrapped her hands around his shoulders, pulling him closer. It felt like an eternity since she'd been able to touch him, and the release of tension she hadn't realized she'd been holding made tears come to her eyes.

Luca caught her tears with his thumbs and pulled back. Cece chased him with her mouth. "Don't stop."

"What's wrong?"

"Nothing."

He looked down at her, and she could tell he was skeptical even though the light was dim. "Really?"

"This all stops if you want it to," Ethan said. She felt powerful in that moment. She'd never liked being in charge during sex. Half the appeal of the act was not having to be in control of everything for once. But the fact that she held two men's pleasure in the palm of her hand was heady. She didn't kid herself into thinking they wouldn't dominate her in bed—she wanted that. But the fact that she was the linchpin of this encounter gave her courage.

"I don't want to stop." She tried to look down, but Luca was still holding her face in his hands. She bit his thumb, but he didn't budge. She had to look him in the eye when she said, "This is exactly what I want. This feels more right than I can possibly describe."

Luca nodded, and Ethan grunted his approval. "Carry on," her husband said.

For that, Luca turned their bodies so Ethan couldn't see her easily. And then he carried on kissing her and walking her back toward the bed until the back of her knees hit the edge and she sat down. She was only wearing her panties and bra. Luca brushed his fingers over her nipples, and she shivered.

She was eye level with his cock, and she wasn't about to ignore the invitation it provided. So, she went for the button on his linen pants. But Luca brushed her fingers away and dropped to his knees. He peppered kisses over the skin on her chest, bit into the flesh above her bra as his hands snaked around her body to unfasten it.

When she was free of that garment, he ravished her as though he wanted to consume her whole. Her eyes wanted to flutter closed, but she met Ethan's gaze over the top of Luca's head. He'd leaned back in the chair and pulled his dick out. He stroked himself slowly, like he was so engrossed in watching them that he could only remember to touch himself intermittently.

He'd never neglected her pleasure, and it had always turned her on how intent he was on taking it. She liked how much he wanted her—so much that he couldn't always wait to get inside her. But that quality about Ethan, his intensity, had always wound her up in and of itself.

But seeing him this way—totally wrapped up in what was happening in front of him—threatened to take her down.

Luca kissed down her belly, and pulled her panties off with one hand, tossing them behind him. She didn't know if he'd intended for them to land on the ottoman in front of where Ethan sat, but his aim made it convenient for her husband to grab the underwear and wrap them around his cock.

"These are soaked," he chided. Cece bit her bottom lip. But that prodded Luca to wrench her legs open and look down at her.

"Need to taste." His mouth was swollen from kissing her mouth and body, and his pupils were blown. He still stared down at her, holding her open like he was committing her whole body to memory. It went on so long that the ache at her center became more like a sharp pain.

"Luca." She didn't mean to sound so breathy, but she needed him to touch her.

"Shhh. I've got you." Then, he leaned down and sucked on her clit. He thrust inside her with two fingers, making her feel pinned open and full. She felt as though she'd jumped out of a plane and was suspended in free fall. The blood running through her vessels and veins rushed in her head like the air that would rush past her face as she hurtled to the earth.

She gripped his curls with her fingers and pulled him closer to her. They were melded, but it wasn't enough—it could never be enough for her. He could crawl inside her skin, and it still wouldn't be close enough.

But her parachute opened—her orgasm hit—and it saved her as it jerked her out of free fall, and she floated.

—

Ethan regretted not asking Cece to masturbate in front of him often enough before tonight. He was always coming with her or between her legs, so he'd never had the pleasure of seeing her fall apart without any skin in the game.

His body might be screaming for release, but he didn't want to chase it right now. It was a totally unfamiliar feeling—just being in a moment and not needing to finish so he could move on to the next thing.

Maybe he'd felt a little bit of it when he'd first met Cece. She didn't take any shit, so it forced him to stop. But he'd fit her right into his busy world. He'd won her, and then she didn't challenge him anymore.

He stood up and walked to the end of the bed. Although he'd allowed Luca to be bossy at the beginning of this encounter, his friend knew it wasn't his true nature—sometimes he liked to see his partners on their knees. And it was rarely as satisfying as it was with Luca.

Luca looked up at him, the bottom half of his face wet from eating Cece out. He grinned up at him. Ethan leaned down and grabbed the back of Luca's head, pulling him close. Their mouths were a breath apart when he looked at Cece. She leaned back on her elbows, staring at them. She didn't look like she was regretting this or wanting to put a stop to it at all. She looked as though she was holding her breath, just waiting to see if Ethan kissed the man at her feet.

They gave her what she wanted, and Ethan realized he'd miscalculated something. He'd forgotten how it felt to kiss Luca.

Maybe he'd put it out of his mind after he'd fucked things up with their friendship—their relationship. But he found himself on his knees alongside his best friend, tasting his wife on the other man's lips.

Luca didn't miss a beat, pulling Ethan closer until their pelvises bumped together and they both groaned into each other's mouths. Luca reached for Ethan's cock, stroking it with enough pressure that it might have been painful, but it wasn't. Ethan cupped Luca through the fabric of his pants, squeezing him and making him pant.

He didn't know how long they kissed—it was sort of out of time—but he knew he wanted to come inside his wife. And he also knew he wouldn't last very long with Luca touching him like this. So, he broke away and looked at Cece, who had her hand between her legs.

"Why did you stop?" She seemed upset to have her orgasm interrupted.

Ethan smiled at her and crawled up on the bed until he was over her on all fours. "Because I want to fuck my wife."

He caught her hand and pulled it up, pinning it next to her head on the bed. He dipped down and licked the fingers she'd been using to masturbate, needing more of her taste on his tongue. She grinned up at him. "But what about Luca? What will he do?"

Luca crawled onto their king-size bed beside them. "I'll figure something out." He'd taken his pants off, and Cece looked down at his lap with something that looked like hunger. "Do you want to suck him off while I fuck you, sweet girl?"

He held his breath before she answered. It was one thing to think about having a threesome—especially one with this much baggage attached to it—and a whole other thing to actually fuck two people at the same time.

But then Cece smiled. "You know, I have been meaning to take a trip to Paris. And this is even better than the shopping I had in mind." Ethan wanted to laugh, but there was something caught in his chest watching Cece and Luca like this. The two people he cared about most in the world, together and happy, shouldn't be so monumental. He shouldn't have taken this from them—their friendship. He shouldn't have taken it from any of them.

But he also didn't want to stop and have a big, emotional conversation, with tears and apologies right now. He wanted them both. "I want to watch you suck him off while I fuck you."

As he said the words, he rolled Cece over beneath him and pulled her ass up so he could get to her. Luca kneeled in front of her, so her face would be at dick-level when she supported herself on her hands. Ethan watched as Luca guided his cock into Cece's mouth, almost forgetting how much he needed to be inside her pussy. He ran his hands over the soft skin of her back, down to her ass, until he could spread her wide open for him.

He could feel her shudder of anticipation and see how her movements and his affected Luca as he thrust himself into her mouth. He was being gentle with her, and Ethan knew she didn't always like that. She liked to feel like she was being used in bed, even if that was a huge issue in their relationship generally.

"You can fuck her mouth. She likes it." His own voice sounded ruined. Before either of them could respond, he started entering Cece slowly, giving her time to adjust. She felt tighter when he fucked her this way, even more so because she was all swollen and satisfied from when Luca had gone down on her before.

If he wasn't balls deep inside her right now, he would have gotten off on the image of them together. He was sure he would do that someday down the road, especially if he didn't manage to keep this from blowing up in all of their faces. All he would have would be this—these stolen moments between the three of them.

He met Luca's gaze, and it was almost too much. There was too much emotion and too much satisfaction written all over his face. This was unlike the other times they'd shared a girl. Back then, they'd been so full of their own egos and ambitions that they hadn't been able to feel anything but wanting more.

Now, they'd been humbled—Luca by almost finding himself out of a sport he'd had to claw his way into, and Ethan by almost losing the one thing he could never bear to live without.

He looked away, down to where he was joined with Cece, where she held him tight even as she gave herself to Luca. He felt her tighten around him, and he knew she was going to come again. He might not know whether this would happen again—the three of them together. And he might not even know whether she would stay with him after this. He didn't know if she would wake up in the morning and decide they were both too much for her.

But he knew enough to reach around and stroke her clit to send her over the edge while she took Luca's come down her throat before he grunted out his release. Coming together felt dirty and clean all at the same time. It felt like an exorcism of his darkest demons and a baptism involving his deepest fears.

When it was over, he was empty of the feeling that he always had to be chasing something he didn't have, that no one in the noble line of fools who had sired him had ever had. He felt as though he had everything.

Monday Before Silverstone

Chapter Twenty-Six

"When I was at Lupo in the nineties," Micaela's father said as he stood in front of Panther's entire factory staff, "the team had already won more championships than any other on the grid. I didn't have a lot of opportunities to give 'inspirational' speeches because the team didn't look to me for inspiration. I was supposed to get in the car and just drive." Jack looked to Liam, expecting to see something supportive on his face, but Micaela could feel her boss/lover's glare homed in on the man who'd raised her.

"Panther hasn't won any championships, but Micaela chose to come here anyway." He paused. "Which shows you just what kind of daughter I have." She half expected him to follow that up with some joke about "stupid broads," but she was pleasantly surprised when he contained himself. "She's always looking to do the hard thing." Not really a compliment, but that was about as close as it got.

Liam leaned slightly toward her, and she fought not to look up at him. It was getting so hard to keep her feelings off her face when it came to him—they'd permeated her whole being—that she didn't look at him at all anymore when they were in public. She savored this moment, when it was totally appropriate for him to say, "I don't know how you turned out so well with a father like him."

She couldn't help but glance at him then. He was smiling at her, and her face just automatically did the same thing. "It was easy. I just watched his actions and did the opposite thing."

Someone snapped a picture, and she remembered where she was. She looked back to her father and pasted an expression of placid acceptance on her face. Women all over the world knew how to avoid looking murderous when forced to listen to someone or something insufferable. She was worried her face would stay that way if this went on much longer.

"After dinner, you are coming home with me." Liam made declarations like this almost every day now. It was rare that he didn't find a way for them to be together, but their ruse—that they were just team boss and driver—was becoming more complicated. She was pretty sure Paola knew they were dating. Her concerned looks and inquiries about "how everything was going" had become more and more frequent in the past few weeks since Monaco.

Micaela had put in a miracle of a lap and put her car on pole. The pit stops had been perfect—economical and precise. By the end of the short race, there'd been a five-second gap between her and the driver behind her. Bendetto and Harrow had come in second and third.

When she'd gotten out of her car, Liam had already been in parc fermé. She'd climbed on top of the engine box and raised her arms above her head, looking to the clear, blue sky. She'd wanted to memorize the clouds at that moment. She'd been sure she'd never feel that happy ever again.

But then, when she'd climbed off the car, Liam had swept her up in his arms, yelling how proud he was of her in her ear. She should probably talk to a psychotherapist about what it meant that she'd soaked up his praise like a plant that had been starved of water for too long. Before long, the team had crowded around them, and they'd been separated by her having to get weighed and go into the cooldown room.

Luca and Ethan had been smiling widely at each other, more at ease than they'd been the entire season, but they immediately congratulated her and complimented her on avoiding debris from a crash that had caused an early safety car.

She wasn't sure if the two other drivers—the ones leading the championship—were actually cool with her or if they were only trying to appear that way in front of the media. After all, there was gossip flying around that they'd reconciled their friendship for the good press.

Micaela knew from growing up in this world that the glossy exterior never told the entire story, and you couldn't believe what people told you to your face.

Her father was a prime example of that. He pretended to be the proud papa to the grid's new racing prodigy when Micaela well knew that he was seething with jealousy toward his own daughter. He'd always hoarded the spotlight and punished her when she'd taken any of his shine.

When she was six, a reporter had spent a paragraph talking about Micaela hurtling down the drive of the manor in her go-kart—a go-kart that her father had purchased to look like a good dad for this profile—and he'd smashed it with a sledgehammer because the reporter had omitted the charity golf tournament he'd wanted to publicize.

He'd gone out and bought her a new one the next day, but still.

It made her constantly wonder if her overwhelming attraction and growing attachment to Liam was simply about her wanting to make her childhood right. He didn't treat her like his daughter at all—especially not when she'd slipped up and called him "Daddy" in bed the other night. Thank God he didn't even stop when that happened; she would have been mortified.

Or maybe she was just so unused to having a man actually care about her feelings that she thought it was a mental health issue when she liked it?

Her father wrapped up his speech—only ten minutes beyond his allotted time—and everyone clapped politely. Then Paola stepped up to the microphone. "Liam has brought in lunch for everyone as a 'thank you' for the win in Monaco."

The whole team clapped louder for that than they did for her father. She was sure there would be repercussions for that later.

Liam made sure Micaela wasn't seated next to her father during lunch. He'd have preferred she be seated next to him, but that wasn't possible. People would start to suspect there was something between them if he had her near him all the time.

As it was, they were playing with fire. He didn't want to lose his job, but he knew that was the likely result of their affair the longer and longer it went on. He'd never been addicted to anything—except for winning—his entire life. But he imagined that the throes of craving felt something like what he wanted from Micaela.

God, he had to fight not to smile when someone said her name.

"How's Mikey doing?" Liam winced at her father's question, knowing how much she hated when he called her that.

"She's winning races," Liam replied. "How do you think she's doing?"

Sir Jack laughed. "I think she's a flash in the pan. She'll be out before the beginning of next season. People think they want a girl on the grid, but that's just all the new fans. Once they lose interest, she won't be able to hold on to her sponsors and she'll lose her seat."

Liam ground his back teeth together to avoid stabbing the man next to him with a fork. He should have seated him far away from anyone he could offend, but that would have required him to sit in the middle of the pond outside the factory and someone confiscating his phone.

"Micaela is probably the most naturally talented driver I've ever worked with." He might be sleeping with her, but that wasn't a lie. "Being a woman on track has nothing to do with it."

Her father gave him a sideways glance. "She's only here because of me."

"Maybe some of her talent was inherited, but I'm glad she ended the generational curse of the Cartwright ego." Liam shouldn't have said it, but it felt good to defend her. He would always defend Micaela, even when she woke up and ended things between the two of them.

Luckily, her father thought he was joking and had no inkling that Liam was fighting not to wrap his hands around the other man's neck. He looked around the room until he spotted Micaela laughing with a group of engineers. They all appeared to be a little bit in love with her, and Liam couldn't even be jealous. She was just like that.

Sitting next to her father, he had to wonder how she ended up being kind and down to earth. Maybe people just naturally became their parents or the opposite of their parents, depending on their choices. Seeing his son, sitting on the opposite side of the room from his teammate, he wondered what he would choose. Liam knew he hadn't been the perfect father—and he definitely wasn't behaving like one now.

Brent was deep in conversation with Paola. He was glad he'd tasked her with looking after him. Something she'd said must have gotten through to him where nothing Liam had done had been able to. He was showing up on time to his press responsibilities and avoiding giving flippant, sarcastic answers. And while he wasn't as fast as Micaela on track, he wasn't throwing tantrums or making mistakes that cost the team points.

Paola even had him wearing a suit and engaging with the sponsor execs they'd invited for Sir Jack's speech and luncheon. She was a miracle worker, as far as he was concerned.

Micaela's laugh echoing through the large room brought his attention back to her. He tried not to stare at her, knowing there were always people watching them when they weren't alone. If anyone was really paying attention, they would know he had feelings for her. He'd always been able to keep his cards close to his vest before, but something about her stripped that ability away. She filled a room with her essence, and he was drawn to it like nothing else.

"Well, she'll stay on the grid if she has 'em looking at her like that." Liam had been trying to ignore his lunch companion, but those leering words brought him back. Sir Jack would think anything about his daughter except that she had the talent and drive to be where she was.

Some of the things that Micaela had said—just offhand comments—had made him think her father was a huge twat. And the man was just proving that over and over. He glanced at Sir Jack and found that he was referring to the way the engineers were hanging on her every word. He was almost relieved the other man hadn't seen the way Liam had been looking at her moments before.

But Sir Jack Cartwright respected Liam—as much as he respected anyone—and so he wouldn't think Liam would be caught up in anyone as insignificant as the girl he'd raised.

"Do you think she's sleeping with all of them? Or just a few?" The other man really didn't know how close he was to losing his life.

Liam put down his fork and gripped the table. He took three deep breaths, hoping he could calm himself down enough to not make a scene. He'd always known the man was an asshole; he'd only hoped he'd grown up a little since they'd raced each other. It was evident he hadn't, and his lack of maturity and toxic attitudes hadn't poisoned his daughter.

It was now clear to him he'd done the worst job as a parent imaginable, simply by being himself. And he could say that as someone carrying on an affair with his son's ex-girlfriend who worked for him.

Although he couldn't imagine a universe without Micaela in it, some people truly shouldn't have children. Liam himself might be going to hell for what he and Micaela were doing, but at least he'd done his best with Brent while he was growing up. It wasn't enough—it was never enough—but his son didn't have stories about him that made people cringe instead of laugh.

Not yet.

Media Day Silverstone

Chapter Twenty-Seven

Jocelyn was on a tear today. She'd insisted on walking into the paddock with Cece to make sure there would be cameras on her after complaining for an hour and a half at dinner last night about how she'd been behind the fold in the *Vogue Italia* piece featuring the wives and girlfriends of the fastest growing sport in the world.

And the dinner—oh God! Ethan's parents had invited her and Heka, neglected to invite Luca, and treated Jocelyn like the daughter-in-law they truly wanted. Jocelyn came from the same type of family—old, moneyed, somewhat inbred—that only occasionally spat out half-functioning adults. More often than not, the results of their careful mating selections were rude, xenophobic, and appeared to be perpetually constipated.

Cece had always thought both Ethan and Jocelyn were in the normal camp, but she was beginning to have her doubts about her longtime friend.

"I think I can convince him to stay another year." Jocelyn clung to Cece's arm. To outside observers, it would seem they were just having a kiki, but this felt more like an interrogation. "Do you think I can get him to stay for another year?"

Heka had seemed thoroughly done with her antics at dinner. A few times, Cece had caught his gaze. He just raised his eyebrows and ate his food, muttering a few things to Ethan's brother about the track and the car he drove this year when asked.

"I think they've already lined up a junior driver for that seat." The team seemed to have moved on. Maybe they would have fired the other driver if Heka had wanted to stay earlier on in the season, but they'd signed a long-term deal right after Heka had announced his retirement.

"You're so negative," Jocelyn said. "It doesn't have to be with his current team. Maybe it could be with Lupo."

That made Cece stop short. "Lupo has two very competent drivers." The thought of Ethan or Luca leaving the team right now was laughable. They were winning most of the races and both on the podium in virtually all of them since Suzuka, and they were also getting along.

All three of them having sex, even though not one of them would put a name to what that meant to their relationships with each other, really seemed to help the harmony within the team.

"Don't you want to get rid of Luca?" The thought made Cece want to vomit, but Jocelyn didn't need to know that. Cece was beginning to think her instinct to avoid sharing Ethan's infidelity with her was spot on. Jocelyn would use anything she could to stay in her WAG job as long as she could, even if it meant throwing someone she called a friend under the bus.

"No. He and Ethan have mended fences." Cece hoped she didn't sound dreamy about the fact that they'd made up. Every time she thought of them—together—something inside her softened. It was beyond the heat and chemistry that had always been there. "They're winning races. A team is not going to be looking for a driver—especially one who's ambivalent about being there—when their current lineup is number one and number three in the championship."

The reporters and photographers were now paying attention to the eight-time world champion who had entered the paddock. His team was currently fighting to stay out of the midfield and were already out of contention for the constructor's championship, but the guy had flair.

He was also the only driver on the grid with any dress sense that didn't come from the careful work, over years, of a wife or girlfriend.

But the diverted attention meant Jocelyn let her mask fall. "I don't get why you're defending Luca. You were the one who came to lunch so distressed at the beginning of the season. Wouldn't you rather spend your time with me than have your husband's teammate leering at you all the time."

Cece was taken aback. She didn't know how to respond. If she defended Luca, Jocelyn would know something was up. But she'd thought they'd been so careful. There were cameras and ears everywhere, though. The nature of the sport made information one of the most valuable commodities. The entire paddock was a conflict of interest, and teams tried to capitalize on that, with varying degrees of success.

"I'm just trying to be real with you. Lupo is not going to replace one of their drivers when he's at the top of the time sheets." Cece shrugged, hoping for nonchalance. "How he looks at me, or doesn't, has nothing to do with their business decisions. I'm just the wife of the other driver, and it's still a boys club. We don't matter all that much."

Jocelyn tugged on her hand, and they started walking again. Cece couldn't wait until she could drop her off at the hospitality trailer for her husband's team. "You know that Heka would have been out years ago without me. People really should know that we're the backbone. We make everything run, on time, according to plan. And we make sure it all looks effortless."

Jocelyn spoke for herself. One thing Cece had always appreciated about Ethan—even when their marriage had been rocky—was that he took care of himself. He did his own laundry and hired an assistant to make his appointments, instead of relying solely on his wife. Maybe because his parents hadn't really paid much attention and shipped him off to boarding school and then the karting circuit, but Ethan had never needed her to mother him. Maybe they would have been more connected if he had.

"That's not what I got married for." Cece thought that statement was neutral enough until Jocelyn sniffed.

"So, your marriage is going better, then?" Jocelyn's question made her wonder when she'd become such a sarcastic bitch, but maybe she'd always been that? Except, until recently, it hadn't been directed at Cece.

"Yes." She wasn't going to share anything else. Nothing about how or why her marriage had improved. How they'd opened up their marriage to precisely one person. How they were happy, but it felt so fragile that talking about it any more than strictly necessary for logistical purposes might break it.

They reached Heka's team's trailer and Jocelyn sighed as though she dreaded entering. Probably because there were fewer cameras in there. "Those pictures of you both with Luca seemed pretty tense."

Cece smiled at her friend, even though she didn't feel any positive sentiment toward her at all. "The pictures were tense because the cameras were all over us. We asked for a private table. Everyone is friends again." The not-quite-lies slipped off of her tongue easily.

In that moment, she realized if they made a go of an actual relationship between the three of them, she would constantly have to lie. They could never be together out in the open. The sport was too steeped in machismo. The sponsors were too conservative. What they were doing was illegal in several countries where Ethan and Luca raced.

She'd been looking forward to this weekend. Having to spend time with Jocelyn this morning had seemed to be an unpleasant blip. But now, it had ruined her entire day.

"You did a very good job during that interview." Brent had the feeling that Paola had been reading some pop psychology book about how to talk to men to get them to do what you wanted them to in the workplace.

Since that moment in his trailer at Imola, she'd been scrupulously professional toward him. And she'd made sure not to be alone with him. He stopped in the middle of the corridor they were walking through and turned to her. "I didn't make you uncomfortable asking you out, did I?"

He was trying not to be as much of a little shit. His tantrum when Micaela had joined the team was something of a wake-up call for him. He didn't want to spend his life proving he was just as good as his father. He knew he never would, because he had so many advantages and privileges due to his father's greatness. But he could be a great man in his own way.

And he didn't know why he needed Paola to think of him as a good and decent person. There were plenty of women who wouldn't care about anything but his job, his looks, and his money.

But Paola's opinion of him mattered more than virtually anyone else's.

"No, but I just don't think we should bring any—chemistry—between us into the office." She looked around to make sure no one could see how close they were to each other. "It doesn't look good for the team."

Brent stepped even closer to remind her of the chemistry she spoke of. The way she smelled made him a little bit hungrier for risk than he normally was off the track. "So, you admit we have chemistry?"

"I'm not admitting anything." The way her breaths came faster, and her lips parted when they were close belied her flaccid denial. "I just think the appearance that we have something could harm the team. This is work. Work is work. Anything else—we don't have time for it anyway."

Brent turned and walked toward his room. Paola kept pace, probably thinking he was going to drop it. "I couldn't disagree more, Paola."

She sighed. "I agreed to go out with you over the summer, when we're not working—and only if you behave."

"You agreed to go out with me, but I don't think you're actually planning on giving me a chance."

"A chance for what?"

He stopped at his door and leaned on the frame. He watched as she looked him up and down. It was almost cute the way she pretended she wasn't into him. But he'd paid attention to her, what she liked and didn't. It was written all over her face, even though no one else seemed to be able to read her. He'd heard a reporter call her a "cold bitch," and the only thing that had stopped him stuffing the microphone down the guy's throat was the promise of getting to spend time alone with Paola, away from the paddock.

He wanted to see what her face looked like when she tasted something delicious. He wanted to feel her shiver because her sun-warmed skin caught a chill in the early evening breeze that came up over the terrace at his father's house in the Cinque Terre. He wanted to listen for what made her breath catch and what made her moan as he feasted on her pretty, tanned skin.

"Stop thinking about that." Her tone was playful, yet there was still a bite to it. She was fighting this as hard as he was.

"I can't stop thinking about it, Paola." Brent had never felt this way before, and it was all because she wouldn't let him get away with shit. They felt right together, if only he could make her see it. "And plenty of people get together in the paddock. We're the traveling circus, and no one living outside of this world is going to understand how we live. We can't just put our lives on hold until we're done with the sport."

She shook her head. "You don't have to worry about your reputation." Though they were physically as close as they'd ever been, he could feel her pulling away from him. "If it gets out that I'm dating a driver, there would be hell to pay."

"So, you lied to me?" Brent didn't know how to salvage this situation, and accusing Paola of being dishonest was probably the worst way to do it, but she made him a little bit crazy.

"I have never lied to you." She wrapped her arms around her waist in an uncharacteristically insecure gesture. And he felt a pang of guilt.

"You said you'd go out with me if I behaved."

"I said I'd have dinner with you. Dinner isn't going out. It's a meal between colleagues." She might be denying it now, but it was more than a "meal between colleagues" for her. Her skin was flushed this perfect shade of peachy pink, and she looked away.

He shook his head and stepped closer to her. "Uh uh. You're not going to wiggle your way out of admitting that you feel something between us too. I wouldn't make you so angry if you didn't feel anything for me."

She looked at the ceiling and huffed out a sigh, dropping her hands and flexing them. She was going to run. He could feel it in his bones. It was a good thing he lived for the chase.

"You're not going to leave this alone, are you?"

He simply smiled back at her.

"Don't you have responsibilities?" She knew he didn't have any media duties for ninety minutes. She always gave him time to decompress from the gauntlet of photographers and fans he walked through before he had to be in the press pen. He had time to greet the engineers and the pit crew and walk around a bit before doing anything else.

But he knew this track better than almost any other, and he wanted to spend his time doing something else.

He reached out and grabbed her hand. She didn't pull away, so he pulled her closer to him, until their bodies were pressed together. He felt her breath brush across his collarbone.

"Tell me that you don't want me to kiss you right now." He didn't want her to tell him that, but he was going to give her every. Single. Out. If something happened between them, it would be clear they both wanted it—needed it. "Tell me that you don't want me to kiss you until we're both too drunk on each other to know that this is a bad idea."

There was a second where he thought she would pull away. She should slap him across the face and tell him to never touch her again. He wouldn't blame her if she did. Instead, she bit her plump bottom lip and looked up at him. He rubbed the back of her hand with his thumb and waited.

He'd never had to wait for anything he'd wanted in his whole life. Actually, his father had tried to instill a modicum of impulse control by delaying rewards. Maybe that was why Paola's bribe had been so appealing. But he'd never waited for something in the knowledge that he might not ever have it.

"You're going to lose interest as soon as anything happens."

Her words took him aback for a second. She would be right about that if they were talking about anyone else. But he'd never been obsessed with a woman before—not like this. Every other thought he had was about what Paola would think. He'd never cared what a woman thought about virtually anything he did outside the bedroom. It had never even been a consideration, which made him a colossal jerk. And he didn't have any way of explaining that Paola was different without demonstrating to her that he was an asshole. And then she really might not let him kiss her.

"I thought about you when I picked out this shirt today," he said. When she looked confused, he added, "I've never thought about how anyone else felt about the way that I dressed before. I think about what you would want to eat for breakfast when I'm eating breakfast. I wanted to send you a picture of a sunset when we had a week off and I went to Madrid for that sponsor thing."

Her eyes grew wide, and he thought she might have caught on to the way he felt about her. Suddenly, he was the one feeling vulnerable. "I don't want to sound like a weird stalker, but you're always in my thoughts."

"That actually makes it sound like *I'm* stalking *you*—in your mind."

He ran his hand up her arm and over her shoulder, until he was cupping her chin. She didn't pull away when he rested his forehead against hers. "You are, but I don't hate it. It feels really good."

"This is still a bad idea." She sounded breathy—like she'd climbed up a big hill on a hot day. She was wavering, and he had no idea how to push her over the edge. He was just as shaky and unsure.

"Of course it is. But my whole life is a bad idea. I get into an open-wheel car that goes over 300 kilometers per hour to drive in circles. Sometimes with assholes who think we're playing bumper cars."

"Please don't remind me that you could die doing this. Every time you get in the car, my stomach turns into knots, and I don't feel better until the session is over." It was the first time she'd admitted more than a professional interest in him, and he savored it as much as he wanted to reassure her.

"I feel that way every time I look at you and I don't know how you feel about me. It feels just as risky to be telling you all the wild thoughts that run through my head about you. All the time."

She looked at his mouth, but he still needed her to make the first move. "I think about you all the time too. Because it's my job." His heart stopped before she continued. "And because it's not. You're not even that charming, and I still like you in a way I haven't liked anyone in a long time."

"I won't let the press vultures get to you." He didn't know if he could keep that promise, but he would try.

"You can't prevent that. And I chose to live this sport instead of a normal life. I'm not sure you actually made that choice or had that choice made for you. But maybe it doesn't mean as much to you as it means to me. And that's fine. But what's not fine is you tempting me to take risks with the life I've chosen."

She had him there. He hadn't chosen to make racing his life. It had been laid out for him from an early age, and he'd luckily had enough talent that he hadn't shit the bed at the first opportunity. But he didn't have as much skin in the game as she had.

"I'm worth the risk, Paola." He looked down at her, willing her to change her mind and just give in. "Even if something bad happens, I promise I'll make it worth all the fallout."

She went up on her tiptoes and leaned into him, her mouth hovering just a millimeter away from his. "I hope so."

And then, she kissed him.

Paola kissed Brent not knowing what to expect. She'd seen pictures of him kissing girls on yachts and at galas. During Paris Fashion Week a few years before, he'd kissed a model of the moment at all the tourist spots in the city, sort of making fun of how people thought Paris was the height of sophistication—all because he thought the City of Lights was plebeian.

And for him it was. He was jaded, spoiled, and he left a trail of broken hearts wherever he went. He was entitled and rude.

She'd hated him at first, and she'd convinced herself that was why she thought about him every second of every day. When that hadn't worked, she'd convinced herself that her interest was purely professional—she only thought about him because it was her job. It was only recently, when he'd stopped vexing her every day when she was just trying work that she'd realized she was infatuated with him.

She thought about his dimples at random times during the day. His father had the same dimples, and she didn't think about them all the time. But he was her boss, and there wasn't this zing of familiarity with Liam.

Brent gave her the feeling of a scary rock climb. Falling might be deadly. She could hit a rock on the way down, go unconscious, and succumb before anyone could find her. The rocks under her feet could crumble at any moment and she could tumble to her death. Or she could keep going to the summit, unharmed.

The man standing in front of her, so stunned she'd kissed him that he hadn't kissed her back, didn't want to crush her. But he might do it without meaning to.

There was a moment when she thought he might change his mind. But then he dipped his head down and brushed her lips with his.

Just his mouth against hers made her want to weep with relief—all the tension she'd been carrying around and the weight of her attraction to him fell away. The attraction felt as light as air when his dry lips moved against her mouth, when his tongue reached out to taste her. She felt as though she was in suspended animation, waiting to come alive again if he decided to touch her.

He'd nearly goaded her into kissing him, but he was hesitating when she finally did. Maybe her doubts had infected him. That wasn't what she'd meant to do. She just knew racing drivers. They dove in, headfirst, heedless of any consequences. It made them effective on the track, but it was a liability everywhere else.

Finally, he wrapped his arms around her and kissed her back. He took her mouth with the ferocity of a base jump. The way he kissed her melted all her fears and doubts, instantaneously. She almost wished he was wearing his fireproofs, because then she could feel more of his body against hers. As it was, the perfectly tailored suit she'd suggested to him made her very aware of his honed body. But still, she reached inside his jacket to feel the heat of him against her fingers.

"I want to taste you everywhere," he said against her mouth. She softened against him, and her legs almost gave out on her. "You taste like sunshine."

She wanted to laugh. He sounded like every hero in every sweet romance novel she'd ever read. If she didn't know him, he could be some small-town cowboy claiming her mouth, despite her better judgment.

She must not have kept her mirth to herself. "Why are you smiling? This is very serious business." He was also smiling. Why had she fought this so hard? This moment was one of the best in her life, which was sad. She'd tried to make all of the best moments about her job, but she'd kept herself from connecting like this. She didn't share in-jokes with anyone—anyone but Brent.

"You're just so much sweeter than I expected. You kiss me and talk to me like you've never watched pornography geared towards men."

He didn't let her go, but he threw his head back against the door and laughed in a way that would alert the entire paddock to their presence. But he didn't let her pull away.

When he stopped laughing, he asked, "Would you prefer I went spicy?"

Paola realized, right then, that he would do pretty much anything for her. And that made her trust him enough to turn over a small piece of her heart. Instead of answering him, she kissed him again, pouring the feelings she wouldn't say out loud.

He wrapped his arms around her, and she let herself bathe in the way he made her feel. The reasons why they shouldn't do this no longer mattered when it was just the two of them.

Brent's hands found their way under her clothes, and she lost the ability to breathe along with the ability to think, which went out the window as soon as he put his mouth on hers.

She shivered, even though two people in this tiny room was one too many, and they'd probably fog up the tiny window if this went much further. She wanted to go further. And he was of the same mind, if the erection he pressed into her lower belly was anything to go by.

He stopped kissing her and looked down at her, perturbed. "I wish you were wearing a skirt."

This was one of the rare occasions that Paola wished she was wearing a skirt too. Usually, she dressed down along with her team kit because she didn't want to court attention. "Why?"

"So I can get in your pants and not go off schedule for the day." He said it like it was the most obvious reason for wearing a skirt in the world. She wished the rest of the world could see him like this—silly and hedonistic but totally focused on his goal at the same time.

"It's so considerate that you don't want to piss off the press officer," she said. "But, in this case, I'd probably be more pissed that you left me hanging."

He laughed again, softer this time. And then he turned them around, so her back was against the door. He didn't waste the precious time they did have, undoing her jeans and pulling them down around her ankles. He was on his knees in front of her, so close to where she ached to him. He looked up at her and said, "Even your panties are sensible, and for some reason that makes me so hard."

Paola chuckled, but it turned into a strangled moan when he pressed his mouth against her, through the panties. He could probably feel and smell how much she wanted him. There would be no keeping secrets about how he affected her physically. He hooked his fingers around the sides of her panties and pulled them down along with her jeans. She probably looked totally ridiculous and unsexy right now, but she didn't care. Brent looked up at her like she was a goddess, and that blew all of her inhibitions away.

"Can I taste you, Paola?" She couldn't even answer. She just nodded her head. "You have to keep quiet, or everyone will hear. And you're the one who cares about whether people know about this." He opened her with his fingers and looked at her. Part of her wanted to squeeze her legs together, because the way he touched her was so intimate. When she couldn't take it any longer, he kissed her. His mouth was more voracious there, like he'd been in polite company when his lips visited her mouth and become famished by the time he made it to her pussy.

She put the back of her hand against her mouth to keep the sounds he was forcing from her body muffled. She stiffened for a moment when the back of her head knocked on the door, thinking someone was looking for Brent. He didn't let her mind leave the room and what he was doing to her, though. He entered her with one finger, and then two. She'd been looking at his hands for months, thinking about how big they would feel against her body. But she hadn't spent nearly enough time thinking about how they would fill her up.

No amount of thinking about it would have prepared her for how it felt to have him touch her this way. She was going to come so hard and so soon that she felt like everything slowed down and stopped for a few moments. It was like the seconds before impact when one of the cars crashed. There was only a moment for a silent prayer that this would not end in disaster.

And then, impact. When the room finally stopped spinning around her, she looked down to see Brent staring up at her, his mouth wet with her, a smile on his face. He stood up and pressed against her, whispering in her ear. "We don't have time to take care of me."

"You should probably wipe off your face." She knew her face had a small smile, and that he knew she was feeling bashful. "I'm sorry."

"Sorry about what?" He nuzzled into her hair and squeezed her still bare hip with one hand. "Sorry that I'm going to taste you on my tongue until I can have you again?"

"Sorry that I couldn't take care of—uh—you." And she wanted more of him, but something kept her from telling him how much hunger he'd awakened.

His voice softened, losing the playfulness it had held earlier. "You take care of my needs every day, and now it's time that I figure out what you need and give it to you."

It almost sounded like he wanted this to be more than a hookup, but he probably just meant her sexual needs. She couldn't read too much into this.

"That was a really good start." She moved away from the wall, thinking of how she could pull up her pants without giving him the ick. But he moved first, squatting down and pulling them up. He touched her with a care that made her realize this was definitely more than just him chasing sex from the one person who wouldn't give it to him.

He wanted to meet all of her needs. She craved him more than anything. She was well and truly screwed.

Race Day
Silverstone

Chapter Twenty-Eight

"And Luca Bendetto, the boy who once dreamed of playing rugby for England, raises the red-and-white English flag on his cooldown lap after winning the British Grand Prix!" The announcer was yelling. It had been years since a British driver had won the British Grand Prix. She knew Ethan had to be seething that it wasn't him. He was incredibly on edge when his parents were at a race. And they only attended the British Grand Prix. And Ethan had been expected to win and had only placed third.

His parents stood next to her near the podium, and it was like standing next to two wax cutouts of what parents should be. His mother wore a cream-colored, vintage Escada suit that might have been the least sensible choice for a racetrack ever. His father wore a full-on suit in July. Beads of sweat formed along his hairline, and yet he never considered going around in his shirtsleeves.

When Cece had first met the Harrows, before his mother had made her feelings known, she hadn't been able to figure out what they'd thought of her. When she'd asked Ethan, he'd said, "Oh, they don't think of you at all." He'd seen the confusion on her face. "They don't think of anyone but themselves and their family name. If I marry you, they'll probably think I'm sullying the entire line—because you're not white and American. Then, they'll think about you. It won't be fondly, but they'll be forced to consider you in moments when they think about their own mortality."

That was a dark assessment of his parents' psyches, but it was accurate. Cece wasn't sure if Elizabeth Harrow ever smiled, but she'd certainly never smiled at her daughter-in-law. Her face was always pinched and assessing, but it became especially so whenever she and Ethan discussed their future—the possibility of children—in front of her.

And Cece was starting to think it was possible she and Ethan had a future, but she couldn't quite conjure the image of it without Luca involved somehow. And she didn't know how he could be involved publicly. But she didn't want to hide what she felt about him.

Ethan stepped out onto the podium; his luxurious dark hair was ruffled with sweat. His face was pink and sweaty, but he looked joyful and beautiful. He wasn't thinking about his parents then.

She wondered whether Luca had whispered something in his ear when they'd hugged after the race—that was acceptable, public, manly affection. Maybe he'd made dark promises of what they could do after dinner at his parents' estate, when they were all alone in a hotel room.

Ethan's parents had balked when Cece had informed them she and Ethan would be staying at a hotel for this visit. It was "tradition" that he stayed with them over the race weekend, even if it was farther away from the track than he'd wanted to be, and Cece couldn't stand it. She'd never gotten used to the staff lurking around every corner. She knew they were spying on her.

But her complaints about staying with the in-laws hadn't penetrated until Luca told him, "Oi, your parents are dicks to *me*, and they wish I was their son instead of your twat of a brother." It was true. They loved Luca for some reason. Maybe because they'd never thought about him as a potential romantic partner for their son, capable of sullying the family line. "They are even worse to Cece, and she deserves to feel comfortable."

Ethan had called his assistant to book them into a separate hotel from the team immediately. To be fair, Cece had never verbalized her issues with her husband's parents. She'd spent time with them, feeling scrutinized at every moment—it seemed like the walls had eyes in that old house—without complaint. She should have said something, but she'd been too busy pretending to be some picture-perfect version of the woman Ethan should have chosen to marry instead of being herself.

Only Luca had seen through it and made it right. And it made her braver and more willing to say the things that needed to be said in her marriage. They'd fought more in the past five weeks than they had in the five months before the cheating. But there were never any gritted teeth or stony silences.

Even if they couldn't keep Luca in their bed or their lives, he'd given them that.

She was totally conscious of Luca's gaze on her face as he walked out onto the podium and collected his trophy. His parents were here too. His dad was shaking hands with a mechanic, whom he'd just met, so hard his teeth likely rattled, but he was several feet away from where she stood with the Harrows while his mom jumped up and down and screamed.

But Luca wasn't looking at them. He was smiling at her. She knew people would notice if she cheered loudly for him. She politely clapped and smiled, appropriate given that he was on her husband's team, and they'd publicly reconciled their friendship. But she couldn't show the joy she was feeling for him.

She met his gaze, pointing to his mum, and mouthed, "Look at them."

He grinned even wider when he saw his mom.

—

Luca walked down the hallway of the hotel to Ethan and Cece's suite. He wanted to celebrate with his two favorite people, and there weren't any obligations to stop them or public appearances to consider.

Ethan had slipped him an extra key to the room before they'd left the track. It was becoming more and more difficult to hide how he felt about both Ethan and Cece when they were out together in public. He was in love with both of them, and he wanted to be able to tell people about it. He hated having to pretend they were all just friends, and the only thing they had to be so happy about was that he and Ethan had put a mysterious beef behind them for the sake of competing together for points in a world championship.

What he felt for Ethan and Cece was about their whole lives, not this tiny slice of time when they were part of one of the most popular sports in the world. Before the season began, he was devastated by the seeming end of his career. He hadn't known who he was without racing. But now, he was pretty sure he could walk away from it all if it meant keeping what he had with Cece and Ethan.

He just wasn't sure they felt the same way.

When Luca walked into the room, Ethan was waiting for him. He pushed Luca up against the door and kissed him. Although they'd hugged and clapped backs after the race, like good teammates and competitors, neither of them had been able to pour the same level of emotion into a public display of affection.

But Ethan's hands burrowing under his clothes and his lips rough against his own told the whole story of how much they'd always felt connected. Even when they'd competed on track as though they didn't care about each other off track. Even when they hadn't spoken for years, there had been something like a constant yearning between them.

"You know, there's fanfic about this," Cece said, a little breathy, as she walked into the room. They stopped kissing as she padded across the floor to them. She didn't step between them because she harbored much less jealousy than her husband. She caressed the back of Ethan's head and gave Luca a small kiss on the cheek. She smelled like sunscreen and a hint of petrol. She still hadn't washed off the track.

He wanted to take a shower with her later, but he wasn't sure the hotel shower was big enough for three. They hadn't been alone together since being together was cheating, and Luca didn't know how to broach the subject. He didn't know how to talk about whether this was just sex—exclusively between the three of them—or whether they were in a relationship with each other and had individual relationships within the triad.

They should really talk about all of those things, but then Cece dropped to her knees and undid his pants. And Ethan kissed him again.

When Cece had his cock out, she stroked it instead of putting it into her mouth like he wanted her to. He also wanted to fuck her, but that would have to wait. He felt like he was always waiting in this relationship—waiting to find out if Cece would leave Ethan and be with him, waiting to see if Ethan would ever talk to him again, waiting to know if this was going to be real or just a passing fling.

Being in a situationship with two people was especially difficult when one of those people hadn't yet put their mouth around your dick. But then, she did. She wasn't tentative about giving him a blow job, but he wouldn't expect her to be. She and Ethan were both relentless and consuming, taking as much pleasure from overwhelming his senses as he was getting.

Ethan broke their kiss to pull off his shirt, and Luca did the same. He wanted to feel everyone's skin against his own. While that was happening, Cece positioned herself between Luca's thighs and sucked him deeper. Caught off guard, he punched his hips forward and hit the back of her throat. She swallowed him down like that was what she'd wanted to happen.

She stroked his abs with one hand as the other one wrapped around his balls, caressing him. Ethan stood back, watching them. He liked to watch. "Has she always been able to deep throat?" Sometimes, Cece liked it when they talked about her as though she wasn't there.

“No. I had to ask for it.” He combed through her hair, gently with his fingers, letting her know they might be talking about her as though she was a thing, but he treasured her. That’s all Luca wanted, to treasure her, along with his best friend, forever.

But he couldn’t think about how they could all turn out to be a happy family for long. Ethan used his hand to force Cece to take him deeper and deeper, fucking Luca with his wife’s mouth. Luca looked down and saw tear tracks of mascara running down her face, but the look in her eyes held zero distress. She wanted this. She wanted both of them to use her and then spoil her. She was theirs, and she belonged to both of them.

Thinking about that made him come.

Chapter Twenty-Nine

Ethan's dick was probably hard enough to cut glass, but he stepped back after Luca came in his wife's mouth. Every time they were together, the experience became more intense. There was so much feeling wrapped up in their dynamic that it always felt as though it would explode. It threatened to engulf him and take him over.

He thought about them all the time. He'd been infatuated with Cece when they'd first met—so much that he'd destroyed his oldest friendship—but he hadn't felt this level of romantic, lustful stupor in his life. He'd tried most of the available drugs, but he couldn't remember ever feeling this high. When he was with Cece and Luca, he felt both animal and more human than he'd ever been.

And he knew it couldn't last. Luca would find someone who could give him more than secret nights in hotel rooms, when they were sure no one would see or hear them. He would fall in love with someone who could love him in public. And it would tear Ethan to pieces. He wouldn't end their friendship like he had the last time, but it would hurt to talk to him, to think about him.

He didn't know if Cece would survive it, and he was especially concerned that their marriage would end right along with this relationship. They needed Luca. Or maybe Cece needed him more, and Ethan could step aside. There would be a scandal, but Luca was the better driver at this point. He would keep his seat and the girl.

Ethan would have to retire eventually, and he would just avoid the sport. He'd see Cece and Luca together and it would break him. But they would be happier than Ethan and Cece alone. Luca would treat her like she deserved.

Even though he felt enormous passion for both of them, he wasn't sure he knew how to love them the way they needed and deserved. Not as long as he was worried about people finding out they were all together.

They couldn't sustain this long-term. He knew that. Spending part of the weekend with his parents had solidified that knowledge. It bothered him all the time, like a pebble in his shoe. Harrows didn't know how to love people properly. It simply wasn't in their DNA. They knew how to manipulate people with their wealth and power. They knew how to protect their social standing, their financial status, and their bloodlines.

If his relationship with Luca and Cece became public, he would put that all at risk. And they were closer than they thought. Before his father had left, he'd pulled Ethan in for a hug. Ethan had been shocked. They were not hugging people—that was far too American. He'd been so shocked he'd almost missed the words his father had whispered in his ear.

"You should watch your wife around Bendetto," he said. "He'll take everything from you—more than just the title—if you let him."

Instead of making him want to be more careful, it made him want to be even more reckless.

When Cece crawled to him and tried to undo his pants, he stopped her. She stuck out her bottom lip and pouted at him. He ignored her. He looked up at Luca. "I have a better idea for how we can reward today's race winner."

Luca raised his brow, and Ethan looked down at Cece. "I promise you'll like it. Stand up."

She followed instructions, which she only did in bed. Both of them followed him to the bedroom. Ethan turned and looked at his wife. "That dress should come off." He stepped toward her and ran his nose up and down her long, slender neck. She smelled like Luca and the air after a good rain. She undid the fastening on her dress, and it floated to the floor. Luca stepped behind her and undid her bra, so her breasts pressed against Ethan's skin as she stepped forward. Luca pulled down her panties, and she stepped out of them.

"These are very wet." His friend sniffed the undergarment. "I think she likes taking a cock down her throat."

Ethan rubbed her clit with his fingers, finding her soaked. "I think you're right." Her knees buckled and she collapsed into him, so he held her up and touched her until he could tell she was about to come.

And then he stopped. Cece let out a soft whine. "Shhh. I think I have an even better idea." Then, he looked up at Luca again. "I think I should eat you out while he fucks my ass."

He could see the heat rise in his friend's eyes and his cock rise to attention. He might be exhausted after a hot afternoon in the car, but he was up for it. They'd never had anal sex before.

Ethan had never been opposed to the idea, but they'd started hooking up because there was always a girl between them. To put it crudely, they had enough orifices to go around. Still, it felt vulnerable to propose the idea. Although, he'd had a finger or toy in his ass, this would be different. They would be different afterward. People did this without commitment all the time, but that's not what it would be here.

"Are you sure?" Luca asked as though he really needed Ethan to be sure.

Ethan nodded. "I want this."

"This is so hot." Cece kissed the side of his jaw.

Luca slapped Cece's ass. "Get on the bed, pretty girl."

Cece lay down, and Luca grabbed him by the face and kissed him. It was mind-numbing and delicious. Before he could think better of any of this, Luca had his pants and boxer briefs off and was steering him toward the bed.

"This is so much hotter than the fic," Cece said from the bed as Ethan crawled toward her.

"Open your legs, Cece." She shivered and followed instructions. "There are condoms and lube in the nightstand." Ethan heard Luca open the nightstand, but Ethan focused on Cece.

She curled her fingers into his hair. "Go slow, I want to come with you."

Ethan shivered when he felt Luca's hand run down his spine. He felt totally and utterly vulnerable in this moment as he felt Luca's lubed fingers at his entrance. He'd sort of expected some pain, but he hadn't been prepared for how good it would feel for Luca to fill him up.

He raised his head. "That feels good." He was surrounded by the smell and taste of his wife while being opened up and pleasured by his best friend. He closed his eyes for a second and committed this to memory.

And then, Luca withdrew his fingers. He heard him open up a condom wrapper, and pins and needles filled him as he waited to feel Luca's cock entering him.

And then he forgot every reason why they shouldn't be together.

Ethan's mouth found her clit again as soon as Luca entered him from behind, and she had to fight not to close her eyes and just focus on how he was making her body feel. The only thing that kept her in that moment and off another planet was the way she could feel what Luca was doing to and with Ethan as it was happening.

She'd always thought of threesomes as kind of skanky and sordid before becoming involved in one with Luca and her husband. But this was like taking an IV of pure connection.

Ethan didn't look at her; he didn't stop trying to make her come. Maybe he was afraid of how she would react to seeing him get fucked by another man. But it was beautiful, and she wished he could see how perfect she thought it was. There was virtually nothing the three of them could do together that was wrong or unclean.

Because she loved them both. As they got more and more lost in each other, the reasons why they shouldn't be together fell away until she couldn't even conjure them anymore. As she met Luca's dark gaze as he fucked Ethan, he bit his bottom lip. He was hard everywhere but his mouth, and it made him look even more debauched than he would have otherwise. And she could see he felt the same way about them as she did—that she wanted more from this than simply the next orgasm. Both of these men were vital for her. She might be able to function without both of them in her life, but she wouldn't be happy.

At least not the perfect kind of happiness that flowed through her after they all came and were silent together.

"Why don't you take her and shower in this bathroom? I need a minute." Luca's chest ached at Ethan's suggestion. He worried that what had just happened was too much, and that this was the best time, but also the last time they would be together.

It had taken them a few minutes to recover. They'd all been sort of stunned into silence. Luca had felt like he'd poured himself into both Ethan and Cece, and he felt full of them in turn. But maybe Ethan was feeling differently. Maybe, now that they'd done something novel to him, he was done with the whole dynamic, and this was the way he was saying goodbye. By slowly withdrawing from one or both of them.

"Are you sure?" Cece was apprehensive as well. It was written all over her face.

Ethan rolled over to look at her and smoothed the small crease between her brows with his thumb. He always did that, and it affected

Luca more than it probably should. Right now, it made him feel like he was intruding on the two of them and should probably leave the room. "I just need a minute. Not more than a minute."

Cece nodded, and they kissed. Luca had to turn away. He was going to get out of bed and leave until Ethan grabbed his hand and pulled him over to kiss him as well. "Take care of our girl."

Ethan saying it—*our girl*—made it seem like it was real, but he was afraid to hope for what this meant. None of the reasons why they couldn't be together, in the public eye, had gone away.

Still, he wasn't going to waste the opportunity to have Cece alone, naked, and soapy. He pulled her out of the bed. He would have thrown her over his shoulder and carried her into the bathroom, but his body ached from the race and what they'd just done, even with the endorphins running through his system.

He turned on the shower and tested the temperature. "How hot do you like it?"

She smiled at him and said, "About as hot as it was watching the two of you together."

He didn't know he'd been worried she'd been put off by watching them do that together before she said that. Relief flowed through him that she'd thought it was hot. "I haven't been with a lot of guys, and that's really intimate. You didn't feel weird about it?"

"Not at all." She cocked her head to the side as he grabbed her hand and pulled her under the scalding water. He turned the hot water down a little so as not to dry out their skin. "Did you think it was weird?"

She resisted a little when he turned her to get her hair wet. He wasn't avoiding her question, but he wanted to take care of her. He needed his hands on her. "Not at all."

He wasn't sure what to say next, and she was silent. "It was kind of new. But maybe just because it was you and Ethan."

She chuckled softly as he lathered shampoo in her hair. "I haven't been with two guys at once, ever. And I've never seen that outside of porn. I thought it would be different. But the two of you together was amazing."

"You didn't feel jealous?" He hadn't realized he'd been worried about that either. The way they'd all come together—the lying and the cheating and the way Ethan had watched them the first time—it all felt precarious. As though they were getting away with something every time they all touched.

"Not even a little bit." He rinsed the shampoo from her hair, and she turned around, putting shower gel into her palm and washing his body. They should be talking more, but they were both silent for a moment. She surprised him by saying, "It feels so right when we're all together. And I don't want it to end."

"Do you think that Ethan would be on board with that?" He was in the other room now, instead of with them. He could easily be thinking about how he could be rid of Luca in their marriage. Luca felt like he was on top of the world, because he'd had them both in bed and the woman who felt more like his very own every time he touched her in his arms.

But he also felt like he was wearing all of his internal organs on the outside. He wasn't afraid of anything—it was his job not to be—but this was all so unnerving and foreign.

He'd always been somewhat of a sexual adventurer, but he now realized he'd never ventured much with his heart.

"I think that's why he's in the other room. You know he likes to think things over—to plot—while he's by himself. He has to close himself off before he opens up. But he's not fighting this. He wouldn't have let you fuck him if he wanted to be totally in control."

He pulled her with him under the shower spray. He needed to kiss her without getting soap or conditioner in their mouths. He always wanted to be close to Cece, and her words were giving him hope that it was possible to keep them. Her wet skin against his, so close he felt as though they were melded together, gave him courage. "I want both of you. I've wanted you forever, but I don't think whatever was between me and Ethan was more than sex and friendship before."

She rested her cheek on his chest as he tangled his fingers through her hair, combing out the conditioner. "We're all in so deep."

He just hoped they wouldn't live to regret it.

Summer Break

Chapter Thirty

Micaela didn't feel at all relaxed even though she'd lounged on the deck of Liam's yacht for three days straight after the Hungarian Grand Prix. If she was racing in any other series, she would have been done with her season by now. Unfortunately, and fortunately, there were ten races to go before the winners would be crowned.

On the one hand, there were still enough races for her to win the driver's championship.

On the other hand, she was more tired than she'd ever been in her life. And she didn't feel like she had much privacy anymore. Back when her father had raced, there were paparazzi and scandals, but there weren't Instagram accounts and content creators parsing news articles and candid photos so that there was a full breakdown of everything she did or wore from her outfit of the day to her skin-care products. It made her feel like she was on the edge of people finding out she was fucking her boss.

Liam acted like he didn't care whether people found out. She even had an inkling that he would be relieved. They went back and forth about how much they cared about the world knowing they were together. After she'd won the Hungarian Grand Prix, she'd wanted nothing more than to kiss him on camera. The urge had been almost impossible to resist. She'd dreamed about it on the plane on the way home. She'd been with members of the team, and they'd made fun of her when she'd said his name in her sleep.

At that point, Liam had been so jumpy that he didn't even hug her after the win. He patted her on the shoulder. But then there had been an article on a motorsports website that speculated that there was discord within the team because of Liam's lack of enthusiasm. Liam's office had to make a statement saying something about how she'd been overheated, and he hadn't wanted to crowd her.

It was all such utter bullshit, and she hadn't wanted to live with it any longer. They either had to break up or go public.

But then—on the day they'd boarded Liam's yacht—a fan had taken pictures of them boarding the boat. Luckily, Paola and Brent had also been boarding along with them, so no one had posited the theory that Micaela and Liam were vacationing together, alone.

Oh yeah, and they were on the verge of being caught out by her ex and Liam's son. Liam didn't seem to care whether Brent saw the way he looked at her. He'd been groping her in the pantry when Paola had walked in to find some crisps. The other woman's eyes had grown to the size of saucers, and she'd walked right back out.

Even a super yacht was tiny when you were sneaking around with your boyfriend.

Paola came on deck with a large Turkish towel and spread it out next to Micaela. She lay down and opened up a book. At first, she didn't say anything, which relieved Micaela. Maybe she wouldn't mention that she'd seen Liam with his hand down the back of her shorts the night before.

Micaela turned on the audiobook she'd been listening to, thinking she could possibly spend a quiet afternoon and pretend her situation wasn't as precarious as it was.

"You need to be more careful," Paola said, and Micaela's blood turned to ice. The other woman was going to bring it up—she was too savvy not to—but there had been a shred of hope that they could just enjoy a peaceful vacation where no one mentioned anything going on right in front of their faces. "You're going to burn if you stay out here much longer."

Micaela sat up and put on the large white linen shirt she'd taken from Liam's closet to cover up. Paola was right. Micaela was fairly pale and close to getting pink. She added a straw hat, not sure if the heat in her face was from the embarrassment of thinking Paola was going to mention her affair with Liam or a developing sunburn. She wasn't sure which she'd prefer at this point.

But it was stupid that they weren't going to talk about this. Paola's whole job was covering the team's ass when shenanigans occurred. She actually *should* know what was going on with Liam.

"I'm sleeping with Liam. I've been sleeping with him for a while—since after my first win."

Paola said nothing at first. She just settled farther into the plush deck chair and pulled her sunglasses down over her face. Micaela didn't dare look at her, so she trained her gaze on the coastline. They were anchored off the coast of Tuscany, in the Ligurian Sea. She'd tagged along on countless of her father's vacations with countless girlfriends, so she'd probably seen this precise landscape a thousand times.

Funny how she'd never really appreciated it until she'd seen it from the deck of Liam's boat.

"No shit," Paola finally responded. "I figured as much when you were making out in the galley. You should really be careful about that too."

Micaela finally turned to her friend. She didn't look upset with Micaela. "Does Brent know?"

She'd figured out something was going on between Brent and Paola after Silverstone, and there was also the fact that they were vacationing together. All signs pointed to romance. "You're sleeping with him. And you work together."

She didn't know why she was defending herself by needling Paola. It was plainly childish, but she didn't want to feel like she was doing something wrong. She was tired of sneaking around, and yet terrified of being found out. The only time she found any real peace was when Liam's mouth found hers, and they got lost in each other. But they were never in sync when it came to coming out and telling people they were together.

"He's not my boss. And he's not my ex-boyfriend's dad." Paola was right to point those things out, but they stung a bit when said aloud. "How did this even happen? He's not harassing you, is he?"

"Only when I ask him to," Micaela said, and Paola gave her a sharp look. "I was the one who pushed it. None of the HR rules were broken."

"You're breaking them now by keeping this a secret." Her efficient friend had likely broken out her highlighter pen and employee handbook before she'd even kissed Brent. So, she would know. "Is it worth it?"

Micaela couldn't answer that at the moment. When she was with Liam, everything else fell away. She shed all of her insecurities and worries, and she could simply be in the moment with him. There was nothing to be afraid of, and no one who could hurt her. She felt safe and cared for.

When she was away from him, she felt like she was missing a piece of herself. Everything she feared came roaring back into her mind if he was out of her sight. That couldn't be healthy, could it? This was probably just lust or infatuation, and they were running the risk of their entire lives blowing up, just for a few minutes of pleasure when they could grab it.

"I don't know." She couldn't see into the future to know whether this would all work out or destroy everything they'd both worked their entire lives for.

"Then, you have to break it off." Paola shook her head, and her long locks brushed her sun-burnished skin. Micaela had never seen her so relaxed, but she was still worried. All because of Micaela's twisted infatuation. "Too many people could get hurt."

"Are you worried about me? Or just your new boyfriend?" Micaela knew that wasn't fair, but it was a bit hypocritical to tell Micaela who she shouldn't be sleeping with at the moment.

Paola sat up and took off her sunglasses. Her dark brown eyes seemed to have sparks coming off them. "I'm worried about everyone involved. If you don't figure out what you want, you know the press is going to find out eventually. And then, everything goes out of your control. It goes out of Liam's control. A board of directors and public sentiment will decide your fate. And that's not you, Micaela. I haven't known you your whole life, but I know that you're a woman who makes her own destiny. You wouldn't be in contention to win a championship if you weren't. But maybe I'm wrong, and you want to throw it all away to be that girl."

"Who's 'that girl'?"

"The girl who could have been great. The girl who could have been a legend."

Micaela had wondered herself if she truly wanted to be a great driver or if she just wanted to prove she could be as great as her dad. But the only other time she felt free from the rest of the world's expectations of her was when she was in the car, on the track. She'd loved racing before she'd realized it was the only way she could get her father's attention or approval. She'd learned on the track that she could equal or best everyone. It had given her confidence in a world that tried to take it away from women and girls at every turn.

Liam understood that about her, and he'd taken her on as a driver anyway. And he wasn't a man who yielded to mere lust and infatuation. He had more integrity than that. Integrity that Micaela had picked at and tested, as though he was an opponent whose tires were badly degraded. She'd worn him down.

He'd been the first man to truly see her and want her. He'd taken huge risks to be with her—both as a driver and as a lover. Risks he wouldn't take if what they had wasn't real.

And she felt more than lust for him. What she'd felt for Brent was attraction mixed with familiarity. What she felt for Liam was so much more—she was in love with him.

"I don't think it's as simple as breaking up with him." Micaela hugged her knees to her chest. "I—care about him way too much to do that."

"So, you're in love with him?" Paola asked. She'd settled back onto her lounge chair and opened a book, dropping that word as though it wasn't a bomb. Really dangerous behavior when they were on a boat. "If you're in love with him, and you're sure he loves you back, then it might make sense for you to ruin your reputation."

Micaela didn't see why her reputation had to be ruined based on who she fell in love with. She got that the only way for women to gain any foothold in this business had been to sleep with someone important who could give them a boost, but that was mostly in the past. It was totally different from two consenting adults deciding their complicated, intertwined situations didn't matter as much as being together.

"Love is not a magical cure-all for how the world will see me," Micaela said. "But Liam is important to me. It's not just sex."

It hurt to admit that, but it was true. The way she wanted to defend him when Paola had insinuated he was a perv for getting involved with her was proof of that. She needed to figure out what she wanted, and she didn't need to deny the truth.

"Brent's going to freak out when he finds out that you're going to be his new mother-in-law."

Spoken like a woman who knew how Brent's mind operated.

When Brent and Micaela had dated, Liam had never been jealous when they spoke with each other at dinner and when they didn't pay any attention to him. Now—as they sat at his table on the deck of his yacht, eating food his staff prepared—he wanted to toss Micaela over his shoulder and take her below so she would only look at him and pay attention to *him*.

This woman had turned him from a doting father and avuncular figure into a raving caveman in a matter of months.

He could barely stand to be without her while she'd been reading on the deck this afternoon, even though he'd had work to do. The factory was closed down over part of summer break to make sure no one team would gain an advantage by working on their car round the clock in the month between races. But he'd had a few calls with team sponsors this afternoon.

Micaela's success in the car was garnering them interest from businesses that Liam never would have dreamed of approaching before she'd joined the team—cosmetics companies and luxury fashion brands that hardly targeted men at all—this was one of the big reasons that he'd stolen her from Lupo in the first place. And it did a small amount to assuage his guilt over the fact that they were involved.

He and Brent had always spent at least part of summer break together. It was the only time they had that wasn't about business and cars, and Liam had always treasured it. But this year, he'd actually been pissed off when Brent had assumed they were going on this weekend yacht excursion together. Liam's greedy, cloying desire to be alone with Micaela had been overwhelming. He'd been tempted to lie and say he was going elsewhere or he had business meetings in Kuala Lumpur to avoid spending his vacation with his son cockblocking him.

He should be happy that Micaela and Brent were actually smiling at each other, and that Micaela wasn't looking at him like she wanted to rip off his clothes at dinner. If he were a better man, he would be grateful that his girlfriend had more self-control and discretion than him.

Instead, he wanted to stand up and dump a cold drink in his son's lap so there would be no chance he was turned on by his ex-girlfriend. It didn't even make sense—something romantic was clearly happening between Brent and Paola. She was good for his son, as she seemed to have chiseled away quite a bit at the boulder-size chip on Brent's shoulder.

Because he was a grown man who didn't immediately act on his impulses, he kept his foul mood to himself. Or at least he thought he did before all three of his dinner companions looked at him expectantly as he tried to murder the asparagus with a fork.

"What?" He hadn't been paying attention to a word they'd been saying when he should have been postulating about racing lines or something like that.

Micaela smiled at him knowingly and then put her hand on his knee under the table. They were close enough that Brent or Paola wouldn't notice, but it was still risky. Until Paola had caught them making out—Jesus, he was back to making out like a teenager—they'd been so careful not to get caught. But he was in too deep to care whether people knew they were together, which probably meant it was time to break things off.

Micaela's longevity in the sport depended on her staying scandal free much more than it did for any other driver on the grid—by virtue of her gender. It wasn't fair, but that was the reality. They were docking tomorrow, so he'd do it tonight. He'd make some excuse for why she had to leave the ship to Brent and Paola, and they would still have a few weeks of summer break to figure out how they were going to conduct themselves professionally once the season resumed.

"We were asking what you thought of the new track layout at Zandvoort," his son asked with a furrowed brow that Liam looked at in the mirror every day. They were so much alike that it scared him sometimes. Down to the cowlick that moved every time the breeze caught it.

He glanced at Micaela then and wondered whether she noticed the same things. He'd stopped thinking she was only attracted to him out of a sense of revenge a long time ago, but he still had bouts of angst that she seemed willing to squander her youth on someone as washed up as him.

He had a fiber supplementation routine when most men her age were just starting to experiment with hard drugs.

He'd never dated anyone so much younger because he frankly didn't approve of it. He failed to understand the logic behind a lot of older men dating women so much younger than them.

"I think it will be safer, and it will give the younger drivers an advantage."

Brent grunted and put a large bite of fish into his mouth. Paola looked everywhere but at the three of them at the head of the table. Liam toyed with just telling his son about him and Micaela. But he wouldn't do that because he hadn't talked about it with her first.

She brought out every emotion in him that he'd trained himself out of acting on—the pettiness, the fear, the anger, the unfettered desires that he tamped down for decades because of his responsibilities. And all of the resentment he'd stored up for all of this time was currently directed at his son.

"You're still a younger driver, Brent." Micaela smiled at him, but it was the smile of a competitor, not a friend. "Just not the younger driver on the team."

Brent sat back and said, "I'm full. Do I still have to ask to be excused?"

"What are you talking about?" Liam's simmering anger was going to boil over. Why hadn't he raised a son with the maturity to ignore being needled by one woman? "You've never had to ask to be excused from the table. That's not what we're like."

Brent nodded and stood up. "Good night." When Paola didn't get up to leave, he looked at her expectantly.

"I'm not finished with my dinner." Paola took another bite. "I'm going to let you go off and pout alone."

Brent stalked off the deck and stomped down the steps to the staterooms below.

"Do you know what's going on with him?" No matter what, he cared about what his son was feeling. He may not be acting like it right now, but it would always be close to the front of his mind. It bothered him that Paola knew more about his feelings than he did at the moment.

Paola shrugged and looked at Micaela before responding. "It's not hard to figure out that you favor Micaela. And, because your son knows you so well—which is a testament to your parenting if you really think about it—it's only a matter of time before he realizes that you're—"

"Just say it, Paola." Micaela put her head in her hands, and Liam froze.

"Sleeping together."

The only thing worse than the world knowing about him and Micaela was his son knowing about him and Micaela. He'd thought about telling Brent, but he couldn't pull the trigger when faced with the reality of it.

Paola looked at him as though he might throw her overboard. He would never. "I'm not mad at you for saying it. I'm just glad you haven't told him."

Micaela pulled her face out of her hands and looked at him. She appeared to be both exasperated and composed. "Or maybe he's just being a dick for no reason. He's been known to do that."

Something in Liam told him that was not the case, that he and Micaela had come to the end of the time when they could just be wrapped up in each other. The time they could feel the recklessness of what they were doing without any consequences.

He didn't think Brent knew about his romantic relationship with Micaela. If he did, there would be theatrics and fireworks, not surliness. No, Brent's jealousy was in the realm of the professional. Too bad the professional was so intertwined with the personal at this point that they couldn't be separated.

"Paola, I need a few minutes with Micaela." Still not done with her fish, she pushed away from the table and followed Brent below deck.

A member of the crew came out to grab their plates as he and Micaela stared at each other in silence. It seemed to take forever for them to pick up the dishes, and Liam could feel his nervous system winding tighter with each passing moment.

Micaela's shoulders crept toward her ears, and he knew the tell. She was about to either burst with anger or disappear into herself. He didn't want either to happen, but there was nothing he could do to stop it.

Chapter Thirty-One

"You're a coward, Liam Sullivan." The wind made the ends of Micaela's hair flip behind her shoulders, adding such a precise end to that statement that she might have thought Mother Nature was on her side. "No wonder you left the sport before winning a championship. You're afraid of your own son."

Liam ran his fingers though his messy dark hair, and it stuck up where the cowlicks had their way with him. She wanted to reach out and brush the strands down, like she had almost done a few weeks before—after the Spanish Grand Prix. But she'd been thinking about the cameras then.

She'd thought this trip would bring some freedom for them—to touch each other the way they liked and act like they were actually in a relationship with one another. But he'd had to let his son and Paola tag along, which ruined everything.

"I don't want to do this, but I don't think we have a choice." She could hear the ache in his voice. He hated disappointing people, and he took the responsibility of the whole team—of everyone in his life—on his shoulders.

But this was ridiculous. "You can't be in charge of anyone else's emotions. As young as I am, I know that." She'd gone to enough therapy to get over her shitty dad to know she wasn't responsible for his bad moods and bursts of anger any more than she was responsible for Brent's cheating.

"We knew this would be difficult when it started." He reached over the table as though he was about to grab her hand, but she snatched it away and stood up, facing the railing and the dark sea.

Between the twinkling lights from the scattered houses on the cliffs along with the breeze and the company, this should have been one of the most romantic nights of her life. But he was going to break up with her because he didn't want to deal with his son's wrath.

Instead of standing behind her, enveloping her in his heat, he stood to the side, grasping the railing with his big hands. She still wanted him to touch her more than anything. She wanted his hands all over her. If he knew the depth of her wanting, he wouldn't be doing this. He'd be hauling her below deck, regardless of the consequences.

But her pride wasn't going to let her beg him to see sense. His mind was made up, and there was nothing for her to do. "He's such a little asshole. Maybe I was wrong, and you aren't a good father."

His grip tightened on the railing, which told her she'd made a direct hit. His ego was so wrapped up in his image of himself as a good man, a good father. Everything in her body hurt from just knowing he wouldn't touch her again and hurting him wasn't making her feel any better.

The sting of tears made the lights on shore dance and distort. The reflection on the sea was a dark mirror for the chill that threatened to overtake her, body and soul. She wasn't tempted to dive into the oblivion, but she wished she could get away right now. She wished she was in a car, on an open track, and could prove she was worthy of not feeling like this.

"I'm sorry, Micaela." She didn't want to hear him broken if he was intent on tearing her apart this way. She wanted him resolved in it. She could handle that. Hearing he was unsure about this was more than she could take.

She turned to him, but he was blurry. The tears fell freely now, but he couldn't see because he was looking away. "Look at me."

To his credit, he followed instructions. "Please don't cry."

"Why shouldn't I cry, Liam?" Her voice faltered, but she wasn't afraid of what she felt for him, and he should have to know before he did this. "The man I'm sleeping with is breaking things off because he's afraid." She let loose a humorless chuckle that echoed over the water. "The man who is in my ear every weekend, telling me not to be scared, to take what I want with both hands and not let go, is so afraid of the small, petty man that he raised that he won't tell him to fuck off."

"He's my son, Micaela." He reached out and grabbed her upper arms. She wanted to push him away, but this might be the last time he touched her. "I can't treat him like your father treated you, or I wouldn't be the man you think I am."

"I know you're not my father." She did. His steadfast caring—the kind that hadn't damaged his masculine image at all—might have been the first thing that attracted her to him. But that wasn't all of it. He spoke to the animal part of her. He was meant to be her mate, not a parental figure. But perhaps he didn't see it that way. Maybe he was trying to work his past out using this affair more than she was.

"But maybe I'm some sort of sick stand-in for Brent, so you don't have to feel like you failed as a parent."

She wiped her tears away with the back of her hand, probably smearing mascara all over her face. It didn't matter because the paparazzi and fans weren't there to see it, and she wanted Liam to see her pain. She wanted him to eat it at every meal, every time he saw her.

"You're better than this, Micaela." Liam's voice was maddeningly calm. "You know that this is not just about Brent. This is about your career, the team, our reputations. Starting this affair was a terrible idea in the first place."

"It was my idea. You don't have to point out how terrible it was."

He surprised her by pulling her close. "You think it was your idea." The desirous edge to his tone sent a shiver down her spine. "But I thought of you differently from the moment I saw you with him this season. I was jealous when you laughed at one of his jokes. After you won that race, I wanted you sweaty and satisfied in my arms even more than I wanted to breathe. I think of little else but making you happy. When you're disappointed, I feel it in my bones. The way your face looks just now—knowing that it's my fault—leaves me without words."

"You love me." He didn't say whether that was true, but she knew it was. She pulled away and looked up at him. He was gathering the strength he needed to make her leave him. "You love me, but you just love him more."

The quiet words sat like a stone at the bottom of the sea. That was the way it should be, but Micaela wanted to be tethered to that stone. To sink. It was the way it should be. He should love his son more than he loved himself. He should be willing to give up love to have his son in his life.

But that didn't change the deep hurt that would take up residence beneath her skin, maybe never letting her go. It didn't change that she would look at him and crave his touch—maybe forever—simply because it was the one thing she couldn't have anymore.

"It's not that." She would have expected him to quietly slink away, given that he was behaving like a coward. "I love him like he's a part of myself. I took too much from him while he was growing up, just by being in this sport. And then I made him obsessed with it when—"

Brent wasn't ever going to be as quick as Liam had been in his heyday, but there was something about him that wouldn't allow him to quit. And Liam wouldn't end his son's quest if he wasn't forced to.

Whatever instinct that had made Micaela think Liam would put his own happiness over his son's had lied to her.

Micaela nodded. "I understand."

Again, she expected him to walk away and leave her broken to collect her thoughts. That's what he would have done if she'd had a disappointing race. But he surprised her by turning her around in his arms, so that he was caging her between his body and the rail. The heat of him permeated her skin and alleviated some of the pain she was feeling. But the knowledge it wasn't permanent made her sting.

He leaned close, brushing her hair away from the back of her neck before placing his lips there. She couldn't stop the moan that left her mouth.

"I shouldn't be doing this. I shouldn't be touching you." His anguish wrote those words, and she couldn't deny them. It eased her to know he couldn't just let go of her either. "But I can't seem to stop myself."

She didn't tell him she never wanted him to stop. That wasn't fair to either of them. But she didn't put a halt to him touching her. Not even when he wrapped one arm around her and pulled her back to him so she could feel how hard he was for her. She felt as though she'd had a whole giant bottle of champagne and was on the comedown from her buzz. Tears formed and dropped before she could do anything about it.

"One more time, Micaela." Liam was pleading with her, and more tears came because she wasn't about to deny him. "Just give me one more time, and we'll leave it alone."

This wouldn't work. She wasn't going to get him out of her system. That wasn't possible, and she wouldn't want that even if it was. She would carry a piece of him inside her forever. She let her head fall back against his shoulder and looked up at his face. He was upside down from this angle, but he was turning her inside out.

"One more time."

He pushed away from the rail, taking her with him. They made their way below deck and to his stateroom. She'd always thrilled entering this room before tonight, and she wondered how large a part of what had drawn her to him was how forbidden their relationship was. She was always seeking out the biggest adrenaline rush, and maybe that was it. Maybe she hurt because being with Liam was the closest she ever got to the feeling she had inside a fast car.

But the way he didn't let her go all the way down to his room told her it wasn't that. He turned her in his arms again when they were below deck. She pressed her face into the soft linen of his shirt, needing to memorize the way he smelled for later. When she couldn't have him.

She wished she'd taken one of his T-shirts when she'd had the chance. His scent immediately comforted and excited her, and she would need it when she got lonely. It astonished her how isolated she'd been before Liam. She had few friends because there were few to be had on the grid. And other young women her age were either fans or completely uninterested in what she did. Her job was so consuming that she'd latched on to the only other people—Brent and then Liam—who shared her obsession.

Liam must have sensed she was somewhere else, ruminating on what she was about to lose. He cupped her face in his hands and said, "I can hear you thinking."

As he looked at her, she was sure he could see everything running through her mind, and the way her heart was breaking. She wanted to break away and run out of the room, but she also couldn't bear the thought of this ending with him.

So, she didn't bear it. She turned in his arms and vaulted up on her toes to kiss him thoroughly. For a second, she thought she would knock him off balance, but she should have known better. Liam was like a tree that had survived centuries of storms and remained standing.

His secret to never falling down was that he was also the storm. And he ravished her right back. Their kiss was a crush of lips and a whirlwind of limbs. Somehow, she crawled up his body, and her face was level with his. He held her up with his giant palms on her ass and groaned into her mouth.

"I have to have you hard and fast and then take you slowly," he said. "It has to be twice." He sat down on the bed with her straddling him, her hair covering them both.

At that point, they didn't even bother to disrobe completely. If she was going to have him twice, she could feel his skin against hers later. He yanked up her dress and put his hand in her panties, finding her so wet that the sounds echoed in the room. He gave her two fingers and then three, filling her up.

But not as full as she would be. She pushed herself to kneeling, balancing her hands on his shoulders, and pulled her underwear down on one side and off one foot. This move put her breasts right in his face, and he bit down lightly on one nipple, through the cloth of her dress and bra. The sensation made her mewl with pleasure. Especially when he added a thumb to her clit.

Sex had never felt this electric before. It had never felt like a feast for her senses. Even as she savored Liam's hands and mouth on her, the way his hair was cool to the touch between her fingers as she held on for dear life, she wondered if she would ever feel this way again.

As though he felt her body leaving this room, right now, he pushed those thoughts away by driving her toward an orgasm that would break her. He knew exactly where to touch her and how. He had enough experience with her body to know exactly how to drive her out of her mind. She dangled for a moment, on the precipice of falling over. And then she looked at him. The intensity in his inky-colored pupils and the way his jaw was set with determination was what finally made her come.

She shook in his arms while he calmed her by stroking his big hands on her back and thighs. He was memorizing her too. And that almost made her cry again. She was done crying for the night. It was a waste of the precious little time they had left together. Instead, she pulled the button on his pants loose and lowered the zipper.

After she pulled his cock out of his boxer briefs, she stroked him for a long moment. They should really make a cast out of it and use it to model sex toys. It would sell out immediately—probably because she would buy all of them and lock them up in storage so that no one else could touch him.

"Are you going to smile at my dick or let me fuck you?" His question held a little bit of humor, but it was ragged. She lined herself up and lowered down until he was fully seated inside her. They both groaned with the pleasure of her wrapped tightly around him. He unbuttoned the top of her dress and lowered the cups of her bra so her breasts were bare for him. They were smallish, but he looked at them as though they were the most perfect breasts he'd ever seen.

When he sucked on her nipple again, she had to move. She posted up and down on his cock, slowly at first. He soon lost patience and flipped her until her back was on the bed. He pulled her dress up again so that he could stare at the place where they were joined as he fucked her.

"You're going to come again," he said, but it was already a foregone conclusion. His hair was messy and over his forehead as he fucked into her. The look of singular concentration on his face was so beautiful to her that she reached up and ran her finger over his jaw.

He didn't break rhythm. Soon he moved at a pace that had her unable to keep her eyes open. She had to squeeze them shut against the wall of flame coming at her. She grabbed his forearms and held on as every muscle in her body tightened, bracing.

When she came, she felt him coating her with his seed, shuddering against her. After it was over, they lay there, still partially dressed and covered with sweat. She felt empty on the inside, but it was the kind of emptiness she felt after a good workout or a half hour in a sauna after a cold plunge. She felt clean and new, as though her worries and fears were entirely outside herself.

Liam stroked her face with his fingers, just like she had moments before, and the spell was partially broken. She could feel the ties between them fraying—not because of time or distance—but because he was sawing through the rope.

This coming together had merely been the first act of their goodbye, and she wasn't sure she would live through the second.

"I just need a second," she said. He pulled out of her, and she choked on a sob. She didn't want him to see her like this—vulnerable and sad. He would only try to fix it. Since he was the one causing her pain, that would only make it worse.

She looked at him lying there, with his eyes closed. "We can take a nap."

"Hmmm." He was already almost asleep. He'd emptied himself into her too.

His breaths evened out after a few minutes. Minutes during which she stared at the ceiling of his stateroom, gathering the strength to leave.

She smiled when he snored softly and somehow forced herself to walk out of the room.

Qualifying Day
Dutch Grand Prix

Chapter Thirty-Two

Cece had woken up with a bad feeling this morning. She put it down to the fact that she hated this track. Actually, she hated the whole country. They might have legal weed, but she was deeply skeptical of any country where blackface was an integral part of their holiday celebrations.

The racing fans were always universally awful. That was especially the case this year, when their national hero hadn't won a single race this season and had announced his retirement on media day, reinitiating silly season during a year that had seen quite enough silliness.

Tension made the air feel heavier than South Beach in August. Ethan must have had a similarly bad feeling, though he would never call it that. A feeling that Luca likely shared. During breakfast in their hotel suite, her two men had shared a terse conversation that didn't require words. At the end of it, they'd told her she needed to get ready fast enough to go to the track with Ethan. Even with the extra security, they didn't trust the fans here.

Cece had made noises of protest, but the fact that she had two people invested in her safety warmed her heart. Walking into the paddock with Ethan, his hand on her lower back, made her feel like she did at the beginning of their relationship. The fact that they'd come to the track with Luca in the same car added to that feeling.

People had noticed the relationship between the three of them had changed, but no one knew the extent to which they'd grown closer. It was wild how people only saw what they wanted to. They didn't expect to see them in a romantic relationship, so Ethan and Luca's dynamic morphed into a friendship in public—and Cece was just the really cool wife.

Her good feelings melted away when they got to the track and saw the puffs of orange smoke and garish wigs behind the barriers. She couldn't speak Dutch, but she'd heard enough over the years to know a lot of words sounded kind of like "slut" without the same meaning.

But then she started hearing it a lot more, and people started throwing trash at them. It all happened so fast that she couldn't get her head around what was going on. One moment, she was walking through a crowded paddock with fans behind barriers, flanked by Ethan and Luca. The next, all three of them were being pelted with garbage, including an almost full beer. And then, staff at the track were ushering them into a side building she had never been inside.

The heavy metal door closed behind them with a few words from the track marshals still echoing inside.

"What the hell just happened?" Ethan yelled.

Cece did what she always did when something went wrong and grabbed her phone. Those things really were an addiction. It usually wasn't lit up with notifications because she only accepted them from important contacts. She'd been with two of her three important contacts the whole day. But her phone was lit up with messages from everyone from her mother to her booking agent.

She clicked on one of the many from her mother first that said, "I can't believe you!" with a link. Shit. She clicked on the link, and it went to the @WAGsandSLAGs Instagram page, where there was a photo of her, Ethan, and Luca on vacation with the caption, "Are Things Way Too Cozy at Scuderia Lupo?"

The photo was not one of the summer break pictures each of them shared on social media. Luca had gone as far as spending a few days with his family in the South of France before joining them in the Maldives for what they thought was a week in a private cabana.

It was a lot less private than they'd thought. The cameras hadn't caught anything naked or sexual, but the way Luca's hand rested on the back of her neck and the way he looked at her made it obvious. Even worse than that, Ethan was bringing food out onto their deck at the same time.

In this dank storage room, Ethan and Luca were both pacing. Ethan tested the door. "We aren't locked in."

"We shouldn't go out there," Luca said.

Cece looked up from her phone, feeling like she'd been punched in the stomach. "I agree. We should stay in here."

What would happen beyond the next few minutes was completely beyond comprehension. Ethan and Luca both stopped pacing and walked toward her. She wanted to pull back, so they could come up with a plan for how to handle this. If they touched her, she wouldn't be able to move forward with a clear head. And she couldn't allow her heart to make the decisions right now. That's what had gotten all three of them here.

But they wouldn't let her pull away from them. They flanked her and cut off her avenues for escape.

"This is all going to be fine," Ethan said.

Luca nodded. "We're ahead in the championship as a team. This isn't going to affect anything."

Cece struggled to find her breath. Neither of them was thinking straight. They couldn't be. This would not be fine. Their families would lose it—Ethan's family would demand that he leave her. She covered her face with her hands. Luca's family would hate her for ruining his life with a scandal. She'd ruined his career—the one they'd given up everything for.

And it's not like they could all be together publicly. Saying no one was cheating would only make things worse. The team wouldn't think twice before showing Ethan and Luca the door and making it so no one would accuse them of being homophobes. No, they'd push that on the team's sponsors, who were probably already on the phone with Lupo, trying to figure out how they could get their money back.

"This is a nightmare." She took a deep breath, not able to bear the thought of looking at either of them in the eye when she said, "I have to get out of here."

They both spoke at once.

"No."

"You're not going anywhere."

She held out her phone to them. "You don't see this? Even the headlines make me look like some slut."

Ethan pulled her to him, and Luca approached her from behind. She closed her eyes against the sight of them up close, comforting her. They were the ones who would lose everything. She could disappear into relative obscurity. They would be followed by this for the rest of their lives.

How could she be so stupid? But when had she been smart? A smart woman would have known this was a scandal waiting to happen when she walked into Luca's apartment on New Year's Eve. A smart woman would have flirted with Ethan for a night and given him the wrong phone number five years ago. There had been something in her gut telling her that this could be disastrous the night they'd met, and she'd ignored it.

She was a dumb woman, but not foolish enough to believe them when they told her things would be okay.

She tried to wiggle her way out so she could get some air, but they just held her and did that thing where they talked without talking again. "I can't breathe, and you have to let me go."

They let her out of their arms, but they stood between her and the door. Ethan spoke first. "You don't get it. We're not letting you go."

"What he means is that if you don't want to be with either or both of us, you don't have to. But you're not walking out of here in a panic. Good decisions never come from that."

She could see their point, but they were wrong. The best thing they could all be doing right now is panicking. That was appropriate for the situation.

Cece rubbed her arms, even though the room they'd been stuck in was hot, and the air was stale. She could see both of them fighting their own battle against grabbing her so she couldn't leave. "I don't see how either or both of you are so calm. And it doesn't matter whether I want to be with you. I won't have your careers—the ones you spent your whole lives fighting for—on my conscience. You may not view it as a big deal right now. Hell, I didn't see it as a big deal when I first met you. I thought it was just rich guys driving in circles. Maybe it is." She threw up her hands and turned away from them. When she couldn't feel either of them approaching her, she knew she was getting through to them.

"I won't let you sacrifice your lifelong dreams for me." For a second, her mind went a few years forward in the future, when Ethan and Luca were off the grid, and their lives could be more anonymous. They could be together, like they were in the Maldives, all the time. In most places in the world, she could hold both of their hands. And no one would care.

But that was years away, and this was always going to be temporary. It didn't matter if they were both written in her soul, indelibly. She wanted to promise them she would wait for them to be done, and then they could be together. But life and timing didn't work that way. She wouldn't fool herself into thinking they had a chance if she walked out of this room.

"You love us." Ethan said the word she'd been avoiding using with both of them. They'd been so busy living in the uncertainty of the present moment—the feelings that fueled their affair—that the words hadn't seemed necessary. And when it came to her husband, she hadn't said them because she wasn't sure their affair with Luca wasn't the only thing holding their marriage together.

"It doesn't matter." She wiped away the tears that had fallen. She probably looked like a swamp creature at the moment, but she didn't care. “Here’s what’s going to happen. I’m going to get out of here, and your agents and managers and press people are going to put out a statement saying that what the cameras captured was entirely innocent. That Ethan and I are happily married and monogamous, and that we’re happy to have renewed our friendship with Luca.”

“I don’t want to do that. It’s not true.” Luca and his penchant for the truth.

Cece shook her head. “It is true. Except for the monogamous part, which I feel like we should really lie about in this situation.” She turned to face them, though they were both blurry given that she couldn’t stop crying. “Ethan is right. I care about you both. Please don’t make me watch you throw your lives away for me.”

She’d always known they were living in this fantasy world on borrowed time. She’d always known she was living in this glamorous, fake cloud of wealth on borrowed time. It had never felt like her home, and it had never felt real. Well, the only times it had felt real were when she was with Ethan or Luca. They’d all been so young when they’d met.

“If you need to divorce me—for your family—I won’t fight it.” Ethan wiped his face, which surprised her. If he was crying, it meant he was done fighting.

“You’re making a mistake, Cecelia.” Luca used her full name, and when she looked at him, she understood it was because he was pissed at her. His anger shimmered in between the dust motes floating about in the slivers of sun that made it into the room.

She wanted to deny that she was making a mistake. If she wanted to make her exit believable, she’d tell him every decision she’d made since she met the two of them at that Miami nightclub had been a mistake. But she couldn’t do that. Those miscalculations and errors had made the sum of her life. If she’d done anything differently, she wouldn’t have experienced the highlights of her life with either of them.

But it was over now, and she had to make them see this was the only right choice. She opened her mouth to say something, but the door to the storage shed opened, and their security walked in.

“We think we can get you all off the premises without cameras seeing.”

She tried to infuse steel into her spine, but she failed. At best, there was aluminum keeping her upright.

“I’m going to go.” Both Ethan and Luca had set jaws and clenched fists when she said that. “They have qualifying, and I have a plane to catch.”

Practice Day

—

Monza

Chapter Thirty-Three

The Temple of Speed was set in a graceful, wooded area that the Hapsburg and Savoy kings once used for hunting. The circuit at Monza was still a hunting ground. However, this weekend, Micaela's quarry was a win. She could still win the driver's championship with her second-place finish between Harrow and Bendetto in the Dutch Grand Prix. She'd been truly impressed that they'd gotten it together to win and podium, respectively, given all the rumors swirling around them. The weekend had been so busy she didn't realize she hadn't seen Cece after the stories dropped until after the race when she wasn't with the team to congratulate her husband.

It had been a weird awards ceremony. Her own team was ecstatic she was still in the hunt. She would be the first-ever rookie driver to win the championship in the modern era.

The attention around her success was overwhelming, and she felt as though she was drowning. Actually, it was worse than drowning. She felt as though she could see all the excited fans and happy sponsor representatives. She could smile and answer the questions asked by interviewers and commentators—giving all the correct, media-trained answers that showed the proper amount of humility. The proper amount of self-effacement for a girl driver was not-surprisingly much higher than it would have been for a female rookie sensation.

But everything was dimmer because Liam barely talked to her when he didn't have to. He didn't hug her after her podium in the Netherlands. He'd patted her shoulder and smiled for the cameras, and no one who hadn't lived inside the heat of their relationship could feel the new chill there.

But the loneliness she'd experienced almost her entire life was somehow more acute and cutting in this moment than it had ever been.

She was a few minutes late for the final engineering briefing before practice. From where she sat, she could see Liam. As per the new usual, he wasn't looking at her. His gaze was intent on the screen in front of him.

He'd always been stern and quiet during these meetings, but she knew he could have a million thoughts running through his head and indicate none of them with a change of expression. At least not one that anyone but her—and maybe Brent—would notice. She could tell when someone wasn't meeting his high expectations when a muscle near his temple twitched.

Brent was paying attention. He was the model driver these days. Ever since summer break, he seemed to have a renewed love for racing cars. When they were together, she'd always suspected he only raced because his father expected him to, and at the beginning of the season, he'd seemed intent on destroying his career.

Now, he was like a whole other person. He was out of the running to win the driver's championship, but he could still place in the top five. It was better than most people expected from a nepo baby driver.

She tried to stay focused on the run plans for the first practice. Monza was a fast and tricky track, with long straights and fast curves, and she was still just a rookie. Even though she'd raced here during her junior career, everything changed with the power of her current car. She needed to absorb all the information flying at her, but she was still behind this wall of water that kept everything but pain out. Her father would be so angry at her that she was even thinking about a broken relationship at all instead of focusing on the fact that she was teetering on the precipice of greatness. She should be feeling fresh and excited instead of wistful and depressed.

But telling herself to focus was practically useless. Her racing engineer stood up and asked, "Are you coming?" and she was still sitting there, pretending to think about the run plan and hoping that Liam would look at her, just once.

Liam was looking at her, but not the way she wanted. He had his brows raised in an expression that could either be worry or mild irritation. They hadn't been together long enough for her to discern the difference between those two brow raises. If she and Brent didn't have the history they did, she'd ask him if he could tell the difference.

She smiled a little at that, and Liam took that as a sign that all was well. Nothing was well, though, when his gaze turned heated for just a split second. It wasn't fair of him to give her even a granule of hope that he still wanted her. Not when he'd broken her heart.

Unfortunately, her body didn't get that memo, and she went liquid between her legs. Her face heated when she realized one look was enough for her to have hard nipples as she walked out of the briefing. And there was Paola with a camera, poised outside the briefing room to get pictures for social media.

Micaela's success seemed to be getting to Paola almost as much as it was affecting Micaela. Paola had four assistants, one of whom was entirely dedicated to capturing social media content for the team, but she was taking these pictures herself right now.

"Can we not?" Micaela crossed her eyes and gave her friend a look she hoped elicited pity.

Paola's smile faded, and she lowered the camera. She turned and walked next to Micaela as she walked into the garage. "That bad?"

"Excruciating." Micaela hadn't been able to hide her sadness from anyone on the boat. Paola had seen it right away, and they'd gone to a café on an island the next afternoon, where Micaela sobbed and poured her heart out.

Even Brent had noticed something was off, but Paola had told him Micaela had her period. He'd scoffed and likely resumed thinking about himself.

Paola put her arm around her shoulders and squeezed. "You'll get through this. I promise. Just keep winning."

But winning didn't feel like victory anymore. It felt like every point ticking up in the standings took her further and further away from the happiness she experienced with Liam.

"We have a little time before practice. Let's go grab one of those awful green drinks from that sports nutrition sponsor to keep up your energy."

Micaela hadn't been eating or drinking enough since summer break, and it probably showed. She'd needed ballasts in the car for the last race to make weight. Liam's mouth had flattened out when he'd heard that, as though it had displeased him.

Good. He should know how much he hurt her. Her pain right now was entirely his fault.

Still, it was a long, hot hour of practice before lunch, and she needed nutrition.

The hospitality wasn't far from the garage, but there would be reporters everywhere. All they were asking about this week was the supposed love triangle or throuple between Bendetto, Harrow, and Cece. They'd all denied the reports—together and separately—but the motorsports gossip mill had to be fed, otherwise the sport would perish entirely. At least one could think that, given the rapacious nature of the pseudo-reporters who spread spicy tidbits about drivers and their personal lives.

The reporters actually left her and Paola alone, such was the power of the team's press officer. She'd told the entire team that no one, under any circumstances, was to comment on the salacious stories going around about anyone on the grid. The look in her eyes when she'd said it could have started a fire in a dry environment. Maybe she'd done the same thing with the press.

It was impressive, regardless.

The only wrinkle in their search for food was Jocelyn Godwinson eating lunch in Panther's cafeteria. Generally, members of one team did not go into another team's facilities. The rules were a bit laxer with wives and girlfriends, but this woman had no reason to be here. Besides, Micaela had always found her kind of odious. By the way Paola's lip curled, she agreed.

"What are you doing here, Jocelyn?" Paola got right to the point. "Heka drove for Panther a decade ago, when it was named a whole other thing. Your team's space is way down the paddock."

It probably wasn't necessary to point out that Jocelyn's husband was going to retire from the sport in a few races' time, but if anyone deserved to be put in their place, it was this woman.

Micaela had known Jocelyn for almost half her life. Before she'd gotten with Heka, she'd been with the former president of the sport's governing body—at least until he was disgraced in a cheating scandal involving his favorite team. He'd received a generous severance package, but that wasn't enough for Jocelyn. And she'd dumped him and snagged Heka within weeks. Micaela had always suspected Jocelyn liked the status and spectacle of being attached to the sport much more than she cared about the actual racing. Heka leaving the sport had to be tough on her. Especially given the fact that they had four kids, and it would be harder to just dump him and find a new model this time.

"I just wanted to check in on all of you, to see how you're doing with all of the rumors. And, you know, to say goodbye."

Paola narrowed her gaze, and Micaela's stomach dropped to the floor. All of the sudden, the smells of the food in the air made her nauseous. She wanted to walk right out, but she couldn't do that, because it would be incredibly suspicious. She made her feet stay on the floor and put everything she had into keeping her game face on.

Even if Jocelyn somehow knew all about Micaela and Liam's affair, she wouldn't balk. She wasn't the one who was embarrassed about them. People would assume that Liam had initiated anything inappropriate.

The two of them would know the truth, and she would defend him if it came to that. She just really hoped it wouldn't come to that.

"Rumors? We don't trade in those here." At least Paola was standing firm. She was looking around the room to see if there were any security personnel to escort her out.

"I'm also a guest of the team. Liam invited me. Personally." Micaela couldn't be more shocked if Jocelyn had told them she was carrying the pope's offspring.

"Well, that's highly irregular," Paola said, looking down at a note on her phone. "I didn't see you on my list of VIPs."

It was probably a bad idea for Paola to be treating a guest of the team poorly, but Jocelyn was probably fibbing. If anything, Liam had probably waved her into the cafeteria as a polite way of ending a passing conversation. He would do something like that.

Unless she was telling the truth, and she was a guest of the team because Liam was thinking of replacing Micaela with Heka in the car next year.

That would have been the kind of passing statement that a commentator would throw out during a really boring season. And Micaela didn't have any reason to believe it other than the fact that Liam refused to look at her. Maybe it didn't matter that she was in the running to win the championship. Liam always cared more about the team game. If anything, Micaela had sown discord in the team because of her past relationship with Brent.

It had been great for sponsors, though, because they kind of loved when drama in a team kept them in the news. Every time their logo flashed on a screen—either in the car or on one of the team racing suits—it was more publicity than they'd paid for. But maybe he'd changed his mind and wanted to go in a more traditional direction. It didn't get more traditional than Heka. The pictures Jocelyn posted on social media of him being adorable with their kids were worth their weight in gold.

As all of these thoughts raced through Micaela's head, Paola made a few more sort of polite comments to Jocelyn and pulled Micaela toward the food.

"Are you okay?"

Micaela would sound crazy and paranoid if she told Paola what she was really thinking—that Liam was going to replace her. And she didn't want Jocelyn to overhear her sounding paranoid and crazy and perhaps take some sort of inspiration from her crazy and paranoid ideas.

So, she took a deep breath and said, "Fine. I'm just thinking about today's run plan."

Chapter Thirty-Four

Liam was losing his mind. He'd made a mistake breaking things off with Micaela. He'd thought he'd been doing it for her own good, but he'd been totally wrong. He'd seen it even moments afterward—the light dimming in her eyes. And now she wasn't taking care of herself the way she should. She was skinny and sad. And it was all his fault.

But he shouldn't be the one to take care of her. He couldn't be. It was inappropriate on both personal and professional levels. Completely unsustainable. But he was the only person she'd let in.

As he sat on the pit wall with his headphones on, he tried to listen to the race director and each of the driver's engineers. They'd brought upgrades to the race, and they only had two chassis, so they had to make it work.

He'd nearly wrung the neck of the team member who'd drawn the short straw of telling him that their third upgraded chassis had been left half finished in the factory. He'd been way too focused on his personal feelings for Micaela in the past few months and not nearly focused enough on the team. That half-finished car and the pressure it put on everyone in the team to be perfect this weekend was evidence he'd done the right thing by ending their relationship.

But then, directly after stopping himself from killing anyone or throwing something, he'd walked into the engineering meeting and smelled Micaela's shampoo. She'd left a bottle of it at his house in England, but nowhere else. After breaking up with her, he'd bought a bottle of it to take with him, so he could take pulls of the fragrance when he was alone.

He was still gone for her. Still addicted to her. Still desperately in love with her. He didn't know if it would ever end. He didn't know if he ever wanted it to.

He kept his eyes on the screen, watching the telemetry. He knew there might be cameras on him at any moment. Some content creator made regular edits of him looking "daddy," whatever that meant. He'd had to ask Micaela, which was just more evidence that he was too old for her.

That didn't mean he didn't still love to watch her drive. Under her hand, the car was performing extremely well in this practice session. Monza was the fastest track on the calendar. Most of the turns were harrowing. As he watched the screen as she did a fast lap, he could almost feel the g-force she was experiencing in his own body. It was the only way he had left to feel close to her.

It was pathetic. He turned his attention to his son's session. He was quicker than he had been during the first fast lap, but he was still lagging behind Micaela. He felt guilty that the healthy competition he'd intended to bring into the team was resulting in Brent falling out of the top five drivers. He'd meant to drive his son forward, not hold him back. But he also hadn't intended to fall in love with his son's ex. So, good intentions and all that.

Even now, he found it difficult to focus. His mind wandered away from the telemetry numbers, and he lost track of which of his cars was where on the track. He looked down and tried to rub the exhaustion out of his eyes. When he saw the crash, he jerked in his seat. He knew it was one of the Panther Yellow cars that hit the wall, but he didn't realize which one it was at first. The car hit the wall at Ascari and then crossed the track and hit the other wall on the straight before the left rear wheel came off and the car rolled to its side. If either of the drivers was hurt, he would never forgive himself. He was responsible for keeping them both safe.

Then, he saw Micaela's racing number and the smoke coming out of the gearbox. He wanted to run out onto the track and pull her out himself, and he barely kept himself from doing it.

His chest tightened, and he wasn't sure if he was experiencing acute panic or a heart attack brought on by stress. The radio was silent except for Micaela's engineer asking her to confirm she was all right. He kept one eye on the TV screen showing the crash in replay after replay, feeling as though someone had punched him in the stomach every time. He didn't know how long it was before her radio crackled to life. "I'm okay. I'm okay."

Finally, he could breathe. The broadcast showed the marshals helping her out of the car. She took a few ginger steps away from the smoking chassis and toward the medical car before raising her arms and waving at the camera, so the fans would know she was fine as well.

In that moment, it didn't matter that she was part of the upstart American team challenging their beloved Scuderia Lupo; everyone at the track cheered. But until he could see she was unharmed, until he could hold her in his arms and know that she was okay, he wouldn't be able to think of anything else.

Regardless of the fact that they still had one car on the track—it was coming into the garage, because they'd waved a red flag for the session—he had to make sure Micaela was okay.

He didn't spare a second to consider how it might look for him to rush out of the garage and over to the medical facility. He didn't think for a minute about how he might be fined for breaking one of a dozen rules against team staff interfering with anything having to do with an accident.

He had to see her.

—

An hour later, the mood in the garage was grim. Everyone might have been acting like she was dead, but she was sitting on the pit wall, uninjured. She would be ready to race and out on the track right now for the second practice session, but for the fact that she didn't have a car to race in. The chassis and gearbox had been a total loss, and Frankie had grimly informed her they didn't have a spare this weekend, due to the upgrades.

Liam, for his part, still refused to look at her. He'd come rushing into the medical center, wide-eyed and desperate looking. As soon as the doctor had informed him she was fine and wouldn't need to go to the hospital for additional checks, it was like he'd been unplugged from a light socket. He was himself again. Unfortunately, that self seemed to be furious with her.

And he had every right to be. The crash was entirely her fault. It was a grim reminder that she was a rookie, and she hadn't driven the track in this series before. Monza was the fastest track on the calendar, and the car had demonstrated significantly more power with the new upgrades. She'd been caught out by the corner, and then everything became a blur. She didn't even have the time to be afraid until the car stopped rolling. She hadn't heard the voices over the radio asking if she was all right, and her only thought had been to get out of the car before it caught fire.

That's when the fear had penetrated. The fastenings on her seat belt had seemed stuck for a few seconds that felt like an eternity as she attempted to extricate herself from the car.

As soon as she felt them loosen, she'd slithered out. By that time, the marshals were at the car with fire extinguishers. The whole thing felt embarrassing, and she wasn't sure if she was intact for a few seconds after she stood and started moving away from the car. She noticed the crowds, out for an uneventful day of practice with the picnic lunches, were eerily silent. She looked over and raised her arms in a wave. The cheer that went up bordered on humiliating. She was the one who had crashed and wrecked a million euros' worth of equipment, and they were cheering her on.

Sitting in the garage a few hours later, she shook her head. Even though her race weekend was ruined—her chance to win the championship gone—she was here for the team. And she would do whatever she could to help Brent get the team points.

Still, a little part of her died when all of the other drivers took the track and left her behind. It was a deep ache that told her one bad crash wasn't going to keep her down for long.

She looked over at Liam, who still hadn't so much as glanced her way. She was sure he regretted bringing her onto the team at this point. Hell, he'd probably regretted it for a long time, even before she'd kissed him and started their affair.

It would have been better had she ignored her attraction for him and focused on learning as much as she could from one of the most brilliant team leaders in motorsports.

The only thing that saved this weekend from being a total bust was that her father had flaked out on his planned trip. He never missed Monza, but the prospect of seeing his daughter race there must have put him off the event. He was probably delighted she'd crashed out. He likely hadn't spent a moment worrying she'd been hurt.

She was never enough to satisfy the men in her orbit.

In the past, Brent'd always had more experienced teammates, whose shadow he could linger in while he learned. He'd never really been meant to be the driver that shone. And while Micaela had spanked him at every race—saving this one, of course—she'd felt like more of an equal. Because of their history and because they were the same age, it felt like they were more competitive than any other teammate.

And he'd grown accustomed to that pressure. It had pushed him to be better. It might only be practice, but he'd topped the time sheets in the second practice session. For once, he got out of the car exhilarated rather than exhausted.

But then, after he'd gotten cleaned up and changed, his father pulled him into the conference room.

Micaela was already sitting at the table, and she looked up at him with a questioning gaze. At the beginning of the season, he would have gloated and given her a ton of shit about the crash. But now, he could even locate a moment of concern for his ex-girlfriend. Almost everyone on the grid had a scary crash at some point, and today was her day. But that didn't make it any easier on her.

Probably the worst race it could happen at—when they didn't have a full complement of spare parts—but these things happened. He just didn't understand why he was being brought in to get yelled at along with her.

His father motioned for him to sit, looking grim.

"We have a problem," his father said, and Brent had to fight not to roll his eyes.

He got that they were a team and all, but the problem seemed to be much bigger for Micaela. "And what does that have to do with me? That seems like a her issue." He pointed at Micaela, who looked like she'd probably been crying, so it was kind of a dick move. "And a you problem." He didn't point at his father—there appeared to be steam coming out of his father's ears, and he didn't want to lose a finger.

"It's a team problem," Liam said. Micaela stayed silent and didn't return the glare Brent gave her. "We have one driver who's been performing extremely well—"

"Yeah, until she crashed into the wall during a practice session." Brent shouldn't feel so smug, but it felt good to not be the fuck-up for once. He hadn't gotten to use his petty muscles very often since hooking up with Paola. She'd look at him like she disapproved of him and then wouldn't have sex with him for a few hours.

His father didn't let the interruption stop him. "And one driver that's been inconsistent, at best, during the course of the season."

That shut Brent up. Despite his cooperation with the publicity part of his job, his race results had barely improved. He'd made it through the latter parts of the qualifying sessions, but Micaela had beaten him during every race this year. If his father wasn't the team principal and majority shareholder in the team, he'd be worried about his seat.

Given the way Liam looked at him right now, he should probably be worried about his seat regardless. At least for this weekend. Brent forgot he was smarter than the way he behaved sometimes, at least when it came to how Liam was going to react to things.

Something in the back of his mind tickled when Liam glanced at Micaela. His father used to look that way at pictures of Brent's mother. Always when he'd thought he was alone. It was the most unguarded he'd ever seen his father.

And he was looking at Micaela the same way.

After that, a lot of pieces fell into place in his head—why Micaela hadn't tried to get him back, the amount of time the two of them spent together, why Micaela came on their summer vacation.

Fuck.

"How long have you been railing her, *Dad*?" He put emphasis on the last word. He wanted his father to really consider the ways in which this was a betrayal.

Something white hot burned in his veins that wasn't jealousy. It was more like humiliation. He felt as though he might throw up. He'd been with Micaela for years. He had to wonder if she had been sneaking around with his father before this season. Before they broke up.

Finally, Micaela spoke up. "It wasn't supposed to—"

"Shut up." Brent didn't want to hear from her.

"Don't talk to her like that," his father said. And this wasn't a dad telling his son how to behave. This was a man who was defending a woman he cared about—a woman he loved.

If it was possible, he felt even sicker, hearing his father talk that way about his ex-girlfriend.

"It's only been a few months, and it's over." His father sighed and leaned back in his chair. He covered his eyes with one hand. This was embarrassing for all of them.

Brent looked like a fool and a cuckhold. Liam looked like an old lech. And Micaela looked like a slut. And it was so surprising and out of character.

"And now you're going to give her my car for the weekend so your girlfriend can win the championship?"

There was a long pause before Liam said, "It's what's best for the team."

Finally, he looked at Micaela. He barely stopped himself from saying exactly what he thought of her. There was no doubt in his mind that he was the wronged party in all of this, but Micaela was almost a second victim. Her father had been such a dick to her for her entire life that she couldn't resist an older man being nice to her. An older man in racing.

"Did you fuck him to get back at me?"

Her eyes were shiny, as though she was going to cry at any moment. He knew what it took for her to cry. Even though he thought she was a scheming whore, he knew she was tough as nails. She'd always had to be. Maybe she felt a little bit of remorse—or more likely, regret.

She shook her head. "No. It was never about that. You didn't even play a part in it."

That was almost worse than her saying she'd seduced his father purely out of revenge. It meant she'd seen them side by side and decided that Liam was better.

That was the core of it for him. He would never measure up to his legendary father—not in racing and not in anything else.

At that moment, he just needed to get out of the room.

"We still need you on the team, son."

Brent sneered. "Like fuck you do." He stood up, and his chair hit the thin walls. In an hour or two, there'd be a story about how he had thrown a chair when his father had told him he couldn't race this weekend.

And Paola probably wouldn't even try to keep it out of the news. It wasn't like she was his girlfriend or anything. They were just fooling around and there'd been no discussion about where it was going. He was utterly and completely on his own.

He wanted to go home. And not his father's house outside London. He wanted to go to the little apartment in New York he'd bought and paid for himself. Sure, his father had given him the seat, but he'd proven he was talented enough to be there. He'd earned his place.

"I'm going to leave on the next flight out." His father hung his head, seeming resigned to the fact that he wouldn't be able to pretend they were a cohesive team in the wake of this disaster. "I'm not going to say anything to anyone." He didn't want the press to find out his father had been fucking his ex any more than the guilty parties did.

"Thank you," Micaela said.

"It's not for your sake." He wished he didn't care that this made him look foolish. A part of him would love to see Micaela ground to dust because of this, but it would just be too humiliating.

He didn't know what he was going to do, but he knew he couldn't spend one more second with either of these people.

Monaco

Chapter Thirty-Five

Cece looked at the boats along the Quai Jean-Charles Rey as she walked along Avenue Albert II to the coffee shop near the apartment she'd shared with Ethan. Despite their statement to the press about remaining happily married, Ethan had stayed away from their shared apartment after Zandvoort. She wasn't sure what that meant. Did it mean he loved her enough to give her up? Or did it mean he'd realized he wasn't in love with her enough to blow up his entire life?

Just thinking about it made her dizzy. And thinking about where she should go made her nauseous. Monaco was probably the best place for her at the moment—given that there weren't paparazzi leaping out of bushes—but she couldn't afford to stay here long-term. Ethan had assured her that he wasn't going to kick her out, but his largesse would run out eventually.

And there were still the racing fans who made pilgrimages to the principality, calling her a whore and snapping pictures on their phone. For the past few weeks, since she'd left Zandvoort, she'd left her apartment during the day exactly once for a walk through the Princess Grace Rose Garden. It only took a few Bendetto fans calling her names while streaming live on TikTok to stop her from going out. That, and the fact that it reminded her of where Ethan had proposed in the English garden on his parents' estate. Being shouted at while crying was a sad contrast to being an honored guest at an anniversary event there a few years ago.

But this was early in the morning. She needed the fresh air, and Paola had asked her to meet. Her curiosity about what the other woman could possibly want outweighed her good sense. It couldn't be for anything good. Now that she'd caused a scandal, no one in the racing world would want anything to do with her—or so she'd assumed.

She walked into the anonymous little café and stopped cold. Micaela Cartwright sat at a table with Paola. They were facing the door, as though they were waiting for her to come in. The young racer looked like she'd been up all night crying. Though Cece could relate, she wondered what had happened.

Paola stood up when Cece got to the table and gave her a half hug and a kiss on both cheeks. Micaela just hugged her so tightly that Cece was about to lose her ability to breathe. What the hell was going on here?

They all sat, and Paola folded her hands in front of her as though she was about to pitch her on a multilevel marketing scheme. "You're probably wondering why we're all here."

"I'll say." Cece was glad the other woman wasn't beating around the bush. She knew she'd always liked her for a reason. "I'd also like to know why Micaela looks 'rode hard and put away wet,' as my one Midwestern grandfather used to say." Micaela's nose scrunched up. "I'm sorry, but it's true."

Micaela shook her head. "No. It's fine. You're right."

"I think we have a common enemy," Paola said.

"What do you mean?" The only enemy Cece had was the person who gave or sold photos of her, Luca, and Ethan to @WAGsandSLAGs.

Paola looked at Micaela, seeming to wordlessly ask for permission to continue. The racer nodded.

"Some anonymous finsta sent me a DM yesterday that the same Instagram account that broke the story about you and your—two men is about to break a story about Micaela's relationship with Liam." Cece didn't say anything, so Paola continued. "I don't think it was at all fair for you to have to leave in the middle of the race weekend as though you'd done something wrong. You're all consenting adults."

"You're in a relationship with Liam?" Cece was still trying to process that part. Micaela had always seemed like she had a good head on her shoulders, so she was a bit shocked.

Micaela nodded. "I *was* in a relationship with Liam. But he got scared that Brent was going to find out, and then he figured it out anyway when Liam gave me Brent's chassis." The racer pushed a hand through her tousled blond hair. "And now the whole world is going to find out."

Cece's mind was racing, and the silence between the three of them felt tight and constricting. A server came to take their order while Cece collected her thoughts. If there was someone in the paddock leaking salacious stories about people's private lives—across two teams—it had the potential to destabilize the entire grid.

She reached a hand across the table to cover Micaela's. "I'm sorry you got your heart broken."

"It's that obvious, isn't it?" The girl truly sounded miserable. "Everyone's going to think I'm a pathetic dum-dum."

Cece had to try not to laugh. What she'd said was funny, but the situation wasn't. There was someone—or someones—spreading personal secrets beyond the paddock. Whoever they were, they were cracking open the glamorous facade of this sport and spilling all of the not-so-pretty guts.

The information ecosystem in this sport was more delicate than one liked to think. Traded information, even gossip that was unrelated to anything that happened on the track, was valuable. Assuming it was the same person who'd leaked both stories, they must have a goal other than chaos. So, the question of their identity was burrowed inside what that person could possibly want.

"What do we know about the person behind this account?"

Paola's shoulders dropped. "I'm surprised that I didn't have to convince you that I'm not some sort of conspiracy theorist."

"You could be, but we've both been around long enough to know that rumors in this sport never surface for no reason."

"I don't think it's Brent." Micaela rubbed her eyes again. The poor girl needed to sleep. She had to race in less than two weeks in Baku. Cece had tried to avoid anything related to motorsports since leaving the Netherlands as though the devil was on her tail, but she hadn't been able to resist watching Luca and Ethan every second she could at Monza. It was her favorite race of the year. Her heart ached watching from afar, but just seeing their faces fed something in her. She was still hopelessly addicted to them both.

Watching the previous race weekend also meant she'd seen Micaela's crash and the fallout. She didn't see Brent in the garage after he'd been ousted from his car. Given Micaela's devastation about what had happened between her and Liam, she couldn't imagine what might have happened behind the scenes. It was entirely possible that Brent had shared with someone who shared with someone who shared with the ghoul behind @WAGsandSLAGs.

"I know what you're thinking, and he didn't tell anyone. He was so embarrassed." Micaela was indignant about it. "And I don't think he knew or cared about your—thing—with Ethan and Luca."

"Maybe it was more than one person feeding information to this asshole?" Cece didn't know Brent that well. He didn't seem like a gossip, unlike some of the drivers, but she couldn't know for sure.

Cece looked at Paola. There'd been whispers around the paddock that she and Brent had taken their professional relationship into very personal realms, but nothing confirmed. Cece raised a brow. She'd thought that Paola was smart enough not to get snowed by a pretty face.

She'd thought that of herself until the beginning of the year.

"I didn't see him before he left." Paola looked haunted. "I packed up some of his things. He rushed to the airport so quickly."

"Have you spoken to him at all?" Cece asked. "How can you be so sure that he wasn't impulsive enough to blow up the team entirely?"

"I've asked myself the same questions, but I just don't think he'd want it public that his ex-girlfriend and his dad were having an affair behind his back." Micaela flinched at Paola's words. It did sound terrible when you put it like that.

Cece felt a twinge in her chest seeing Micaela's pain. Even if it turned out they'd been targeted by two different people, they were in the same boat. "You're the only person who can understand what I'm going through. I can't believe this is going to come out, and we're not even together anymore."

"It sucks that the worst part about all of this going public is that we don't even get to be with the people we love."

"So, you love them?" Paola asked. "It was never just a sex thing?"

They were being really honest, then? Cece didn't have any reason to hide anymore. Her pride wouldn't be preserved if she denied loving them. "I do love them. I think I have from the second that we met. The issues in our marriage—they weren't caused by the fact that we weren't involved with Luca all along. But something was missing without him. We didn't communicate the way we should before him. I'm not sorry it happened."

"Did they send you away in Zandvoort?" That was what some of the blogs had speculated. It made Cece feel cheap to even think about that possibility.

"No, I insisted on leaving. I knew that if I took myself out of the picture, things would calm down."

"But they haven't," Micaela said.

Cece's heart sunk. "What do you mean?"

"They are getting harassed by fans who want to replace you." Paola shrugged. "It turns out that you were living the dream that a lot of fans didn't know they had."

"I would not want to be involved with two drivers." Micaela shook her head. "One team boss was enough."

After a beat, they all grinned at each other.

True to character, Paola went right back to business. "Who has something to gain from two different teams in chaos?"

Micaela shrugged. "Anyone who doesn't have a seat. Silly season is over, so there are a couple of desperate guys on the grid."

They went through the drivers who wouldn't have a place on the grid next season. Cece threw out a couple of names. Paola shook her head. "Hendriks has a seat. It hasn't been announced. And Majors is going to drive ovals in the US next season."

"That only leaves Heka," Micaela said, though her tone lacked confidence. "But he's ready to retire."

"Cece, did you tell Jocelyn about your relationship with Luca and Ethan?" Paola asked.

"Absolutely not." She didn't know why she responded with such vehemence until she remembered all the times Jocelyn had mentioned the account. Hell, she was the one who'd shown it to her first. "I haven't even enjoyed her company very much lately. I certainly don't trust her. But I did hear about the account from her." They all looked at each other.

"She's your good friend, though," Paola said.

Micaela cocked her head. "She was lurking around the Panther garage during Monza," she said. "Do you think she would do something like this? Heka seems to want to retire."

"Jocelyn wants to stay in the paddock more than anything in the world. And this is the first time that Heka hasn't cooperated with that." The more she thought about it, the more it made sense. "She's trying to get Micaela or one of the Lupo guys fired. This late in the season, either Panther or Lupo would have limited options—Heka would be one of the only reasonable ones."

"How do we stop her?" Paola said, ever the goal-oriented pragmatist.

—

Not that Luca minded having his cock in Ethan's mouth, but he missed Cece. If he closed his eyes, he could imagine her sitting on the bathroom counter, horny beyond belief, as her husband sucked him off in the shower.

She wouldn't be able to resist joining them, and she'd slip off one of those silky nightshirts she liked to wear, step out of her lacy panties—they were white in his fantasy, even though she liked black underwear—and step inside the steamy glass enclosure. She'd claim it was for a better look because the glass was cloudy, but she'd start touching them both.

Luca would cup her breast when she leaned over and told Ethan how Luca liked to be sucked. Then, she'd reach between his legs and tug on his balls.

In this reality, Luca opened his eyes and looked down to find Ethan stroking himself as he took Luca's cock all the way to the back of his throat. He was torn between watching what was happening in the present moment and the scenario he couldn't have.

The speculative scenario—the one in which Cece was with them—won out. He closed his eyes again and watched as Cece knelt down behind Ethan and took over fucking him with her hand. In both realms, he sawed in and out of Ethan's mouth faster, until he gagged but didn't push Luca away. Instead, he dug the fingernails of one hand into Luca's thigh so hard, pulling him closer, until he likely drew blood.

In his mind, Cece stood up and stepped closer to him, pressing her full lips along his jaw as she threaded her long, delicate fingers through his hair. He wanted to taste her, so he reached between her legs and speared into her wet, soft cunt. He could smell her arousal in the humid air as the tension in his body approached the breaking point.

"Fuck." He was so close. When the memory of her taste on his lips came, so did he. It seemed to go on and on because his mind wanted her back so badly, but it was also over too soon.

He'd had to fight not to say her name when he shot down Ethan's throat. He and Ethan had tried very hard not to talk about her during the Dutch Grand Prix. It was all they could do to get through the weekend. The following race, they'd been shoved out of the spotlight by the controversy after Micaela Cartwright's crash during practice and the drama that ensued.

And then they'd taken P1 and P2 in the race. The celebration had been weird. None of the mainstream broadcasters had wanted to ask about their scandal, and yet it was right there, the whole time.

But now that they had a week off, staying silent on the matter of Cece was getting harder. It wasn't like they could avoid each other. Ethan was right here, in the apartment with him. He was kneeling at his feet, recovering from an orgasm that had felt almost like an exorcism. Except the ghost of Cece was still right in the room with them.

Ethan stood up, and Luca pulled him close. They kissed, and it was like they weren't both missing an integral piece of themselves for a short moment. But then Ethan pulled back. "Are we going to talk about her?"

Luca nodded, and they finished their shower. They hadn't talked about anything really important since she'd left them. He'd overheard Ethan telling her to stay in their apartment as long as she needed. When he'd hung up the phone, he'd looked at Luca and said, "She's not going anywhere."

The way he said it, Luca believed Ethan would move heaven and earth to keep his wife. And, although they'd been inseparable, they hadn't talked about their future all together. Luca didn't want to seem insecure, so he didn't bring it up. But it was getting to the point that silence on the matter was stifling.

So, they dressed, and Ethan made them both coffees. They sat at the island where Cece had sat and poured her heart out over Ethan's infidelity over eggs and looked at one another warily.

That the team didn't care about them being in a relationship, as long as they were winning, had surprised Luca, because they were an

Italian team that had priests saying masses in favor of their victory every weekend. But, after a woman that Luca and Ethan had hooked up with together before Cece had gone to the press, they'd been called into a meeting.

Both of them thought they'd be sacked, but the team's CEO had said something about the stock being up and his experiences at boarding school—*"Who hasn't hooked up with their best mate?"* And they seemed more excited about the possibilities for sponsorship by Grindr or Scruff more than anything. That would probably make the team more money than the saint candles depicting Luca and Ethan.

"I want her back," Ethan finally said. "And I'm not giving you up either."

Something that had been coiled inside Luca's chest for weeks unspooled. Ethan wanted to be with him *and* Cece. But the problem of Cece not wanting to be with—or even talk to—either of them still hung over his head like a cloud.

"I want that too."

Ethan dropped his gaze to his coffee. "We should have talked about this sooner."

"It was easier to ignore it during the race weekends. And then fuck every time we had the opportunity to discuss it thereafter."

It was strange they'd never been intimate together alone before—not without a woman they were both with in the next room. But, after Cece left, neither of them questioned the attraction they'd always had for one another. They'd taken too much comfort in one another to break things off, even though that's what would have happened before.

"I don't hate that approach. It gave us both time to think." Ethan smiled at him, and it felt like they were fourteen again. Maybe he'd been a little bit in love with his friend this whole time, and it had taken their girl to unlock it. But it was out of the bag now.

Luca grabbed the back of Ethan's neck and pulled his mouth to his. Even though he'd just gotten off, he wanted him again. The absence of the other part of them made their need that much more urgent. Soon, they were both on the same side of the island and grinding their hips together.

Ethan had the presence of mind to pull back before one of them had the other bent over the back of the couch. "We need to figure out how to get her back, though."

"She was so convinced that us being together in public would ruin our lives. It won't be easy." Luca rubbed the damp hair at the back of his head. Ethan put his arms on either side of his hips. He wasn't going to let Luca get away with avoiding this any longer. Where it might have made Luca feel caged-in and dying for an out before, it made him feel safe in that moment. He wasn't used to seeking that feeling out, but it was okay because it was his oldest friend.

"My parents are assholes, so they are going to disinherit me regardless." Ethan didn't seem as emotional about that as Luca would have been, but then Ethan's parents were cunts.

"And my parents don't care." They'd called Luca after the news broke, but they were only concerned that he was okay. They'd checked in on Cece and Ethan too. He didn't know what he'd done in a past life to deserve the two people who'd raised him, but he was grateful every day. "They'll be happy if we figure this out. They'll be your family."

Ethan kissed his jaw, and said, "It wouldn't matter if they wouldn't. You and Cece are my family. You have been for a long time. And I think I could be happy if it were just us. But I don't want that. I want more. The two of you are everything."

Those words choked Luca up. He cupped Ethan's face in his hands. "I love you. Not just because you and Cece are a package deal. You need to know that."

Ethan nodded. "How are we going to get her back, though?"

"She has to be absolutely sure that this is not going to affect our careers negatively." They separated and were silent for a few long moments. They both took drinks of their coffees and looked out the window, over the Mediterranean. He didn't think the ocean was as blue anywhere but here.

The weather was perfect that morning, barely any clouds. The only way today could be better was if Cece was with them.

Ethan looked over at him and smiled. "I have an idea."

New York City

Chapter Thirty-Six

The car pulled up in front of a nondescript SoHo warehouse building. Well, it wasn't anything to write home about on the outside. The building had housed a commercial laundry for about a hundred years, until the offers from real estate developers got too rich. Paola knew that a couple of billionaires, several A-list actors, and three or four professional athletes owned apartments there. One of those professional athletes was Brent.

If he truly wanted privacy, he'd have to move someplace that didn't have tourists and paps hanging out by the door, hoping to get a glimpse of Harry Styles.

He'd been avoiding her calls long enough. It was only four days, but she was going to have to put out a press release regarding who would be driving his car in Baku by next week—him or the very talented reserve driver who would be only too happy to take Brent's seat for good.

And that didn't even touch how she felt about him avoiding her calls as his girlfriend. If that's what she was. They hadn't talked about it, thinking they had all the time in the world to define their relationship. And she'd been resistant to defining their relationship as anything before Monza.

She didn't stop at the concierge desk, and he didn't try to stop her. Either Brent had put her on the approved guest list and given them a picture or she looked as though she might just stomp over anyone who got in her way. It was probably the latter, because Brent's silence made it clear he didn't want to see her.

So, she'd done what she had trained to do. She'd pried this address from Liam, even though he hadn't wanted to give it to her. He wanted to let his son sulk in peace. Well, he was actually afraid of what would happen if he poked the bear—his own son—too quickly after his relationship with Micaela had been revealed.

That controversy had actually died before it had started. Paola put out a press release denying the relationship had ever taken place. The account didn't have photos or any other evidence—only a blind item—so no one else had picked up the story.

And they wouldn't if Paola could get Brent to come back to the team and pretend that nothing had happened. Paola could tell reporters that the team had taken the decision to let him leave the race at Monza, and that everything was harmonious. She almost laughed thinking that line of bullshit, but she didn't.

It wasn't funny that Brent was making every effort to throw his life away.

At this point, she didn't care. Both her personal and professional lives were colliding and making it impossible for her to put those crisp lines of separation between her logical thoughts and her very illogical feelings. She'd felt pity for Micaela and Cece, and how they'd fallen prey to something as stupid as love.

But she hadn't been willing to admit to anyone, including herself, that she was just as vulnerable. She didn't know when it had happened or why the guardrails she'd so carefully constructed around her heart had failed when it came to Brent.

He was good looking, but he was far from the best-looking man she'd dated. He was funny, but his humor was so bro-y that she found it embarrassing when she laughed at one of his jokes. He was sweet, but he could turn sullen and entitled on a dime.

He wasn't her type at all. But he made her feel like she was the smartest and most beautiful woman in the world. His attention on her was like sitting on a sunny beach with a fruity cocktail in one hand and a book in the other. It didn't matter if she was in the middle of answering ten thousand press inquiries and teetering on the edge of a meltdown.

He made her feel free.

Four days without that was too long.

She didn't have to wave a key card in front of the sensor on the elevator, so he must be home and have approved her entry. Good. She wouldn't have to try to find a window washer to help her break into his fifth-floor loft.

The elevator opened into Brent's living room. Paola had never been there, so she took a moment to take it in. Brent had mentioned them coming here after the season was over and seeing New York during the Christmas season. Paola had never seen the Rockefeller Center tree up close. And she'd only been ice-skating a few times. Brent had told her that he'd teach her.

He lived on the top floor, and the elevator opened facing three large, arched windows looking out over the city. Light played over the deep leather couches in the open loft space. Brent obviously hadn't decorated it himself, but everything about the place spoke comfort to her.

He'd also talked about how this place was the only thing that truly felt like his. He'd purchased it with money from a trust fund set up by his mother's father and his racing earnings—making sure it was only performance bonuses. It was important to him that his father hadn't bought this place for him. He felt like he could be his own man here.

A heavy dining room table that looked like it had been made with reclaimed wood dominated the center of the room. It was big enough to seat at least ten people. Big enough for friends and family. It said that he wanted to invite people into his space, even though inviting people in made him vulnerable.

As much as he wanted to be his own man, separate from his father, he was a testament to the man who raised him. He didn't know she could see that—probably didn't think anyone saw it—but she saw him.

That was probably the moment she'd realized she was in love with him.

Her eyes stopped roaming the giant loft when her gaze met his in the kitchen off to the right. He looked happy to see her, unsurprised.

"Are you hungry?" For a second, she let herself think about what it would be like if that was an everyday occurrence—her coming home to him and him asking what she wanted to eat. But just for a second. They didn't have an ordinary life, and both of them would grow bored with the domesticity.

Her stomach growled, answering for her. "What's for dinner, honey?"

Now that she was here and saw he wasn't attempting to destroy his liver or drown in pussy—not that she'd thought that, but she didn't know if it would even be cheating if he did—she could relax a little and let him open up to her in his own time.

Well, unless she got impatient, which was extremely likely.

"You're in New York, so we're having pizza. I called in an order when I saw you in the lobby cameras." He rounded the island and walked toward her. She expected him to crowd her against the door to the elevators or one of the rustic wooden posts that held up the high concrete ceilings, but he stopped at the giant, sun-soaked, leather sectional. He perched on the back of the couch and waited for her to come to him.

She'd come all the way to New York for him, so he could cross the room for her. She stayed put.

"You don't seem surprised to see me at all."

He shrugged. "I figured you would come find me and try to sort me out. You're not going to get me to come back, though."

Despite herself, she stepped forward. Now she was close enough he could reach her. She wasn't sure if she wanted him to do that. It would be so easy for him to pull her in and soften her up. Then, she could make all of his little PR problems go away and smooth things over with his father so he could—what?

"What are you going to do?" Paola asked. "Are you just going to quit, midseason? You'll never get another drive, no matter the series, if you do that."

He looked down. "So, you're going to start right in about how I'm an irresponsible, ungrateful prick then? You're here as an employee of the team and not my girlfriend?"

"I tried to be both, Brent." Her whole body tightened in anger. He knew how important her job was to her, and he was throwing it in her face like the asshole he pretended to be for the rest of the world. "But you're making it extremely difficult."

"I'm not jealous of them," he said.

"What?"

"I'm not jealous that my father was with Micaela. I didn't love her, and I don't love her."

Paola hadn't entertained that idea any more than she had the idea he was holed up with someone else to lick his wounds for him. "I know that. And I'm here because of you. Not the team. Not your father."

"You managed to kill the story?" There was a hint of disappointment mixed with pride in his voice.

"You don't want to see your father's life ruined. And you might hate Micaela for a lot of reasons, but I know that you respect her."

He was silent for a beat, and then the intercom went off. He pushed off the couch and walked close to her. So close she thought he was going to gather her in his arms and kiss her. Part of her wanted that—had wanted that as soon as she'd walked through the door. She vibrated with wanting him as he got near her, as she could smell him.

But then he passed her and walked to the panel near the elevators. When he turned around, he smiled at her as though he knew what she was thinking and said, "Pizza's here."

"That was fast."

He snagged her hand as he came up next to her. "That's what I love about New York. You can get whatever you want within fifteen minutes." He looked down at her and bit his lower lip. "Almost anything you want."

She wanted to slap him on the shoulder—or the face—and tell him she would have come running had he answered any of her calls. "I'll keep that in mind."

The elevator doors opened, and the delivery guy handed Brent the pizza. "Thanks." He never let go of her hand.

When they were alone again, he pulled her into the kitchen and put the pizza down on the island. It looked like soapstone. He'd bypassed the table, choosing intimacy. They were silent as he grabbed the plates and poured the wine while she nearly burned the tips of her fingers off serving the pizza.

"Ouch." She blew on the burns until he grabbed her again and pulled her toward the sink. This was more leading than he'd ever done with her, and she'd be lying if she said she didn't like it. If this was what he was like when he was away from the glaring cameras and his father, she couldn't say it was necessarily a bad thing.

But it was a thing that conflicted with her professional duties. That kept her from fully enjoying the way he soothed her irritated skin with cold water and then dried her off. She looked up at him, waiting for him to kiss her and turn this into a romantic date instead of a business meeting over pizza.

He didn't do that, though. Instead, he smiled at her and said, "It should be cool enough not to burn the roof of your mouth now."

She was hungrier than she'd realized, but then she'd been too nervous to eat at the airport or on the plane. Halfway through her second slice, she stopped herself before she got sick. He had a slice of pizza halfway to his mouth when she asked, point-blank, "What are you going to do? It honestly doesn't matter to me whether you go back to the team, we just need an answer."

He put his food down and raised one brow. She wouldn't say it because it would piss him off to know he looked just like Liam when he did that. "It doesn't matter to you at all? You were the one making an impassioned case for me to go all in on the team and my career. All of the sudden, you don't care?"

"Professionally, no." She was being honest. It would be a headache if he quit midseason, and it would likely reignite the rumors about Micaela and Liam. But that could be handled. "I'll make it work, no matter what you do. It's the speculation and uncertainty that's hurting the team."

"I'm sorry that I walked out at Monza." He took a sip of wine. "That had to have been a rough couple of days."

"Sorry to me or to the team?" She couldn't help having her personal feelings for him leak through in that question.

There was a long pause of them staring at each other before he said, "Both."

"So, what are you going to do about it?"

"What do you want me to do about it?"

"Why does that matter?" Neither of them was eating at this point, and they weren't answering each other's questions. Both of them were being stubborn, and she wasn't going to be the one to falter. She'd felt like she had been faltering since giving in to his charms a few months ago.

He looked away first. "You are as tough as nails, and it makes my cock so happy. You know that?"

"I don't care about your cock right now." Untrue. "I care about what you're going to do with your life."

"You'll care about my cock later?" He grinned at her, and she was a goner.

She still rolled her eyes and said, "Yeah. Later. But, right now, I want you to tell me that you'll finish out the season and play happy families."

He didn't seem shocked by her statement. "I knew I could get you to tell me what you wanted me to do."

"Are you going to do it, or are you going to be an asshole about it?"

"My father is the only asshole. And Micaela's at least half an asshole." He picked up his pizza again. "But I'll do it because you want me to."

"Not even a little bit for you?" She wanted him to do it if he loved racing, not out of duty to his family or even wanting to please her. She wanted him to be doing this for himself.

Brent's loft was spacious, but he'd felt the walls closing in on him before Paola had shown up this afternoon. He'd thought about picking up the phone the first three or four times she'd called after he'd stormed off. But then, he'd turned off his phone to avoid the temptation at all.

He'd needed a few days to think on his own. The things he needed and the things he didn't became clear to him when racing and Paola were out of reach. He hadn't once been tempted to turn on the qualifying sessions or the race. He hadn't even checked the results because they didn't really matter to him.

Somewhere along the way, and he didn't know where, his love for racing—or what he'd thought was a love for racing—had gone away. For a while, it had been replaced with his desire to please his father. And then, with his need to beat Micaela and save face in their little nepo baby war. But the pure love for it he'd felt on the karting track? That was long gone.

It wasn't the same way he felt when he thought about Paola. When he knew she was on her way up to his apartment, adrenaline had pumped through his veins. He'd known he had to keep his cool because he had to win her. She was better than any trophy sitting in his father's overstuffed case, though.

When he was with her, every problem he had seemed manageable because she expected him to manage. He'd known she wanted him to return to the team and at least finish out the season. Because that's what he'd promised he would do.

"I'll go back, but I have a condition."

"And that is?" Paola froze.

"You know," he said, softly. "But I'm going to spell it out for you. I'm in love with you, Paola Rodriguez. And I want you to be with me, out in the open. And I want you to be next to me when I decide whether I can find my love for racing again. But I don't know if I will. You might take up all the room in my heart."

She sat in front of him, looking stunned. He didn't think anyone had ever rendered her speechless before. Even if he wasn't the first man to declare his love for her, he was the first to do that.

"Are you going to respond at all? Or am I going to have to await a press release?" He didn't know if teasing her was a good idea at the moment.

She looked down, and he was worried she was going to walk out of the apartment and probably file a sexual harassment complaint. If she didn't return his feelings, he deserved it. But then she looked up at him and smiled. "You don't have to wait for a press release."

He stood up and rounded the counter almost before she finished her sentence. Her "I love you" was claimed by his mouth on hers. He pulled her up to standing flush against his body. His hands couldn't fill themselves with her curves fast enough.

When he pulled away a little for air, she said, "I must smell awful; I've been flying."

He ran his nose up the side of her neck. "You smell perfect. We can shower after I have you."

She pulled him even closer with her hands on his ass and said, "How could I forget?"

"You said you'd care about him later, and it needs to be later now." He pushed his fingers through her lush hair, pulling it down from the messy knot he'd been wanting to undo since she walked in the door.

"Shut up before you make me take it back."

He pulled his fingers across his mouth as though he was closing a zipper and put his mouth to work peppering kisses down her neck instead.

Her stomach growled again, and he wondered for a second whether they should stop so she could finish eating. What he had in mind for them would require a lot of energy. "Do we need to stop so you can fuel up?"

Instead of answering right away, she pulled his shirt over his head and started kissing her way down his chest. "Pizza is better cold anyway."

Before she could get to his belt, he picked her up using his hands under her thighs. She felt so good against him that he groaned with pleasure. She wrapped her legs around his waist as he carried her to his bed.

"I love the way you think."

She laughed and whispered in his ear. "I love *you*."

Wednesday Before the Grand Prix

—

Singapore

Chapter Thirty-Seven

Cece didn't *want* to be in Singapore the same week as the race. Unlike Monaco, it was a big city-state, and she probably wouldn't see Ethan or Luca, but there was always a chance. The problem was she couldn't afford to turn down a job at this point. And a *Vanity Fair* shoot with a world-renowned photographer was a job that could very well lead to more jobs.

Editorial shoots usually didn't pay well, but this was a partnership with a label she'd worked with before. Alexander had made sure she would be compensated at a rate that was well above her market value as a model.

And the location was frankly to die for—the SkyPark at the top of the Marina Bay Sands hotel. The iconic pool deck spanning the three towers was the first thing she'd wanted to see when she'd attended the race for the first time. Ethan had teased her about being a tourist, but Luca had defended her. He'd always had to hide his awe at the cool things his wealthier compatriots found pedestrian. Ethan had shut up after that reminder, and they'd stayed there every time he'd raced in Singapore.

Anxiety rose in her throat as she ascended the elevator. She wasn't nervous about the job—all she had to do was move around in beautiful clothes after being made up and styled by the most talented people she knew. The makeup artist they'd hired was so good she could definitely cover up the bags under Cece's eyes. She was nervous about her life.

She caught a glimpse of herself in the reflective elevator doors. Yikes.

But she hadn't been sleeping well. She couldn't sleep without Ethan and Luca next to her or the promise of them being next to her soon. With time, she was sure it would pass, but she couldn't wait for the day it didn't hurt to exist without them to continue on with her life.

When the elevators reached the SkyPark level, she took a deep breath and prepared herself to be the professional she was before she'd been a wife or a lover or a scandal. She'd been through so much in the last ten months that she should be prepared for anything.

The one thing she wasn't prepared for was seeing Ethan and Luca waiting for her when the elevator doors opened.

"What the fuck are you doing here?" The words were out of her mouth before she could do anything to keep them back. Her mind couldn't compute their presence and panic welled up inside her chest before she could tamp it down. Why would they be here? Did they care at all about their careers? Although the rumors had died down in the face of the drama with the Panther Motors team, the one way to reignite gossip about the three of them was for them to show up here.

Both of them smiled at her, beamed really, as though they were simply happy to see her. Neither of them was dim, but they were just giving her these stupid happy grins she couldn't understand.

"You're not happy to see us?" Luca took the first step toward her, and she almost made a dive for the elevator doors closing behind her. She looked around at all the people working to set up what was a real photo shoot and composed herself. They would simply leave and discuss this privately before they took their leave. And none of them would speak of this again.

"I told you that I needed space." She walked between them toward the tent the staff had set up as a dressing room. "This is not giving me space."

"Well, we would give you space, but that's not why you're here," Ethan said, and even more alarm bells started going off in her brain.

"I'm here to work." Maybe if she told herself that, they would leave. But they were here for a reason. Something in her brain had told her that this job was too good to be true, that there had to be a catch. Six figures for an editorial shoot wasn't something that happened to wives of real celebrities. But no, she'd told herself that it was probably the one benefit of being involved in a sex scandal—people wanted to look at pictures of you.

Luca grabbed her arm and turned her toward him. He didn't manhandle her, but his touch was insistent—the way you'd touch someone if they were on the edge of losing their cool. She hated the way her body calmed instantly when he took her in hand. It wasn't fair he had this effect on her. Ethan stepped closer too. She fought the urge to push them both away. Partially because she'd probably land in the long pool bordering the walkway. That would be more embarrassing than just standing here and hearing them out.

She indulged herself by taking a moment to drink Luca in. He had more of a tan than he had in the Netherlands. No one had been there to remind him to reapply sunscreen. She'd been doing that since earlier in the season. He also looked about as tired as she felt. She'd wanted more for him this season. She'd wanted him to be free of the kind of extraneous bullshit that dogged drivers when their offtrack life intruded.

Then, she turned to her husband. He looked tired as well, but there was something hopeful about the way he looked at her. She loved that he was so sanguine about the fifty people staring at them, waiting for something to happen.

"Are you going to hear us out?" Ethan asked. "Or does Luca have to toss you over his shoulder and drag you away like a caveman?"

His mouth quirked and she barely kept herself from smiling back at him. How could they be so cool and collected? They hadn't all been together for almost a month, and she vibrated with both the need for them to touch her more and the fear about what would happen if they did. But she guessed that was why they drove the cars at the limit—they didn't experience the drive for self-preservation the way everyone else did.

She nodded. "I'll hear what you have to say."

"Do you want to go downstairs so that we can speak in private?" Luca asked. She was torn. If she went downstairs with them, there would be photos of the three of them walking into a hotel on social media within minutes. But neither of them seemed to care. And if the rumors weren't going to faze them, why should she sacrifice a few more moments with them for the sake of her already-tattered reputation?

Together, they walked back to the elevators. Both of them put a hand on her lower back as the car descended three floors. Less than a minute passed, but it felt like forever. She didn't know what they were going to say or what they had planned for her. She was equal parts afraid they were going to break up with her for good and excited they'd possibly—maybe—figured out a way for them to be together.

Ethan took her hand as they made their way to the room and Luca keyed them in. As soon as the door closed, Ethan turned and kissed her. It wasn't rushed or frantic. He kissed her as though he had all the time in the world. But at the same time, he didn't wait for permission. He had it, though. She told him as much as she drank from the desire he poured into his kiss. Luca stepped behind her and moved the hair off the back of her neck, claiming that spot with his lips. She was stone-cold sober and yet completely intoxicated by their touch—surrounded in it, swimming in it.

But they'd brought her down here to talk, and they all still had so much to say. Their entire relationship had been initiated because of this electric thing between the three of them. It had exploded in their faces over and over. It was time for them to think things through, talk things out, before falling into bed.

Reluctantly, she extricated herself from their embrace and moved to a chair facing a sofa in the suite. She didn't dare choose the couch, where one or both of them could sit next to her, and their nearness would destroy her good sense.

They exchanged a look that spoke a language they'd been honing since they were teens. She just hoped this—entanglement—wouldn't destroy a friendship that long and deep. Again.

They mirrored each other, sitting with their legs spread, their elbows on their knees, leaning as close to her as they could get while still being across the room. She wanted to reach out to both of them too. But she had to be strong. She could be the strong one, for once.

"Why are you here? What is happening?" She likely sounded bonkers, but she was disoriented. They grinned at each other, and it kind of pissed her off. "Was this entire photo shoot staged just to get me to hear you out?"

She would have thought Luca was more sensible than that, but it seemed like something Ethan would do. It was self-aggrandizing, foolish, and wasteful. She was about to tell them all of that when Luca said, "We planned it because we thought it would be the only way to get you here."

"You knew where I was this whole time!" Cece squeezed the arms of the chair so hard her knuckles turned white. "I didn't leave the apartment for weeks. And now the two of you drag me across the globe to say what? What could you possibly have to say that would change things? We can't just magically transport ourselves to the future or an alternate universe, where no one in a zillion-dollar-per-year sport is going to blink at two queer drivers and their shared wife."

When she stopped talking, she had to take in a deep inhale. That gave them an opening. "The team is fine with it."

Her grip on the arms of the chair loosened, but she still wasn't convinced. "The most Italian team on the grid is fine with their drivers fucking? Be so fucking for real."

Luca grinned at her, and she wasn't sure if she wanted to kiss him or slap him. "Turns out, when you're winning races, you can do whatever you want."

She looked to Ethan—uptight, staid Ethan—and waited for him to contradict Luca. But he shocked her. "He's right. The team actually has new sponsors because of the whole thing. Alessandro told us that he doesn't care what's happening in our bedrooms as long as we're bringing in more points than anyone else."

"But your family." At this point, Cece was grasping for things that would kill her hope. She didn't know why she was doing it. If she was hearing them correctly, they were telling her they could all be together. But she still felt like she had to fight the urge to believe this was all going to work out.

"They are being themselves about the whole thing." She wanted to cross the small distance between them and sit in his lap, comfort him. "But it doesn't matter to me whether they never speak to me again or I'm never to darken the door of their hallowed home. They are not my family in any sense of the word that matters. You are my family. You have been since the day we met." Then, he reached over and grabbed Luca's hand. Something inside Cece broke at seeing the way Luca stroked the back of Ethan's fingers with his thumb. "Luca is my family. And the two of you and any children we might have are all I need."

"You're not worried about the money? Or Luca, your family?" She really couldn't think of anything else. Her mother would give the whole situation a hearty side-eye, but she would live with it. She might even enjoy taking a corner of the spotlight bestowed by her daughter's scandalous lifestyle.

"News flash, babe. We're both rich. And we're going to be fine." Ethan paused. "We just really need you to say that you'll give this a chance and not run off. We know it isn't fair to you that people will paint you as something you're not just because you're the woman in this whole situation. And we can't guarantee that there won't be fans who call you names and shitty reporters butting into our business. We just hope that being with us—how much we love you—is worth taking it on the chin for."

It was worth it, no question. If they wanted her without reservation—the way it seemed they did—she could take hits from the outside world as long as she could live inside the protection of their love.

God. They actually loved her.

"You love me, don't you? Both of you." Ethan wouldn't give up his family for a trophy. He would let her go if she was simply a possession. He wouldn't be out with Luca unless there was real love—the kind that lasted—there.

"I love you both in a way that makes me feel like I'm bleeding it out all the time. Being without you for even a day is hell for me." Ethan said. "The only way I've survived is because this guy made sure I ate and slept and didn't get too bogged down in what it would mean to lose you."

Ethan had never been this effusive before, and she knew how much it hurt him to show this much of himself to anyone. She was honored he gave that to her—the gift of knowing him deeply and intimately. It was all she'd ever wanted when they got married, but it took Luca joining their relationship to make them whole.

"I've loved you for a long time, Cece. I would wait forever for you, but I hope I don't have to." Luca's words were more straightforward than Ethan's but no less powerful.

She stood and crossed to the couch. She went to sit between them, but Ethan pulled her into his lap. In an instant, she was straddling his hips, positioned against his cock in a way that made her curse the clothing she wore.

He held her face in his hands. "Do you love us too?"

Her eyes and heart were both full to the brim. She nodded. "Yes. I love you so much." She glanced at Luca, who'd turned and moved closer to them—touching them both. "Both of you own my heart."

Ethan grinned. "We've missed you so much. And we've thought about you all the time." He stroked both of her sides with his hands until he cupped her breasts. "We have plans for what we want to do with this body."

"Please tell me you didn't arrange an entire photo shoot so that you could fuck me. There are fifty people waiting up in the SkyPark."

"We had your call time set ninety minutes early." Luca kissed the side of her neck. "Kind of hoping we could convince you to be with us and make you come a few times. But there really is a photo shoot."

The way they were both touching her, she was starting not to care. Let them wait until the sun went down. Her whole world was about this. "A whole ninety minutes to win me back and make me come?"

"We can work fast," Luca whispered in her ear as he undid the tie at the back of her neck, holding her halter dress up. It was so hot and humid in Singapore that she hadn't worn a bra, so her breasts spilled into Ethan's hands. He sucked one of her nipples into his mouth while he pinched the other, setting her body ablaze.

She ground down into his cock, needing their clothes off immediately. Luca's hands left her, and she could hear his clothes hit the floor as he removed them. Cece retained barely enough focus to unbutton Ethan's shirt as he pulled her dress down farther, kissing skin as he revealed it.

She pushed Ethan's shirt off his shoulders before Luca picked her up by the waist and stood her in front of him. She shuddered as she felt Luca's skin against her bare back. He pushed her dress the rest of the way down, and she was naked in front of Ethan and Luca.

Luca's hand reached between her legs and went straight for her clit. Her knees buckled, but he held her up, opening her to Ethan's shuddered gaze.

"Pants off." Luca's order was gruff, and Cece could feel herself grow softer and wetter under his hands, even though his order wasn't for her. Feeling Luca's cock against her hip wasn't hurting matters in that department either. Ethan lifted his hips and pulled off his pants and shorts, kicking them off when they got to his ankles.

His cock was so hard it sat against his stomach. Cece licked her lips, almost wanting him to order her to suck it. She wanted to give herself over to these two men who were her entire world. She wanted to show them they had her heart and her body for as long as they'd care for it.

Luca leaned close and said, "You know what I've been thinking about the most?"

"Hmmm?" His hand working between her legs made it impossible for her to form words.

One of Luca's hands clutched her hip and the other rubbed her clit, keeping her open to Ethan's gaze while he stroked his cock. "I've been thinking about how we haven't both been inside you at the same time enough."

Cece's skin tightened and flushed. They'd only done that a few times, but it had been so intense. The intimacy of it was out of the realm of anything she'd ever experienced before.

"Do you want that?" he asked. He wouldn't push for that if she said it was too much, but she couldn't think of anything that she wanted more at that moment.

"I do. I want it." As soon as she said that the hand clutching her hip moved around and grasped her ass cheek. Was he going to bend her over right there and take her from behind? He took some of her wetness on one finger and started toying with her back there. She choked on how good it felt. All of her senses were overwhelmed.

"You're going to straddle his cock like a good girl while I get you ready."

Cece nodded as he walked her over to the couch. She was so mindless that he picked her up again by the waist and sat her on Ethan's lap. He took one hand loosely across her throat as he positioned his cock at her entrance. "That's my pretty girl."

She knew he loved her, but he knew she loved it when he treated her like a thing in bed. That thought lingered for a moment, making the simmering pleasure in her body threaten to boil over until he was fully seated inside her.

A bottle of what she assumed was lube popped open behind her. Ethan didn't move, waiting for her to adjust to him inside her at this angle. She was already so full. It was already so good.

When Ethan started to move, she felt Luca's finger at her back entrance. She pushed back against him with as much space as she had to maneuver to take him in. He added another finger, and she almost passed out with the mix of pain and pleasure. She was pinned and strung out on the sensation of the two of them moving inside her—the way they coordinated and worked her up made her feel cared for.

From the outside, what they were doing would look obscene, but it felt almost sacred to her.

"She's ready for us both," Luca said. Cece wasn't sure she could take more pleasure, but she needed to come so badly she would do whatever they wanted to get there.

Ethan pulled her close to him and he kissed her as he slid farther down the sizable couch to give Luca room. She felt Luca for just a split second before they were both inside her. "Fuck. Please," was all she could say. Pinned like this between them, she felt as though she couldn't breathe, couldn't think, couldn't do anything. If they didn't move, she might die.

She thought it was the kind of fear they might feel before going for a gap—the hope they'd time it just right, the fear it would end their race.

Cece clutched Ethan's shoulders as he pumped inside of her in tandem with Luca. When they were like this, all three of them were fucking each other. It was heady and almost so sweet it made her back teeth hurt. She wanted it to last forever. It had been so long since they were together, and Luca's torturing touch had her so close before they were inside her that she went up like a firework almost instantaneously. The way her body squeezed down on both of them made it so they came almost immediately after.

None of them moved for a long time, but they were sweaty and sticky, and Luca had to take care of his condom. She was still coming back to the world, laid out on the couch on top of Ethan when Luca came and sat on the ottoman next to them, stroking one hand up and down her back.

She kissed Ethan's damp chest where her nails had left a mark. "What were you guys going to do if I hadn't shown up for the photo shoot? Or if I'd shot you down?"

"We've already done an interview with the reporter talking about how much we love you." Ethan kissed the top of her head. "We were hoping that you'd read it and then take pity on us."

"You both have such egos on you. How am I ever going to cope?"

Ethan slapped her ass, lightly. "Yeah, but we're worth it."

Thinking about how lonely and empty the future had felt this morning and how full and joyful it promised to be now—they certainly were.

Race Day

—

Las Vegas

Chapter Thirty-Eight

While she could do without some of the glittery spectacle, Micaela officially loved this race and this track. From the first practice, late Thursday night, she'd felt completely hooked up and at one with the car. The floodlights kept her hyper-focused as she maneuvered the car through the speedy turns and drove flat-out past the casinos on the Strip. She'd taken her second pole position, ever. If she won the race, she would have P2 in the driver's championship and her pick of seats after her contract was up at the end of next season.

And she was going to leave Panther at the end of next season. Things with Liam had settled into a new normal—one where neither of them spoke to the other unless it was absolutely necessary—after Brent had shown up in Baku ready to race. Thanks to his efforts during the back end of the season, the team would also get second in the constructor's championship.

As far as the world was concerned, all was well in the orbit of Panther Motors. But it still felt like a bit of her insides had come loose every time she felt Liam come into a room. It didn't seem to get better, and she couldn't imagine it ending. He didn't even talk to her in the car anymore. She knew certain messages came from the team, and she was sure there were others in the garage who suspected they'd been together and broken up because of the state of affairs. But no one said anything.

And it was the absence of any acknowledgment they'd meant anything to each other that hurt so much. But it was her fault she'd started a doomed relationship that had to stay a secret. Part of her always knew it would end this way. The way everything they'd shared together had simply been erased by a tacit agreement made her wonder if it was worth it.

The only time she wasn't swamped by memories was when she was working. She could push her love for Liam and how it had ended out of her mind when she was meeting with the engineers and strategists. She didn't ruminate while she was eating the meals her dietician basically forced down her throat or going through the grueling workouts she'd demanded from her trainer. Her mind was so disciplined that she didn't even dream of him anymore.

But when she was in the car, she was truly free.

Ironically, the ice-cold racer she'd become would be one who could make her father proud. Only she didn't care whether her father was proud of her anymore. She didn't even care about what Liam had to say about her as a racer. She knew she was quick, and she knew this was what she wanted to do.

But she wanted Liam too. Without him as her person, the pole positions and victories felt hollow.

She just had to get through the driver's parade and the crush of celebrities in the paddock and on the grid until she could be free again. This particular driver's parade, under the lights of the Vegas Strip, might actually destroy her, though.

She stood on the flatbed of a truck across from Luca and Ethan. Since they'd opened up about their relationship with Cece in *Vanity Fair*, they'd received a lot of press attention. But they'd also seemed lighter and more relaxed. Better than almost anyone, she knew secrets could weigh you down. And being happy and in love hadn't made them any less hungry for wins. Luca had already clinched the championship, and she was fighting it out with Ethan for third. The results of tonight's race would determine the top three drivers.

Brent came to stand next to her. He'd surprised her by not being an asshole since he came back. His good mood likely had more to do with he and Paola being officially in a relationship, but she'd take what she could get. Even if the number of happy relationships around her made her a little sick to her stomach.

"Usually, getting pole position would make you happy," Brent said. "I'm guessing this has something to do with my dad."

That made Micaela look around. There were cameras everywhere during the race weekend, and they were especially astute at catching everything at this particular track. "I don't want to talk about it."

"Chill out, the boom mics are pointed at Heka right now."

Micaela glanced over at the Finnish driver. He was leaning at the back of the truck, and she hoped he didn't jump off to avoid answering questions about why he was divorcing his wife. They'd been the golden couple of the sport for so long—until Heka had discovered his wife was feeding gossip to @WAGsandSLAGs in hopes that a seat would fall into their lap, and she could convince him not to retire.

No one—other than Paola, Cece, and Micaela—knew where Heka had gotten the tip to check his wife's emails.

Apparently, along with her terrible parenting skills, this had been the last straw for Heka. Unfortunately, getting rid of Jocelyn was going to be expensive. So, Heka had to unretire for at least two more seasons.

Micaela looked at Brent. "You don't really want to have a heart-to-heart about me and your dad, do you?"

He screwed up his face in mock disgust. "Not really, but my girlfriend tells me that I need to show you that I'm over the fact that you and my father did the nasty rather than tell you."

Micaela rolled her eyes. She wasn't sure how long he could last, pretending to be nice for the sake of his relationship, but she was happy for the reprieve from asshole Brent.

"C'mon. We were always better as friends, and no one knows my dad better than I do." The first part was true, and she bit her tongue to avoid stating there was one way she did know his father extremely well.

It was the least she could do, even though she was the walking wounded right now, and it would be nice to spread the pain a little bit.

"We're working together. Sort of. That's all this is, now."

It was Brent's turn to scoff. "You're both miserable. The two of you are just moping around the garage like we aren't having the most successful season in team history. Just tell him that you're still crazy about him and get on with it."

"You're seriously suggesting that I fuck your dad?" She reached out and felt his forehead as though she was checking him for a fever. They both cracked a smile. "Did you hit your head? Or is Paola's vajayjay just made of pure gold?"

They both laughed and then sobered.

After a beat, he said, "Listen, I'm sorry I was such a douche when we were together. You didn't deserve that. And I don't think you *only* got with my dad to get back at me. It took being with Paola to realize that I needed to grow up, though. It took loving her to realize that I'd wasted your time and taken advantage of you."

"I'm sorry that I fell in love with your dad." She looked down. "I didn't mean to. It didn't feel like a choice."

Brent clapped a hand on her shoulder, which jolted her whole body forward enough that he had to pull her back. She bumped into him, which made them both giggle. "My dad's an easy guy to love. He deserves to be happy. You both do."

Micaela wished someone would convince Liam of that. Or at least let him know he wouldn't turn to stone if he looked at her.

Liam would be glad when this season ended. Then, he would only have to spend twelve more months unable to look at one of his drivers in the face. At least Brent had forgiven him, so he was only on the outs with Micaela.

He'd fucked up in ending things with her. And now, he'd been living in his mistake for months. He was so fucked up over it all that he actually got jealous when the big screen showed her laughing about something with Brent during the drivers parade, even though that was the reason they'd broken up.

Unfortunately, he couldn't do anything about it. He had to get through the crush of press and of VIPs crowding the grid to ensure both cars were ready.

He couldn't stop everything and tell Micaela that he'd been a fool, and he was deeply and irrevocably in love with her. Especially not with her father here, gloating about how he'd always known his daughter was destined to be a champion. He wouldn't kick the guy's ass, and he wasn't going to reveal he was in love with the man's daughter. All she'd ever wanted was for her father to be proud of her, and he wasn't going to take even an iota of shine that it had finally happened.

"I'm here with Sir Jack Cartwright and Liam Sullivan," the broadcaster said. "And we're talking about the amazing strides that Micaela and Panther have taken throughout the season. Both of you must be very proud parents right now." The reporter put the microphone in front of Liam first, but Micaela's father spoke instead.

"I'm so proud of our girl and thankful that Liam gave her a shot and a really fast car during her first season." He didn't care about any of that. He was just glad to have a reason to be in front of the cameras again. He'd probably attribute Micaela's success to his super sperm and not her own hard work and talent if allowed to keep talking.

Liam leaned toward the microphone, happy to point out that Jack was so much shorter than him with his gesture. "We're so happy to have Micaela with the team. Her talent and dedication to getting every detail right, every weekend, has elevated everyone in the garage and back at the factory. She lit a fire under her teammate, and she has the kind of energy that creates dynasties in this sport. She's going to be very important, far into the future. We're so proud of both of our drivers."

"Thank you, Liam," the broadcaster said. "Looking to the future, do you think you have a chance of keeping Micaela with you after her contract expires at the end of next year?"

The idea that Micaela might leave hit him in the chest. He'd put it out of his mind until now, comforting himself with the idea that while he might not be able to have her as his woman, he would be able to see her almost every day.

Jack took the microphone again. "My daughter is going to have every option in the world."

Liam looked to where Micaela was lowering the balaclava over her face and putting her hand out for her helmet. Soon, everyone would have to leave the grid for the formation lap. She would get in the car, and he would have to put his professional face on and forget she owned his heart and probably always would.

He was struck by how ridiculous this was. She should be with him. She belonged with him. It didn't matter that he was her boss, and there were a million conflicts of interest. But he believed the team needed her energy. The team needed her almost as much as Liam needed her. Pushing her away had put everything he'd worked his entire life for at risk.

She wouldn't hear what he was about to say on the broadcast, and she might not want him anymore. She would see this after the race, and then she would decide. But he needed her to know that he loved her and needed her, regardless of the result.

"Actually, I think there's a really good chance of her staying with the team, considering the fact that I'm in love with her, and I plan to marry her."

The team took the tire blankets off and vacated the track in something that resembled a choreographed dance. There was nothing but the first turn in front of her and the other drivers behind her. She started the formation lap and did final checks with Frankie. The car roared underneath her as she made her way around. She took in the fact that she was racing down the Vegas Strip now, starting right in front of the Venetian, so the excitement of that wouldn't interfere with her race.

By the time the lights went out, her car leaped forward under her, and she cut in front of Luca behind her before the first turn, the only thought in her mind was winning. Everything hooked up, and she took a twenty-second lead before pitting. She came out behind Luca and Ethan, but neither of them had stopped yet and she was on the faster tire.

Her engineer told her the Scuderia Lupo drivers had made a miscalculation and waited for a safety car that didn't come, so they had to double-stack in the pits, which meant they came back on the track behind her.

Taking care of her tires, she still managed to extend her lead before the second pit stop, so she came out in clean air, with the Scuderia Lupo drivers well behind her.

The race's perfection ensured that it wasn't the most exciting for the viewers, but it was the most exciting result of her career. Of course, she'd always imagined herself as a champion, even as a rookie. She wouldn't be a racing driver if she didn't dream of dominating every single moment on the track, but this was sweet.

She levered herself out of the car, and one of the stewards grabbed her before she could jump into the arms of her waiting team to be weighed. The crowd around the parc fermé and the podium roared as she stood and raised both arms in victory.

When she turned to see who was there from the Panther team, she was shocked to see Liam there, looking at her, smiling. He opened his arms, and she didn't think about the implications before taking a running leap at him.

He caught her and lifted her up. She almost thought this must be a dream. It couldn't be real, because this was better than any make-believe she'd ever played.

Of course, it wasn't going to last forever. Nothing this beautiful ever could.

When he pulled back and put her on her feet, she saw her dad. He didn't look happy, which somehow didn't surprise her. Still, he hugged and kissed her for the sake of the cameras.

With that duty complete, she gathered hugs and high fives from Frankie and the pit crew before she was led back into the cooldown room.

There was a screen that showed clips from the race along with water, towels, chairs, and the tire company hats they wore with their finishing positions in the race. She sat down and cracked open a bottle of water—Las Vegas was chilly in November, but the car was still hot—and didn't realize what she was looking at until they played it again.

It wasn't a clip from the race, it was a clip of Liam telling a broadcaster, "I love her, and I'm going to marry her."

Her heart sank, and she thought for a second he fell in love with someone else and was going to marry this person until they played the clip from the beginning again. Then, she saw he said this in response to a question about Micaela remaining with the team.

Her mouth fell open, and she stared at the screen until they started playing clips from a close call at the race start between two of the backmarker teams. She noticed Ethan and Luca both looking at her speculatively at that point.

"And here I was thinking our declaration of undying love for Cece was dramatic." They looked at each other and laughed. Then they hugged, and Micaela looked away once Luca started whispering something in Ethan's ear. It seemed like a private moment, and she needed a second or a million to gather her thoughts.

Her skin flushed when she realized cameras were watching her react to this moment. Part of her wished Liam had said this to her privately, but a bigger part of her was glad he'd said it at all.

She didn't really register what was happening until there was a microphone in her face and someone was asking about her thoughts on the race. Given what Liam had said just before the formation lap, she had to commend the journalist on his professionalism. She would not have been able to resist making some sort of comment.

The podium itself was a blur, and she was probably in a bit of a fog until Liam grabbed her and pulled her aside before she could walk into the press conference.

She wasn't ready to talk to him yet. She wasn't sure what she should say. The way he'd done this was bizarre. But, at the same time, being in his arms again was everything she wanted.

"I'm sorry," he said, before she could respond. "I shouldn't have said that the way that I did, but your dad said something about you having the opportunity to move to another team, and I couldn't stand the thought of it."

He looked desperate and wild eyed, and she decided to have pity on him. "I wish you would have told me in private. I wish you would have told me months ago."

"I know. I know. I fucked up, and I'll do anything if you'll forgive me."

"Anything?" An idea formed in her mind, a surefire way Liam wouldn't get cold feet before she made him follow through on his very public commitment.

He pulled her close to him and laid kisses all over her sweaty hair and flushed face. "Anything."

And that's how Liam Sullivan and Micaela Cartwright ended up getting married by an Elvis at six o'clock on a Sunday morning in November.

Acknowledgments

First off, I have to thank Holly Root and Taylor Haggerty for getting really excited—instead of really scared—when I told them that my new project was a cross between *Drive to Survive*, a *Real Housewives* franchise, and a Jackie Collins novel. And then I really have to thank Maria Gomez and Megan Sakoi for taking the chance to acquire the book and bringing on Krista Stroever—who *got* my creative choices and voice from the very beginning of our work together.

There is a long list of folks who read the book and loved it enough to keep me believing in it. Sanjana Basker gave such smart notes that helped me make the characters more embodied. And Becca Hensley Mysoor gave me notes that helped me amp up the emotional resonance and angst. Adriana Herrera, Adriana Anders, Alexa Martin, Rachel Hawkins, and Elle Diaz read early versions and made me believe that I was truly onto something. And Kennedy Ryan and Sarah MacLean—thank you both for getting excited when I told you I was doing something wildly different.

Turns out, I really needed their words of encouragement when trying to revive a subgenre. Thank you to Erin Leafe—who I read *Lucky* by Jackie Collins along with as I was diving into the book. It sparked the idea to turn my idea into a "bonkbuster" and buck current genre conventions. And I have so much gratitude for Serena Golden, who said, "Oh, like Jilly Cooper's *Riders* series?" when I told her about the project.

I would also be remiss if I didn't thank the originators of the high-glam "sex and shopping" subgenre of romance that practically invented the girlboss as she exists today—Judith Krantz, Dame Jilly Cooper, Danielle Steele, and the Lady Boss herself, Jackie Collins. This book would not exist but for theirs, and the fact that my mom let me read her hardbacks before returning them to the library.

This book also wouldn't exist without the font of information available from female content creators in motorsports. My friend, Lily Herman, and her newsletter, *Engine Failure*, provided invaluable analysis and context for how I approached the book. And Toni Cowan-Brown is a primary source of information on the history, technology, and politics behind Formula 1.

About the Author

Andie J. Christopher is the *USA Today* bestselling author of *Unrealistic Expectations*, *Not the Girl You Marry*, *Not That Kind of Guy*, and *Thank You, Next*, among others. She writes sharp, witty, sexy contemporary romance about complex people finding happily ever after. Her work has been featured on *NPR* and in *Cosmopolitan*, *The Washington Post*, *Entertainment Weekly*, and the *New York Post*. Prickly heroines are her hallmark, and she is the originator of the Stern Brunch Daddy. Andie lives with two French bulldogs, a stockpile of Campari, and way too many books. For more information, visit www.andiejchristopher.com.